VALENTINE'S VOW

AVENGING LORDS - BOOK 3

ADELE CLEE

Valentine's Vow
Copyright © 2018 Adele Clee
All rights reserved.
ISBN-13: 978-1-9164336–0-1

Cover by **Jay Aheer**
Cover art by **Midnight Muse Designs**

Books by Adele Clee

To Save a Sinner

A Curse of the Heart

What Every Lord Wants

The Secret To Your Surrender

A Simple Case of Seduction

Anything for Love Series

What You Desire

What You Propose

What You Deserve

What You Promised

Lost Ladies of London

The Mysterious Miss Flint

The Deceptive Lady Darby

The Scandalous Lady Sandford

The Daring Miss Darcy

Avenging Lords

At Last the Rogue Returns

A Wicked Wager

Valentine's Vow

A Gentleman's Curse

CHAPTER ONE

SOUTH OF CHALK FARM, LONDON 1820

The secluded area near Primrose Hill was the perfect place to fight a duel. The road lay hidden behind a screen of trees and thick hedgerows. There were no houses in the vicinity, no farmers up with the larks on this cold November morning, no chance of a constable stumbling upon the violent scene.

Lucius Valentine stared out across the field to the wooded knoll blocking his view of the notorious Chalk Farm Tavern. The mere sight of a gentleman huddled in a booth, trembling hands clasped around a bottle of brandy, prompted the landlord to take bets as to whether the fellow might live to see nightfall. But Valentine did not need to down copious amounts of liquor to give him courage. Nor did he need people prying into his affairs.

"Your partner in crime, he is late, no?" Dariell's voice broke the tense silence. The Frenchman was Valentine's second even though his skill in combat lay with his fists, not a pistol.

"Is it a crime for a gentleman to seek satisfaction?" Valentine said, although he was not the injured party, nor the challenger ready to risk his life to salvage his reputation.

"Duelling, it is illegal in your country, as is murder."

"I have no intention of murdering Mr Kendall."

1

Despite Dariell's numerous conversations with Kendall's second, an apology in the *Times* was the price Valentine must pay to restore the man's honour. But only a weak man grovelled when innocent. Did Kendall not know that Valentine was an expert marksman? That he could shoot the fellow through the eye from two hundred yards?

Valentine dragged his watch from his pocket and checked the time. Why would Kendall issue a challenge only to suffer the humiliation of failing to attend? It made no sense.

Suspicion flared.

"Perhaps Kendall is playing a dangerous game." Valentine drew his greatcoat across his chest. Cold muscles led to slow reactions. "Perhaps he is hiding up on the knoll waiting for me to leave. His witnesses will testify he arrived at the appointed time, will inform the world that I am the coward."

Mr Kendall was like an annoying terrier snapping at Valentine's heels. Worse, a thorn in his side. The man appeared at every ball and soirée, attended the same club, occupied the adjacent box at the theatre. Kendall might be handsome and charming, but he had the brains of a trout.

Valentine chuckled to himself. This battle had nothing to do with an imagined slight and everything to do with the right to court the widow Lady Durrant. Never in his life had he fought for a woman's affection. And he'd be damned if he would do so now. Kendall lacked the courage to fire. Valentine would wrap the man round and round in a spool of words until the fool struggled to recall the day let alone the month.

"The duel, it will commence soon I think." Dariell's comment dragged Valentine from his reverie. The man had a mystical insight, could predict events long before they occurred.

"Let us hope you're right." The dullard was already thirty minutes late. "My fingers are numb. Lord knows how I am expected to fire a damn pistol. Perhaps that is Kendall's plan. Wait until my blood freezes in my veins and then attack."

"There is no chance of your blood freezing today, my friend," Dariell said with some amusement. "I suspect it will be quite the opposite."

Valentine was about to question his friend's logic when a sudden movement drew his gaze to the row of trees bordering the road. A lone figure slipped between the tall trunks, greatcoat flapping about his thighs as he advanced towards them with short, hurried steps.

Valentine observed Kendall's approach with interest. There was something of the dandy in his walk, a swagger that cast doubt over the man's masculinity. Evidently, he had dressed in a hurry. Three times his top hat slipped down to obscure his eyes. The pistol in his gloved hand dangled carelessly at his side as if the object were not a means to end a man's life but a lady's reticule filled with curiosities.

Why the hell had Kendall come alone?

Where the hell was his second?

And why had he not brought a doctor?

Was this all a ruse? Did the fellow long for a bed six feet under and lack the courage to take the muzzle into his mouth and fire?

"Are you ready to meet your destiny, my friend?" Dariell said in the mysterious voice of a fortune teller at the fair. "Ready to discover what fate has in store?"

"Ready? It takes more than a pistol pointing at my head to unsettle me." After a childhood wrought with chaos and instability, few things fazed him now.

Kendall was twenty feet away when Valentine realised his mistake. A woman's soft thighs filled the gentlemen's breeches. The flare of a woman's hips drew his gaze up to the rumpled cravat that looked to have been tied by a monkey. There he noted ample breasts squashed into the fine silk waistcoat.

"Lord Valentine?" The lady kept her dainty chin high, her

shoulders straight, but he heard the nervous tremble in every misty white puff of breath. "Lucius Valentine?"

Valentine inclined his head. "Lucius Montford Harcourt Valentine," he said, "in case there is any mistake."

The lady's sharp gaze studied his face as she moved closer, so close he caught a whiff of her perfume. The image of her sitting in a silk robe at her dressing table flashed into his mind. Who thought of perfume when preparing for a duel? Scents of iris, rose and jasmine stimulated his senses along with the earthy aroma of musk. In its entirety, the fragrance spoke of elegance, of contradiction, of a woman who was as self-assured as she was feminine.

"Floris?" he said, inhaling deeply.

She blinked in surprise. "Yes. White Rose."

"It's exquisite."

"It is my one and only indulgence."

For a reason unbeknown, the last word played havoc with his insides. He was not a man held hostage by his wants and desires. And yet something about the way the word slipped sensually from her lips sent his head spinning. Perhaps it was the cold, the confusion, the confounding notion that he stood opposite a woman brandishing a pistol.

"You have me at a disadvantage, Miss …" Valentine considered her rich brown eyes fringed with the longest lashes he had ever seen, considered the faint pink blush that coloured her milky-white skin, the resolute chin that showed a steely determination.

"Miss Kendall." She dipped a quick curtsy. "You're here to fight a duel with my brother."

Her brother!

The trout had a sister!

Was this beauty Kendall's secret weapon? Had he deployed this alluring creature to unsettle Valentine's composure? Did Kendall not know that it took more than impressive breasts and kissable lips to entice him?

"Just Miss Kendall?" he teased, intrigued to know more about the woman who would risk her life and her reputation for a bumbling buffoon.

"Aveline Kendall, but I prefer Ava." She looked down her dainty nose at him. "Not that you will have the need to call me either."

Was that a challenge? Did she think him a man who craved the unobtainable?

Dariell cleared his throat. "You have come alone, madame. Are we to assume your brother has withdrawn his complaint?"

Miss Kendall firmed her jaw and breathed a frustrated sigh. "My brother finds himself incapacitated this morning, monsieur."

More like too inebriated to stand.

"And so I act in his stead," the lady continued.

In his stead?

What the hell was she about?

Lord Sterling was named as Kendall's second. Why had he not come to withdraw the complaint? The fact Miss Kendall thought Valentine capable of shooting a woman was insulting enough for him to offer a challenge of his own. If she wanted to degrade him, she might as well rip his shirt off his back, chain him to the pillory and pelt him with cabbages.

"Miss Kendall," he began in the tone of a disapproving parent, "clearly, you have never wielded a pistol let alone fired one from twenty paces." She had made the mistake of bringing one weapon. At least she had no intention of taking a second shot.

"How difficult can it be?" She studied the object in her hand with obvious disinterest, although he noted the slight tremble in her fingers. "As long as one has a steady aim, I imagine it is a relatively straightforward process."

Straightforward?

"There is nothing straightforward about killing a man."

"Oh, I have no intention of killing you, my lord."

"I'm pleased to hear it because you are playing a high stakes game you cannot hope to win." How was it that Mr Kendall had been a prickly pain in his arse this last week and yet Valentine had never laid eyes on his sister? "So, if you have no intention of killing me, pray tell me what you're doing in a field near Chalk Farm wearing your brother's breeches and carrying a pistol."

A brief silence ensued. It gave Valentine an opportunity to study her, though he could not decide if she was the most courageous woman he had ever met or the most foolish.

"As I have already explained," she said with an air of hauteur, "I shall take my brother's place. Hopefully, we will conclude the matter swiftly and with minimum fuss. By all accounts, you're a gentleman of honour and high principles."

Valentine snorted even though Miss Kendall spoke the truth. "Who told you that?"

"Lady Honora Valentine."

"My mother!" God's teeth. So, Miss Kendall did move among those in Society. Who acted as her chaperone? Her brother clearly had no conscience when it came to her welfare. "You know her well?"

"I attend her club." Miss Kendall shook her head, impatience evident in her tone. "Now, let us get back to the matter of—"

"Her club?"

While Valentine had spent the last five years abroad, he knew with absolute certainty that women were not permitted entrance to White's. Then again, his mother was progressive in both attitude and mind. It would not surprise him to learn she had petitioned parliament regarding the inequality.

"The Association of Enlightened Ladies. We meet on Fridays." Miss Kendall drew the oversized greatcoat across her chest. "May we proceed, my lord? My nose is numb, and I can barely feel my toes. And I should like to return home before my absence is noted."

Valentine stared at Miss Kendall, dumbstruck. Judging by Dariell's snorts of amusement, his friend found the whole scene comical. He would, too, had the lady not seemed so determined in her cause.

Purely to sate his curiosity, Valentine decided to oblige her whim. "Very well. Let us proceed. Are you familiar with the order of events?"

"Do I look like a lady skilled at fighting duels?"

She looked like a lady who would challenge the devil if need be.

"As you act as your brother's second, Miss Kendall, Dariell will inspect both weapons. Once he is satisfied—"

"How do I know I can trust him?"

Dariell stepped forward. He captured her gloved hand and bowed low. "Madame, you may trust that fate will intervene no matter what interference a man might make. It is my wish that you both walk away from the battlefield with your honour restored."

Miss Kendall looked Dariell keenly in the eyes before scanning his unconventional attire—the long trousers and tunic of a man used to living in hotter climates. A curious hum left her lips. "You believe a person's destiny is already written?"

"Indeed, I do."

She gave a curt nod and handed Dariell her pistol. "Then I trust you, monsieur."

"And did you load the weapon yourself, madame?"

"Of course."

Dariell took the lady aside. He spoke about the striking mechanism and what she might expect once she pulled the trigger. His friend then checked Valentine's pistol, before taking both weapons into his possession.

"Shall we fight to draw first blood, Miss Kendall?" Valentine asked with a menacing undertone. He hoped to scare the woman enough that she might drop to her knees a quivering wreck and plead for an end to this nonsense. "Shall we fight to maim or fight to the death?"

"I do not intend to fight at all." The hat—being too large for her head—slipped down over her brow, and she gave a huff of frustration as she pushed it back into place. "I intend to delope. I believe that is the correct term."

"Delope?" Valentine bit back a smirk. "And what will you do when I fire, Miss Kendall? I am accurate to within half a centimetre, and that is being modest. I will most certainly hit the intended target."

A brief flash of uncertainty passed across her features, so brief a less observant man might have missed it. "But you won't fire, my lord." Those magnificent brown eyes journeyed over his face. Despite many women finding his physical appearance pleasing, this lady's gaze was more inquisitive than lustful. "Sources say you are a gentleman above reproach."

Valentine scoffed. "My mother is a little biased."

"She said you are a man of few vices. And a man with your unblemished reputation would never harm a woman."

Damn. Was there anything his mother hadn't told her? Did she know which side of the bed he preferred, how he liked his eggs in the morning? The urge to unsettle her confident composure took hold.

"No. I am not a drunk or a gambler, Miss Kendall. I am not obsessed with collecting snuff boxes or Arabian stallions. If I am to name a vice, then perhaps my *weakness* lies in the bedchamber, but that would leave an inaccurate picture of my ability to perform." He spoke in the licentious drawl no gently bred lady should ever be permitted to hear. Then again, gently bred ladies did not attend duels at dawn. "Not that I would expect a woman of your limited experience to comprehend my meaning."

Valentine expected to see her cheeks flame red with a blush, expected a nervous quiver at the least, but Miss Kendall's luscious lips curled up in amusement, and she laughed.

"Limited experience?" Her voice brimmed with mockery. "My lord, I have travelled the world, watched the sunset over the

Aegean Sea, explored deep into the Mines of Lavrion. I am well versed in Greek philosophy, in geological theory. And I have borne witness to the fact that it is easy to mistake the groans of pleasure for pain."

Valentine stared at her. To say he was aroused was an understatement. This woman possessed the power to unsettle his calm composure, to wreak havoc with his disciplined mind.

"Forgive me," he said, eager to put an end to this meeting, eager to restore the natural order of things, "for making an assumption that proved wholly incorrect."

"You're forgiven," she said in the light-hearted way one might expect from a lady born of privilege with nothing to do all day but play the pianoforte and sip tea.

Valentine found the contradiction baffling. Fascinating. Intriguing.

Despite the bitter chill in the air, the lady shrugged out of her greatcoat. She wrestled with the heavy garment, struggled to free her arm from the sleeve. Without thought, he moved to assist her.

It was his second mistake.

The potent scent she wore teased his nostrils. His fingers brushed against her arm, and his stomach muscles tightened in response.

Damnation.

"Oh, the ridiculous thing." She tossed the coat on the ground, gripped the top hat by the brim and threw it as if skimming a stone. A mass of brown curls tumbled down around her shoulders, softening the hard set of her jaw.

Valentine closed his eyes.

The saying "out of sight out of mind" was a fallacy. He pictured the curls brushing her cheek, dancing provocatively on her shoulders. He pictured himself looking down on her, the glossy tendrils spread wide across his pillow as he educated her in what it meant to groan with pleasure.

"Shall we get to it?" Her sweet voice sent a jolt of desire straight to his cock.

He needed to leave. He needed a stiff drink. He needed to dunk his head—and another part of his anatomy—in an ice-cold water trough.

Valentine opened his eyes. Anger flared for no rational reason. "Let us conclude this matter, Miss Kendall. I am in want of my bed."

"As am I, my lord. It has been an extremely tiring morning."

"Thoroughly exhausting," Valentine agreed as he shrugged out of his greatcoat and dropped the garment on the ground. He gestured to Dariell, who stepped forward and returned their pistols.

"You must stand back-to-back," Dariell instructed.

They did as Dariell asked.

Valentine cursed inwardly. He felt the warmth of Miss Kendall's body radiating through his waistcoat. Although he had avoided looking at her figure since she had removed her coat, he felt her soft buttocks pressing against the tops of his thighs.

Good God, how the hell was he to turn around when his cock was ready to burst out of his breeches? How the hell was he to fire a weapon when his fingers shook like those of a man in his dotage?

"I only hope she is worth the trouble," Miss Kendall whispered.

"Who?"

"The widow you and my brother are determined to marry."

"Lady Durrant?"

"Indeed."

In his youth, Valentine had paid court to Portia Durrant, known then as Miss Briscoe. Marriage was presumed to be the inevitable outcome. But how was a man to know his heart when he was detached from all emotion? How was a man to make a lifelong commitment when there was a chance he would turn out like his father? Mad. Deranged. Dangerous.

And so Miss Briscoe had married the decrepit Lord Durrant—out of spite, to teach Valentine a lesson.

"I have told no one of my intentions," he said, though that was not entirely true. He had made a vow, a solemn promise to his mother that he would take a wife, sire an heir.

"Jonathan said the lady is having a devil of a time deciding between the two of you."

Valentine did not give a damn what the trout said. Jonathan *bloody* Kendall could rot in hell for all he cared. Besides, he suspected Lady Durrant enjoyed manipulating events, took pleasure in showing Valentine what he had missed by not taking her as his bride.

"I wonder if the lady prompted my brother to call you out." Miss Kendall continued to bait him. "Hoping fate might decide the outcome."

Valentine gritted his teeth. The remark made him sound weak, made him sound like a lovesick puppy eager to sit, to beg, to wag his tail, to do his mistress' bidding.

"We walk twenty paces and then fire." Valentine hurled the comment like a ball of ice, hoping the reality of the situation hit hard, hoping she felt the coldness of his words trickle down her spine.

He caught Dariell's curious gaze. At no time in the last five years had his friend seen him so agitated. Valentine was known for his control under pressure, and yet this lady's presence ruffled his calm demeanour, gnawed his insides, nagged his mind.

"You may cock your weapons." Dariell's words were met with deathly silence, the stillness broken only by the clicks of their hammers. "Twenty paces. I shall count. One. Two …"

As Valentine walked the required number of paces, he considered the fact that he may have made his third mistake. A logical man did not place his life in the hands of a stranger, did not place his trust in a woman. What was to stop Miss Kendall turning on the count of ten and putting a lead ball in his back?

Relief rushed through him when Dariell called, "Twenty!" His friend paused, and they turned around. "Attend. Present." The Frenchman looked to Miss Kendall. "That means raise your weapon, madame."

Miss Kendall smiled at him. "Oh! Thank you, monsieur." The lady closed one eye and pointed her pistol at Valentine's heart. "When do we fire?"

Valentine raised his arm aloft and fired into the adjacent field —he would rather die than shoot a woman. A loud crack rent the air. Crows cawed as they scattered. A stream of white smoke burst from the muzzle and the sharp smell of sulphur reached his nostrils.

Miss Kendall arched a brow as he lowered his weapon. The corners of her mouth curled up in amusement. Although he had deloped, she did not fire or lower her weapon.

"Did I mention that my father taught me to shoot at the age of twelve?" she said, watching him keenly. "I would line glass bottles on the fence and practise with one eye closed."

God damn!

Valentine's pulse pounded hard in his throat. Had Jonathan Kendall sent an assassin in his stead? Had this angel come to do the devil's work?

"And what do you intend to do now, Miss Kendall? Shoot me?" Pushing aside his nerves, he drew on the arrogance beaten into all aristocrats from boyhood. "If you wanted to kill me, you could have done so upon your arrival."

Valentine handed Dariell his pistol and stepped forward.

"Perhaps I want to win with honour." Miss Kendall's aim remained trained on Valentine's chest. "Or is it that I want to teach you a lesson, my lord?"

"And what lesson would that be?" Valentine stalked towards her. The imagined drum of a death knell rang in his ears.

"That it is dangerous to make assumptions."

Valentine closed the gap between them until the muzzle of her pistol pressed into the fine silk of his waistcoat. From such close quarters, the ball would rip a hole right through his heart. Their gazes locked. He wasn't sure if he wanted to throttle her or kiss the smirk off her face, such was the nature of these new and confounding emotions.

"Assumptions about what?"

Her hand never faltered despite the fact it took strength to point a pistol straight for so long. "Assumptions based on my sex. You should not presume, that because I am a woman, I lack the skill to compete with you. Remember the lesson should you ever find yourself in a similar predicament."

Valentine snorted. "I am unlikely to forget." No woman alive possessed Miss Kendall's courage and audacity.

Miss Kendall raised her arm aloft and fired. Despite the deafening sound, she did not flinch. Instead, she waited for the air to settle before stepping away and bending down to gather her greatcoat and top hat.

"I trust the matter is resolved." Valentine could not tear his gaze away from the soft curves imprisoned within those damn breeches.

"Indeed." She straightened. "Though in future, I beg you to disregard my brother's childish tantrums."

"You expect me to ignore his slanderous remarks? Honour is everything to a gentleman."

"I expect you to be a man, my lord, and rise above the foolish antics of a boy."

Valentine wasn't sure if he should be flattered or offended. Either way, Mr Kendall was hardly a boy.

"Well, my hackney is waiting. The driver has already added three shillings to the fare. Apparently, it is the price one must pay for leaving a man waiting in the cold." She turned to him and offered her hand.

With a sudden eagerness to touch her, Valentine took it without hesitation. The essence of this beguiling creature penetrated his gloves to infuse his body with a warm glow. "Am I to press a kiss to your knuckles, Miss Kendall, or shake your hand in a gentlemanly fashion?"

She shrugged. "I am told you're a man who follows his instincts."

His instincts told him to run, told him to put a hundred miles between them lest she bring turmoil and mayhem to his ordered and structured world.

"Then I shall kiss you, Miss Kendall, and bid you good day." He bent his head and kissed her gloved hand, resisted the urge to linger there for longer than necessary.

"Good day, my lord."

They walked to the road in companionable silence.

The hackney was parked a little further along from Valentine's carriage. Dariell bowed to Miss Kendall, strode off along the lane and climbed into Valentine's conveyance.

Valentine stood rooted to the spot and watched Miss Kendall walk away. He could not resist one last look at the woman who defied all expectations, who broke down and reconstructed what it meant to be a lady.

CHAPTER TWO

Once nestled safely inside the hackney cab, a relieved sigh burst from Ava's lips. Only now could she release the anxiety she had kept at bay. Her heart pounded in her chest, wild and erratic. With trembling fingers, she tugged down the blinds for she did not wish to glimpse Lord Valentine's carriage.

How she had held her nerve, she would never know.

And yet the worst was far from over.

With luck, she would make it home before Jonathan woke from his drug-induced slumber. Lord knows what he would do then. Ava would have to justify her actions, face the hurling accusations of a man who had lost his mind to his addiction.

But laudanum did not feed the hunger crawling through her brother's veins. Gambling was his new love, the thing that gave him purpose, the thing that destroyed every aspect of the man she knew and loved.

Still, she had saved his life this morning, and that brought some comfort.

Gathering her composure, Ava sat forward and was about to instruct the driver to depart when a loud rap on the window sent her heart racing. Drat. On this lonely country lane, one did not need a high level of perception to know who demanded her attention.

"Miss Kendall?" Lord Valentine's rich voice reached her ears.

Oh, hell's bells! What the devil did he want?

"Miss Kendall?" The gentleman sounded most determined.

With reluctance, Ava sat forward. She opened the door mere inches and peered through the gap. "Can I help you, my lord? Have you a problem with a wheel?" What other reason could he have for delaying her departure?

Glacial-blue eyes studied her face though she found nothing cold in his gaze. It was alert, attentive, assessing. Honora was not biased in her appraisal of her only son. Lucius Montford Harcourt Valentine must have stolen into God's box of gifts, for in Ava's experience men were rarely intelligent, handsome and honourable.

"My problem is my conscience, Miss Kendall," he said in the suave way that no doubt made women clutch their hands to their breasts and sigh. "I cannot permit you to ride home alone in a hackney."

Ava imagined ladies swooned at the prospect of sitting in a closed carriage with Lord Valentine. "Why? I arrived alone in a hackney," she said, dismissing the thought of sharing a ride with the viscount. "I have a pistol and have no qualms shooting the driver if necessary."

The corners of Lord Valentine's mouth twitched. "And I trust you have the box and powder with you to reload."

"Do not mistake me for a fool, my lord. The box is under the seat."

Why did men go out of their way to appear superior?

"Oh, you are by no means a fool, Miss Kendall." The rich tone of his voice slid over her shoulders like the smoothest silk. He was teasing her, luring her into his trap until she had no option but to accept.

Being a woman uncomfortable with flattery and interfering

gentlemen, she said, "I must insist that you step back and close the door. I really cannot delay a moment longer."

If Jonathan woke before she returned home, there was no telling what trouble he would cause. Lord Valentine might find himself pacing the field again at dawn tomorrow.

A tense moment of silence ensued before the lord clambered into the hackney and slammed the door shut. He dropped into the seat opposite and rapped once on the roof. The cab rocked with the extra weight and lurched forward before Ava could protest.

"I don't know what you think you're about." Anger burned in her veins.

"Have I not already made my point, Miss Kendall? I cannot permit you to ride alone."

For the love of— She was not a simpering miss in need of a man's protection.

Ava knocked on the roof. "Stop, I say. Driver. Stop this vehicle at once." The cab jolted and jerked to a halt.

The look of shock and uncertainty on Lord Valentine's face was a sight to behold. A gentleman with such an attractive countenance was probably unused to ladies challenging his commands.

Ava straightened. "I have not asked for an escort. I have not begged or pleaded for your assistance. The journey is relatively short, and my welfare is not your concern."

In the dark confines of the carriage, Lord Valentine studied her. Twice his gaze dropped to her thighs, encased in gentlemen's breeches, and still, he said nothing. He stared at her poorly tied cravat, seemed mesmerised by the swirling pattern on her waistcoat.

Heat rose to Ava's cheeks. Anyone would struggle under such scrutiny. She reached for the greatcoat folded on the seat beside her and drew the garment across her lap.

"Have you always possessed the need to command and domineer, my lord? Do you belong to the school of men who fail to value a lady's opinion? Do you believe me too weak to make calculated judgements?"

The viscount laughed. "I *am* an aristocrat. Dominance is in the blood. Pomposity is spoon-fed from an early age. But one might argue that my chivalrous need to accompany you highlights a weakness on my part, Miss Kendall, not yours."

Oh!

Well, at least he could admit his error. "I suppose I should give you credit for your honesty. Nevertheless, I demand freedom from your company."

The lord smiled, and her stomach somersaulted. Damn. Did he have to be so dreadfully handsome? Not that it mattered. She had no need to lay eyes on him again.

"Freedom comes from understanding that some things are within your control, Miss Kendall, and some things are not."

Oh, the rogue! So he had decided to play on her weakness for philosophy. "Do not think to win me over by quoting Epictetus." Was he refusing to remove himself from her conveyance? "Will you not obey my request?"

"Obey?" Lord Valentine snorted. He sat back and pushed his hand through his wavy golden locks. "Perhaps you might prefer a different quote."

"What? You know more than one?"

Heat flashed in his eyes at her set down. It was similar to the look of admiration she had seen in Mr Fairfax's eyes when the scoundrel thought to ply her with port so she might lose the use of her mental faculties.

"It is not what happens in any given situation, but how you react to it that matters." Lord Valentine folded his muscular arms across his chest. His arrogant grin conveyed satisfaction in delivering yet another Epictetus blow.

Ava scrambled to recall a quote to throw back in retaliation, but his comment gave her pause. Being in such a desperate hurry, she did not have time to sit and argue. Of the many battles she would invariably face today, this one held no real importance.

"Very well. Sit there if you must." Ava tapped on the roof of the hackney. She sighed with relief when they rolled forward and were soon on their way.

"So, you spent time in Greece?" Lord Valentine said, breaking the prolonged silence.

Still secretly seething, Ava lacked the enthusiasm for conversation, but it would be rude not to answer. "Five years."

He raised a brow as if impressed that a woman of her breeding had survived without the luxuries afforded one living in town.

"My brother and I returned to London eighteen months ago, following the deaths of our parents."

"Allow me to express my condolences on your misfortune."

"Thank you."

"I also recently returned from a five-year stint abroad. I worked in India and the Far East."

"Worked?" Lord Valentine certainly knew how to shock and surprise. Why would a gentleman with his wealth and fortune seek to soil his soft hands? "Your mother said you went with friends, that you returned together to pursue important goals."

"We were in partnership, bartering and trading goods, mostly. Lord Greystone was the mastermind behind the venture." Nothing in his manner or voice conveyed shame for having demeaned his position.

Ava found that she admired his honesty. But had he told her because it made him appear more progressive? Had he told her because it showed he differed from the rest of his ilk?

"Well, I imagine your work gave you purpose else you would have returned home sooner." At least he had not spent five years on a Grand Tour as an excuse to live a life of debauchery.

"I cannot recall another time when I felt more fulfilled." The lord glanced briefly at the window although the drawn blinds prevented his gaze from lingering there for long.

"And so you have come home to claim the hand of your one true love." Ava's tone carried a hint of mockery. She couldn't help herself. In her experience, wealthy men rarely married for love. Lady Valentine made no secret that she wanted her son to sire an heir, that she wanted grandchildren to dote on, to carry the family name for generations.

"I came home to support my friends who were eager to address their grievances," he corrected.

Confusion clouded Ava's mind. Was he not attending a dawn appointment to prove he was worthy of Lady Durrant's affections? Had he not come home to do his duty?

"But that is not the only reason you came home," she said, pressing him for information.

A faint groan left his lips. "No. I made a vow."

"A vow? To your friends?"

"To my mother." He wore his frustration like a moth-eaten coat—with embarrassment, with a hint of annoyance that he had fallen foul to such a demanding creature. "She wants me to marry."

"To marry Lady Durrant?"

He nodded. "My mother encouraged an alliance with the lady before I left for India."

"You do not strike me as a man who does his mother's bidding." He seemed so strong, so self-assured. A man wholly in charge of his own destiny.

Ava waited for him to chastise her, to insist she kept her untamed tongue on a leash. She expected the cock of a reprimanding brow at the very least. But no. Deep furrows appeared on his forehead. His gaze turned meditative, distant, as if witnessing a scene long since passed, one that caused immense pain.

"A man cannot run from the past forever," he suddenly said, though offered no further explanation.

Run? What did a man of his wealth and exceptional looks have to fear?

The need to soothe him took hold. "Except that my brother is intent on making things difficult. Lady Durrant has captured him in her web, and he has himself in a terrible tangle."

Lord Valentine snorted in agreement. "I get the distinct impression Lady Durrant enjoys the drama. I once heard her say that the trick to capturing a man's heart is to make him think he must climb obstacles to have you."

And this was the woman he wanted to marry?

Honora Valentine must be desperate for an heir to consider such a lady a suitable wife for her son.

"Personally, I prefer honesty to deception," she said. "And while I understand the need for primogeniture, I could only ever marry for love."

"Ah, that mystical emotion that eludes the best of us." Lord Valentine cocked his head and narrowed his gaze. "And what is love to you, Miss Kendall?"

"Love?" Goodness. He was extremely direct. Had she finally met her match? "Well, I suppose at first one must feel an undeniable attraction, a physical lust that goes beyond anything one has experienced before."

Covertly, she scanned the breadth of his chest, the sculpted line of his jaw, and those bewitching blue eyes that made her stomach flip. No doubt many women found themselves a little in love with Lucius Valentine.

"And yet you do not strike me as a woman who values the superficial."

"Desire is a potent thing, my lord, necessary in any relationship." But that was just a small part of what drew two people together. "Of course, I would have to admire a man's mind as much as his body."

"Of course," he said with a sinful grin. "A woman needs more than one means of stimulation."

Heat rose to Ava's cheeks. The conversation grew more inappropriate by the minute. The other enlightened ladies would commend her for speaking so openly, for not shying away from the awkward topic.

"Some say one feels love when aroused to the point of madness." Mr Fairfax had certainly appeared mildly insane when making his declaration. "For me, true love is finding a man who can be my friend and my lover. A man who can accept I am strong enough to be his partner, not open to judge or ridicule me during those moments of weakness when I need his support." This was the most progressive conversation she had ever had. "I would need to trust him implicitly, be ready to lay down my life for him if necessary." Was she not describing her parents' perfect marriage? Few people found such a deep, abiding love. "As you may have gathered, my wants might be considered excessive by most ladies' standards."

"Oh, I am certain there is a man capable of meeting your long list of criteria." The silky, rich tone of his voice slid across the carriage to stroke and caress her senses. "Have you ever been in love, Miss Kendall?"

Ava swallowed. She had no desire to speak of Mr Fairfax or his lascivious antics, but her need for honesty forced her to answer. "I thought so, once, but believe I was mistaken."

"Mistaken or mistreated?"

Good Lord! Lucius Valentine was the most perceptive man she had ever met.

"Does it matter?"

"A great deal. I can only surmise that the gentleman was not worthy of your good opinion or your affection."

Ava floundered under the heat of his stare. His perfect blue eyes penetrated the barrier she had constructed as a means of protection, raising her pulse to leave her hot, slightly breathless.

Memories of Mr Fairfax's assault came flooding back. The dark room, the lack of air, his hot, slimy hands slipping over her skin. She had lacked the strength to ward off his advances. Thank heavens Jonathan had arrived to save her virtue. It was why she could never abandon her brother, no matter how low he stooped.

"Are you unwell, Miss Kendall?"

Outside, the hum of early morning activity reached her ears. Ava shot forward and raised the blind. They had left the peace of the countryside behind, entered the bustling streets of London. Costermongers were journeying across town with their barrows. The hackney swerved and swayed, navigating the carts and wagons eager to make their deliveries before the roads became congested.

"You should hold on to the strap," Lord Valentine suggested when she almost slipped off the seat. "Unless you're happy to end up sprawled across my lap."

One look at his muscular thighs sent her nerves skittering. She needed air. She needed out of this enclosed space.

Ava was about to lower the window when Lord Valentine spoke again.

"Open the window at your peril," he said as if accustomed to riding the streets at dawn. "At this time, the salop sellers are out offering hot drinks, their cure for those with a pounding head from a night spent in drunken merriment. They'll think nothing of thrusting their hands into the vehicle to force you to purchase their wares."

"Then I pray they have fat fingers." Ava lowered the window a fraction and inhaled the stench of manure and rotten vegetables. It was the tonic she needed to banish the ghosts of the past. "We're approaching Mount Street which is where I shall alight."

"Mount Street?" Lord Valentine frowned. "But I was under the impression your brother owned a house on Newman Street."

Oh, dear! Lord Valentine was not as radical as he would have her believe. "My brother does own a house in Newman Street which is currently let to Lord Sterling. I own a house in Park

Street, directly opposite your mother. My brother resides with me for the time being."

"*You* own a house opposite my mother?" The lord arched a brow and gave an odd hum. Ava wasn't sure if it was a sound of surprise or admiration. "And you are alighting on Mount Street because?"

"My neighbours like to gossip, and I hope to return home unnoticed." Even enlightened ladies had to mind their reputations to a certain degree.

"I suspect most of them are still snoring in their beds."

"Trust me. Your mother has a keen eye and misses nothing. Besides, the driver will attempt to fleece me for a few extra shillings and an argument at this hour will most certainly rouse attention."

Lord Valentine sat forward and with a look of steely determination said, "I shall pay the driver, Miss Kendall. There will be no complaint regarding his fare."

Ava sighed inwardly. Chivalrous men were far too assertive. There was a fine line between considerate and controlling.

"I couldn't possibly permit it." This time, the topic was not open to negotiation.

As the hackney rolled to a halt on the corner of Mount Street, Ava reached under the seat and retrieved the mahogany case. She flicked the catch and raised the lid before placing the pistol on the velvet inlay next to its identical counterpart. Then she gathered her hair on top of her head and tucked it into her brother's top hat.

"You missed a tendril." Without warning, the viscount captured the stray lock of her hair. He studied the texture, caressed it between his fingers. His eyes turned the colour of the Aegean Sea on a summer's morning, so blue she imagined diving into their mesmerising depths. "Allow me to assist you."

All the air left Ava's lungs. Her heart slammed against her ribs.

Lord Valentine wound the lock slowly around his finger as if it were a prelude to something far more salacious. His knuckles brushed against her cheek as he tucked her hair into her hat. "There. We would not wish to give the game away."

"No," Ava breathed as she struggled to find her voice.

"Should you ever face a dawn appointment again, Miss Kendall," the viscount said, gesturing to the weapons resting on their plush bed, "I suggest you take both pistols. It pays to be careful."

The thrum of desire hung in the air, thick and heavy.

"In my limited experience," she began, scrambling to regain her composure, "it does not matter how good a shot you are or how well equipped. What matters is reading your opponent, researching their character. After all, it is merely by chance that you are not bleeding to death in a field near Chalk Farm."

The viscount's jaw slackened though he made a quick recovery. Before he could offer another word, Ava gathered the box and her greatcoat, opened the door and climbed down to the pavement. Removing the coins from her waistcoat pocket, she thrust them into the driver's outstretched and rather grubby hand.

"You'll get no more from me," she said to the stout fellow. "That covers the inconvenience of waiting in the cold."

She turned to find that Lord Valentine had alighted, too.

"I presume that when your brother has recovered from his ailment, he will deem the matter satisfied." As the lord pushed his muscular arms into his greatcoat, his bright blue gaze slid sensually over her body. "After all, he would not want the *ton* to know his sister came to his rescue."

"You do yourself a disservice, my lord. Veiled threats are beneath you," she said, feeling somewhat unnerved by his probing stare. She would rather see the flare of anger than the heated look that made it hard to swallow. "After all, you would not want the *ton* to know you fought a duel with a lady. I may have to tell your peers that I almost shot you."

"Had I been anything but a gentleman, the outcome might

have been vastly different." Rather than appear affronted, the viscount laughed. "But as we have both escaped a lead ball in the chest, I shall bid you a good day, Miss Kendall. I have an odd feeling our paths will cross again."

Ava gave a little snort. "Good day, my lord. Let us hope our paths do not cross often. With your obsession for chivalry, you will have a hell of a game keeping up with me."

CHAPTER THREE

Despite being aware of Lord Valentine's stare boring into her back, Ava did not turn around. Oh, she wanted to, wanted one last glimpse of the dashing viscount, wanted to fall under the spell of those mesmerising eyes—so calm, so blue, so full of depth and restrained power.

Who would not want to admire perfection?

But men of his ilk only toyed with women of inferior lineage. Education counted for little when a member of the aristocracy took a wife. Other than the job of a serving wench in the roughest tavern in town, there was but one calling for a woman with a sharp tongue and a point to prove—that of a spinster.

Ava ferreted around in the pocket of her coat, looking for the door key. She fought the urge to glance towards the corner of Mount Street. Enlightened ladies did not dream of falling in love, of being whisked away by a hero capable of banishing every awful memory, capable of fixing every aspect of one's miserable life. Enlightened ladies were strong enough to deal with problems on their own, knew that love was blind, fickle, and soon wore off like any other potent drug.

The last thought roused a mild sense of panic.

Jonathan.

Had the effects of the laudanum diminished? Was he pacing the floor ready to unleash the devil's own wrath on the sister who had betrayed him? At least he couldn't shoot her. The only pistols available were in a box wedged under her arm.

Ava's hand shook as she tried to slip the key into the lock. Just as she seemed close to mastering the simple task, the door swung open.

Twitchett stepped back. "Thank the Lord you're alive, madam."

Bless him. The man's face was as white as his hair and cavalier-style beard.

"It was as I suspected," Ava whispered as she crossed the threshold and handed the butler her hat, gloves and coat. "Lord Valentine is a true gentleman." She glanced at the stairs, listened for the rants of a madman, but the house was silent. "I trust my brother is still abed."

Twitchett placed the hat and gloves on the console table and gave a weary sigh. "He woke some twenty minutes ago, madam, and was not best pleased."

Ava's heartbeat pounded hard in her throat. "Tell me he is still here." She imagined Jonathan snatching paper from her escritoire to scribble another challenge, racing around to Lord Sterling's abode and insisting he deliver the letter to Lord Valentine's second at once.

Twitchett nodded. "It seems the effects of the laudanum left him unsteady on his feet, and so Mrs Stagg put him back to bed."

Thank heavens!

When he found his strength, it would be a different matter.

"Then I had best visit him in his room." Ava had to make him see sense before he did something foolish. "Hide the pistols." She handed the butler the mahogany box. "Lord knows what he will do when he learns I fought in his stead."

Jonathan had every right to be angry. After her intervention this morning his peers would think him craven. But what else could she do? Lord Valentine was the best shot in England. Thankfully, he was not a man to boast or brag. Blessed with a host of impressive attributes, he had nothing to prove.

"Can I arrange for refreshment, madam? Coffee, perhaps?"

"Coffee would be wonderful. It's bitter outside this morning."

"Evidently. Your lips are an odd shade of blue."

Ava pressed her fingers to her lips. Was that what had caught Lord Valentine's attention? His gaze had dropped to her mouth more times than she cared to count.

"Perhaps a hot bath is in order," Twitchett said, the deep lines on his brow evidence of worry as well as his growing years. "Shall I arrange for Mrs Stagg to heat the water?"

"There is no need." What if her brother left the house while she was otherwise engaged? "But have Mrs Stagg prepare a tisane. Something to ward off a chill."

That seemed to appease Twitchett for the time being.

"Now, wish me luck." Ava summoned a smile. "I am about to enter the lion's den."

"Ring if you need assistance, madam. I shall send Bernice up with a taming stick."

Ava patted Twitchett on the arm. "My brother's roar is far worse than his bite."

In essence, Jonathan was more a lion cub—boisterous and playful some of the time, quick to bite and nip for the most part, lovable when asleep. And yet none of those descriptions matched the dark mood of the man lying still, but wide-eyed, in bed.

"Oh, you're awake." Despite her best effort, she could not keep the nervous thread from her voice.

Jonathan's cold, grey eyes flicked in her direction. He lay propped up on a mound of pillows, had a deathly pallor that had nothing to do with illness and everything to do with the effects of the drug, coupled with a hatred for interfering sisters.

"No doubt you're surprised." Jonathan's words carried the

depth of his contempt. "Perhaps you failed to add enough laudanum to my port last night. A few more drops and you might have been rid of me for good."

"Don't be ridiculous." Ava swallowed. The tension in the air was like a prelude to a violent storm. She stepped farther into the room, gripped the gilt chair next to the armoire and brought it closer to the bed. "I saved your life this morning. Had I wanted rid of you, I would have let you meet Lord Valentine on the battlefield." She dropped into the padded seat and gave an exasperated sigh.

"Do you know what you've done?" The words slipped from lips drawn into a scowl.

While the effects of the laudanum made him more subdued, Ava sensed a threatening undercurrent. "I am not in the habit of repeating myself, Jonathan. You're alive. That's all that matters."

"All that matters?" Jonathan sat up and tugged to straighten his nightshirt. "Do you know what happens to a man who misses his dawn appointment? He is mocked and ridiculed. He cannot walk the streets without people pointing and sneering." With each sentence his voice grew louder, more impassioned. "No doubt there will be a caricature of me fleeing the battle, flapping like a distressed hen."

"Trust me. Lord Valentine has no intention of discussing the incident with anyone." The viscount was not a man to gloat. "What part of 'I saved your life' do you not understand?"

"You did not save my life, Ava," he yelled, "as I had no intention of bloody firing."

She winced at his sudden outburst. "But what if Lord Valentine fired first?"

A groan resonated in her brother's throat. "It was a matter of principle," he said as if she were the idiotic child in this relationship. "I exaggerated the slight, called him out merely to show I am serious in my desire to court Lady Durrant. We would have fired into the air. Valentine would have saved himself the embarrassment of having to post an apology in the *Times*."

Only a buffoon risked his life to prove a point. Lady Durrant must be a diamond of the first water to have so many men vying for her attention. No doubt she had a brain the size of a pea. Well, it would only be fair if she did.

Jonathan pushed his hand through his mop of dark hair and growled in frustration. "Sterling must have been livid when he arrived this morning. The fellow lacks the courage to stand in my stead. Devil take it, thanks to your meddling he would have gone to that peculiar French fellow and withdrawn my complaint." Jonathan shook his head, but the effort forced him to press his fingers to his temple and grimace. "God damn, it feels as though someone has taken an axe and cleaved my brain in two."

"Must you curse?" Ava sighed. Jonathan's temper was as erratic as a candle flame on a gusty night.

Jonathan's curious gaze focused on her cravat—or his cravat to be more precise. "What the hell are you wearing?" he said as if only seeing her for the first time. He considered her breeches and snorted. "Do enlightened ladies dress in gentlemen's clothes now? Mother would be so proud."

"There is no need for sarcasm." Now was the moment to inform him of the role she had played this morning. Ava took a second to steel herself. "There is something I must tell you. It is the reason I am dressed in this ridiculous attire."

"Good God!" He blinked rapidly. "You've applied to attend one of those institutes for scientific studies. Let me tell you there are some feminine assets a lady cannot hide."

"Certainly not. I refuse to study in an establishment where they believe women have an inferior mind."

Jonathan frowned. "Is it that your friendship with Miss Faversham goes beyond the conventional? The lady's admiration of you is highly inappropriate."

"Good heavens, no!" Miss Faversham loved anyone who

showed her the remotest kindness. Ava inhaled deeply. "It concerns the duel. When Lord Sterling arrived this morning, I told him the matter had already been resolved. I told him there was no need to speak to Lord Valentine's second and that he was to go home to bed. He didn't believe me, of course, and insisted on trying to rouse you."

Jonathan stared in stupefied silence.

It took a little time for him to process the information.

"You did what?" He cursed again beneath his breath. "Why the hell did you say that?" Jonathan flung back the coverlet and sprang to his feet but misjudged the distance and tumbled to the floor.

Ava rushed to assist him. She grabbed his elbow. "Because *I* took your place this morning. I attended the duel with Lord Valentine. Honour is restored. Satisfaction achieved."

Jonathan's eyes turned a dark gunmetal-grey. His hard gaze focused on her face. "What the blazes? Tell me I misheard you." Anger infused his tone. "Tell me that a woman of your intelligence wouldn't be so stupid."

"I—I cannot." Ava stood and looked down at the pathetic creature who was supposed to care for her in their parents' absence. "I fought the duel with Lord Valentine, and the matter is resolved."

"Like hell it is." Jonathan scrambled to his feet. "Did the devil fire at you?"

"Of course not. He is a gentleman in every regard."

Except in the bedchamber. Had he not alluded to his prowess, hinted he was a man of great passion? An odd pulse in her core sent an image of the handsome lord crashing into her mind. Oh, now was not the time for moments of fancy.

"A gentleman? Unlike me, I suppose." Jonathan threw open the armoire and almost pulled the door off its hinges. "I'm just the fool betrayed by his own family."

"I was trying to help."

"What? By giving the *ton* a reason to mock me? By ruining any chance I have with Lady Durrant?"

Doubt crept into her mind. Perhaps she was overprotective. Perhaps she had no right to interfere. But it was too late now.

"Where are you going?" she said as she watched him drag on a pair of breeches as if the garment had wronged him in some way. "The matter is settled. Lord Valentine would suffer embarrassment, too, should anyone discover the truth."

Just as he was about to draw his nightshirt over his head, Jonathan stopped. "Yes," he said. A wicked grin stretched across the width of his face. "Duelling with a woman is more shameful than failing to wake up on time. I shall use the information to my advantage."

Ava groaned inwardly. Why could he not put the matter to bed? What was this powerful hold Lady Durrant had over him? Ava did not have the heart to tell him, but Jonathan was no match for a man like Lucius Valentine. And yet a part of her wished her brother every success in pursuing the widow.

"Lady Durrant must be an exceptional woman," she said, surprised at the faint hint of jealousy in her tone. "She seems to be the focus of everything you do." Was she not the one encouraging his gambling?

"When a man is in love what hope is there?"

"Forgive me if I sound cynical, but she hardly has your interests at heart else she would have stopped you challenging the best shot in England to a duel."

Jonathan poured water from the jug into the porcelain bowl on the stand. He washed his face and dried it on the towel before saying, "Love makes us reckless. Not that you would know. With you, a man is doomed before he's had a chance to prove himself worthy."

Ava watched the ungrateful wretch shrug into his shirt. Disappointment hung heavy in her chest. She had helped Jonathan more times than she could count, suspected he was the one guilty of pilfering items from her home. And he had the audacity to criticise.

"Do you not think I might like to be reckless?" She was tired of playing mother to a spoilt brat, tired of being the sensible one who had to correct his mistakes. "Perhaps I might like to ignore my troubles and wallow in a pleasure pit."

"You?" Jonathan turned up his nose and stared into the looking glass to tie his cravat. "You've not smiled since the accident. Our parents are dead. When are you going to stop mourning and start living? When are you going to stop interfering in my life and concentrate on your own?"

A hard lump formed in Ava's throat. Water welled in her eyes and she blinked it away.

Eighteen months ago, her perfect life had shattered into pieces. Try as she might, she could not patch the broken fragments together, not when there were missing pieces, not without cutting her finger and drawing blood.

"I ought to change out of these silly clothes," she said, though her voice sounded distant to her own ears. She backed away from him, shuffled towards the door. She thought to ask where he was going at this early hour. Instead, she said, "Will you be home for dinner this evening?"

"Dinner? Lord, no. I am attending the Rockford ball. Don't wait up. I might spend the night elsewhere." Elsewhere with Lady Durrant, gambling? Or in the house he had been forced to lease to his friend Lord Sterling due to mounting debts? "Have Twitchett send my evening clothes over to Newman Street." After tugging on his boots, he retrieved his black coat, breeches, shoes and stockings from the armoire and laid them on the bed.

She could have argued, made the point that Twitchett had enough to deal with in his role as butler, footman and gardener, but she was tired of being the constant voice of reason.

"Then I shall bid you a good evening." With a heavy heart, Ava left the room.

Heaven knows what Jonathan would do in the interim, but she felt it necessary to write to Lord Valentine and warn him that her brother was not a man who counted his blessings but one who sought to manipulate others in the hope of gathering more.

An hour passed.

The house fell silent, so silent it proved deafening.

Having paid a boy to deliver the letter to Lord Valentine in Hanover Square, she stood at the drawing room window and stared out across the street. Were it not for Honora's weekly meetings and Jonathan's endless problems life held little meaning.

One accident had destroyed Ava's hopes and dreams, her plans for the future. While her father had mined for crystals and gems, her mother crafted unique, breathtaking jewellery. Ava loved the bohemian lifestyle, the freedom, the independence, the stunning scenery along the Aegean coast.

Now, she was suffocating in the smog-filled city.

In London, a woman of means did not work. She did not mine alone in dark caves or discuss the healing benefits of crystals. A woman did not barter and trade with importers or charter ships to foreign lands.

Thoughts of her parents filled Ava's head—people so loving, so happy, so carefree. The memories were so powerful that tears choked her throat. When grief wrapped its hands around her heart and squeezed there was but one thing to do.

She hurried up to her bedchamber.

As soon as she opened the door to her room, she knew something was wrong. The clawing scent of Jonathan's spicy cologne irritated her nostrils.

No! He wouldn't have. He couldn't have known of her hiding place.

Ava raced around the bed, stared at the pretty red and gold Turkish rug. The tasselled border no longer ran parallel with the edges of the boards. She dropped to her knees, moved the carpet and lifted the wooden plank.

Relief flooded through her when she saw the two jewel-encrusted boxes. She opened the first, gazed upon the rainbow of stones, their unusual shapes, vibrant colours. They were worthless —chipped, faulty, too small to be of any use—yet her father mined them with his own hands, and that made them priceless.

When she opened the second box, the sudden pang in her chest told her something was amiss. The box contained her mother's jewellery—sapphire earrings, an unusual ruby pendant. Ava searched the box looking for the rare pink diamond her mother had crafted into a ring for her twenty-first birthday—the last gift, the last token of her love.

It wasn't there.

Ava's heart thumped so hard she thought it might burst from her chest. Tears trickled down her cheeks, and she struggled to catch her breath. Three times she emptied the box onto the bed and checked the contents. But in her heart, she knew Jonathan had stolen into her room, knew he was the light-fingered culprit.

Ava packed away the jewellery and rang for Twitchett. She should find a different place to hide her treasures.

The butler arrived moments later. He drew in a sharp breath when he noted the obvious evidence of her distress.

"My brother is no longer permitted in this house. He is not to set a foot over the threshold." Every word carved out a piece of her heart. Never had she felt so betrayed. Never had she felt so lost, so alone. But while she would not abandon him completely, neither would she permit him to take liberties with her precious possessions. "I want his clothes packed and sent to his house on Newman Street."

Family is everything.

Guilt twisted the blade a little deeper as she recalled her mother's words.

"Packed, madam?" Twitchett paused. "Are you certain you want me to deal with the matter today?"

No doubt he thought the decision rash, the result of a heated argument, the need to prove she had the upper hand.

"I'm certain. And have my mother's trunk brought down from the attic."

Twitchett frowned. "You wish me to send it to Newman Street?"

"Of course not." She did not mean to be so sharp, but her steely resolve had returned. "I need to find a suitable gown. Tonight, I am going to the Rockford ball."

Tonight, she would hold her weasel of a brother to account. Tonight, she would drag the truth from his lips even if she had to shame him in front of that vixen, Lady Durrant.

CHAPTER FOUR

"Have you come to offer your mother assistance or to stare at the house across the street? Lucius? Is there something wrong with your hearing?"

"Forgive me." Valentine tore his gaze away from the window, from the house he presumed belonged to Miss Kendall. Something strange was afoot. "I am curious. Are your neighbours adjourning to the country for the winter?"

The question gave him the opportunity to take another furtive glance at the odd comings and goings. He caught sight of the butler loading the last valise into the hackney cab before climbing inside the vehicle.

The thought that Miss Kendall might be going on a trip played havoc with Valentine's mind. The woman held him in a spell. An odd sense of excitement had flitted about in his chest upon receiving her note this morning. The alluring aroma of her perfume clung to the paper, so much so, he could not resist bringing the letter to his nose and inhaling deeply. He had not crumpled the missive into a ball or thrown it into the grate but had placed it with care inside the top drawer of his desk. Twice in the space of five minutes he'd opened the drawer to catch a whiff of Miss Kendall's potent scent.

Was that not a sign of sorcery at work?

His mother raised her chin and cast a suspicious eye at the house across the street. "Ah, you speak of Miss Kendall. She has not mentioned a trip, but when one has an adventurous spirit, anything is possible."

Adventurous? The lady was as daring as she was dangerous.

"You know her well?" Valentine hoped his mother would tell him something unsavoury to help shake this peculiar craving. It went beyond lust, was more a desire for interesting conversation, a need to rise to the challenge and prove he was more than a match when it came to progressive attitudes.

"Yes. I knew her mother. Bright girl. The youngest daughter of Lord Moseley." His mother reached into the side table drawer and removed a slip of paper. "We came out the same year."

A host of questions bombarded Valentine's mind. The need to discover more about the woman who had bested him on the duelling field held him in a vice-like grip. But his mother was as sharp as a hatpin, and so he had to be subtle.

"Will you attend the Rockford ball this evening?" Valentine said, quick to change the subject. At fifty, Honora Valentine still held her good looks. With golden hair, a trim figure and a mischievous glint in her sapphire-blue eyes, there were many gentlemen eager to fill his father's long-abandoned shoes.

"A ball? I cannot think of that now, not when there is treachery afoot."

"Treachery?" That got Valentine's undivided attention. His mother was not prone to exaggeration or flights of fancy.

"I explained everything in my note." A deep frown lined her brow. "Is that not why you're here?"

"No." Valentine paused. He could hardly say he had come merely to spy on Miss Kendall. "I had business in Brooke Street and decided to call here on my way home. Your letter must be with the unopened correspondence on my desk."

"Oh, then I have distressing news to depart."

Valentine sat forward. After twenty years spent in a volatile marriage, it took something monumental to unsettle his mother's calm composure.

"They are all listed here." Honora flapped the paper she had removed from the drawer. "The names of the suspects."

"Suspects?" Intrigued, Valentine stood. He crossed the room and took the list before returning to his seat. He scanned it briefly. It took every ounce of willpower he possessed to stop his eyes bulging when he noted Miss Kendall's name. "Of what are they accused?"

If it was wielding a pistol with intent to injure a man's pride, he knew who to blame.

"One of the ladies listed is a thief."

Valentine's gaze fell once again to the name of the lady who had stolen into his mind, who had slipped like a shadow beyond his well-constructed defences.

His mother came to her feet and strolled over to the gilt display cabinet. The lock clicked as she turned the red-tasselled key. Carefully prising open the glass door, she reached up to the top shelf, captured the gold lidded goblet in her cupped hands and brought it over to rest on the side table.

"Hamilton Kendall sold me this when he purchased the property opposite almost two years ago." Gently, she raised the ornate lid to reveal a large oval ruby. The largest ruby Valentine had ever seen. "Pigeon blood."

"I beg your pardon?"

"It's referred to as a pigeon blood ruby. Don't ask me why. Perhaps because it has the most vivid, most precious hue of all such stones."

Valentine stared at the vibrant gem. "Perhaps I am being

obtuse," he said, wondering what this had to do with treachery, "but I fail to see the problem. Has there been a theft or are you anticipating one?"

Honora gripped the stone between her thumb and forefinger and held it up to the light. "Do you not see it lacks clarity for such a rare object? Can you not see the absence of natural flaws? This is not the blood ruby I purchased, but a paste imitation."

An imitation?

Valentine held out his hand, and his mother dropped the ruby into his palm. Unless one was an expert in facets, knew how to measure and assess the refraction of light, knew how to spot inclusions, then it was almost impossible to tell a real gem from paste.

"I trust you have taken it to an expert," he said, running his fingertip over the smooth surface.

"Would I stand ready to discredit a lady without first checking my facts?"

"No, you would not." Valentine sighed. "And you think a lady on the list had a copy made and switched it for the real ruby." It sounded implausible. One would need to have access to the cabinet, be able to move about the house unnoticed. Of course, there was another explanation. "And you are certain Mr Kendall sold you the genuine article?"

Honora Valentine arched an elegant brow in response. "Without a doubt. Hamilton Kendall would never risk his reputation as one of the most sought-after jewellers by selling fake gems."

Miss Kendall's father was a jeweller?

"Hamilton Kendall worked for a living? Surely Lord Moseley disapproved of such an unconventional match for his daughter."

Had Moseley forced his daughter to elope?

Is that where Miss Kendall gained her romantic notions of love?

"Some men can rise above prejudice." Honora's blue eyes turned a little dreamy. "Hamilton Kendall was the most charismatic man I have ever met. His lineage boasts of an earl, a hero of the Seven Years' War, one of the greatest poets ever to grace King Charles' court. Lord Moseley would have found it impossible to say no."

Having met Miss Kendall for all of an hour, Valentine recognised certain family traits. The lady carried herself with the grace of an aristocrat. It took the courage of a war hero to meet the best shot in England on the duelling field. And something about the way words left her mouth affected him more than anyone skilled in rhythmic meter.

"While your respect for Mr Kendall is evident," Valentine said, handing the fake gem back to his mother, "that did not stop you adding his daughter to the list of suspects."

Honora placed the ruby into the goblet and returned the object to the display cabinet before removing to her seat.

"Every drop of blood in my body tells me Miss Kendall is innocent. But I believe she was here when the thief made the switch." Disappointment marred his mother's countenance. "I am convinced it was during one of our weekly sessions."

"Weekly sessions?" Was she referring to a meeting of The Association of Enlightened Ladies?

"I have a gathering every Friday. A small group of ladies who share similar interests. We discuss politics, literature and otherworldly subjects."

Valentine considered the last topic on the list. "You discuss worldly matters—wars, famine, or do you contemplate the ideology of mysticism?"

His mother raised her chin defiantly and yet he had offered no challenge. "Not that I would expect you to understand, but we attempted to prove that the living could contact the dead. Enlightened ladies must—"

"You did what?" Valentine almost shot out of the chair. "It is dangerous to dabble in the unknown." Though some held a keen interest in the macabre, he'd heard enough eerie stories of malevolent spirits to put him off the practice for life.

"We were not dabbling, Lucius. We hired a professional. Mr Cassiel."

"Cassiel?" After the archangel? Valentine had seen an illustration of the figure in *The Magus*, sitting astride a dragon. While the name proved appropriate for a man claiming to possess a godlike ability, no doubt it was as fake as the paste ruby. "And his first name?"

He would make a few enquiries regarding the legitimacy of the man's *otherworldly* powers.

Honora pursed her lips. "Angelo."

"Angelo Cassiel? Of course."

"I know that tone, Lucius. You think it foolish. But one must keep an open mind to such possibilities."

When the mind was open to possibilities, it was open to manipulation. Some people knew how to pray on those looking for an answer to the question that had plagued humanity for centuries.

"Personally, I need to *see* something to believe it. The philosophy has served me well."

The corners of Honora's mouth curled into a smirk. "Has it? I beg to differ. Faith and love are two of the strongest emotions known to man—besides hatred. You cannot see them, but that does not mean they don't exist."

Dear God. The last thing he needed was a lecture on love, marriage and responsibility.

"Have you proposed to Lady Durrant?" his mother said bluntly. "No, of course you haven't as that would mean believing in something you cannot see or touch. It would involve things like trust and hope."

Valentine shrugged. He refused to be drawn into a discussion about his failings. Something prevented him from making the final leap into matrimony, though he knew not what. Perhaps Miss Kendall had the right of it. Perhaps some people needed more than a life partner. Some people needed a friend, a lover, a trustworthy confidant. Perhaps his list of criteria would prove longest of all.

"Forgive me, Lucius. I did not invite you here to argue." Honora came to her feet. She closed the gap between them and placed a comforting hand on his shoulder. "It's just that you have so much to give and it breaks my heart to see you alone. After what happened with your father … well, I fear it has affected you more deeply than you think."

Valentine placed his hand on hers and rubbed gently. It was a gesture of solidarity shared many times over the years, when his father's delusional mind had resulted in another irrational episode.

"What happened affected us both," he said. After a lifetime of trauma, he wished to ease his mother's burden not add to it. "I understand your concerns and will do what Society demands of a man in my privileged position."

She pushed a lock of hair from his brow and cupped his cheek. "I want you to be happy. Is that so wrong?"

Valentine sighed inwardly. What was happiness? It was winning at cards, the purchase of a new curricle, a passionate moment of ecstasy. The task was to make it last longer than an hour, to make it last a lifetime.

"Let us get back to the matter of treachery," he said in a light-hearted tone to banish the air of melancholy. "What do you want me to do with this list?"

His mother leant down, kissed his forehead as if he were a boy of five and then returned to her seat. "I want you to investigate all four ladies. Miss Kendall lives across the street, though I doubt she would disgrace her father's name by doing the unthinkable."

Deep in his gut, Valentine knew Miss Kendall was as honourable as she was courageous. Theft was beneath a woman willing to fight a duel out of principle. "What about Miss Faversham?"

"Major Faversham's daughter lives with her family on Mount Street. A nervous girl terrified of her own shadow. We are encouraging her to find her voice."

Valentine knew the short-tempered major but not his daughter. "As to the other ladies listed, I am acquainted with Mrs Madeley and Lady Cartwright." Valentine glanced at the ornate goblet in the display case. "And you think one of these ladies stole into the cabinet?"

Honora pursed her lips and nodded. "I believe someone was brazen enough to steal the ruby while attending our weekly meeting. We always sit in the day room. One of them could have snuck in here under the guise of using the pot."

Valentine refused to form a mental image of the ladies going about their ministrations, and yet in his mind's eye, he saw Miss Kendall hike up her skirts to reveal soft, milky-white thighs.

Damnation.

"And what of Mr Cassiel's visit? When did you attempt to correspond with the dead?" Valentine wondered what Miss Kendall thought of the mystic. Would a woman with her logical mind possess the ability to recognise a fraud?

"Mr Cassiel came two weeks ago. He arrived at midnight and left before dawn. Apparitional experiences are more common during the witching hour."

Most probably because tired minds were weak minds.

"And did you make contact with a so-called spirit?" Scepticism dripped from every word.

"That is not important," his mother chided. "Perhaps you should speak to Miss Kendall as she seemed to have the most success communicating with souls on a higher plane."

Suspicion flared.

Had his mother received a message from his father? Was the deceased lord keen to torment his wife from beyond the grave? Was that the reason for her reluctance to discuss her findings?

"Can *you* not tell me? It would save me troubling the lady." And yet Valentine could think of nothing he would enjoy more than probing Miss Kendall's mind.

"I cannot, as I am not party to that information. Mr Cassiel placed us all in different rooms so as not to confuse the messages."

"I see." Most people imagined strange noises when alone in the dark. When alone, there were no witnesses to challenge any eerie observations. "And who did Mr Cassiel place in this room?"

"Erm … Miss Kendall spent an hour alone in this room."

An odd pang in Valentine's stomach forced him to take a deep breath. "Then the lady had ample opportunity to make the exchange."

His mother winced as if unwilling to accept his theory. "Well, yes, but she is such an honest sort. I cannot see her risking everything when she must have a house brimming with precious gems."

Valentine held a similar view of the lady he had met only this morning. "Who suggested hiring Mr Cassiel?" It was an unusual way for anyone to spend an evening, even for a lady seeking enlightenment.

A blush touched his mother's cheeks. "Miss Kendall made the initial suggestion, but we were all in agreement."

Yet more reason to suspect his mother's alluring neighbour. Valentine sat back in the chair and took a moment to consider why he had the sudden urge to prove Aveline Kendall's innocence.

"Very well," he said. "I shall make a few enquiries."

An investigation would distract his mind from thoughts of marriage. Assisting his mother might ease the crippling guilt he invariably felt every time he failed to offer for Lady Durrant. It would also give him an opportunity to cross paths with Miss Kendall.

"You understand that my eagerness to find the culprit has nothing to do with money," his mother said. "It is not the value but the manner in which the theft occurred."

"Of course." He understood that when one had lived on a knife edge for years, trust and confidence in one's friends mattered more than expensive gems. "Where might I find Mr Cassiel? The man had opportunity, after all."

Anyone who dabbled in the occult for a living had motive, though the mystic would have needed prior knowledge of the ruby, an etching or detailed description at the least.

"You will need to ask Miss Kendall. She was responsible for hiring someone suitable."

So, the lady knew the mystic.

Were Miss Kendall and Mr Cassiel partners in crime? Surely not. Was Cassiel the gentleman who had mistreated her, the gentleman who made her doubt her love?

Annoyance turned to anger for no reason at all. "And how am I to do that without alerting Miss Kendall of our suspicions?"

Honora Valentine smiled. "You're an intelligent man. I am sure you will think of something."

"In my current unmarried status, I can hardly knock on her door." In the eyes of the gossips that would mark the lady as his mistress.

Hmm ... the idea proved tempting.

Perhaps an affair with Miss Kendall was exactly what he needed. No doubt, the liaison would be fraught with tension and trauma, much like his friendship with Lady Durrant, and might make him long for the quiet indifference that came with an arranged marriage to a wallflower.

His mother craned her neck and narrowed her gaze as she

stared at a point beyond his shoulder. "There is no need to worry about disturbing Miss Kendall." Honora's sapphire-blue eyes widened. "Here she comes now. I shall make the introductions, and you may reveal your interest in hiring Mr Cassiel."

Valentine's gaze shot to the window—and his heart shot to his mouth.

Wearing an elegant blue pelisse and matching bonnet swathed in burgundy ribbon, Miss Kendall crossed the street. There was an elegance in her bearing that instilled confidence in her ability to conquer the world if she so desired. Intelligence, grace and beauty radiated to make a captivating package. And yet the urge to weaken her position—to see a glimpse of vulnerability —took hold.

Valentine stood, straightened his waistcoat and brushed the sleeves of his coat. "I'm afraid I cannot stay. I have an appointment across town." He would not risk his mother noting his amorous interest in her neighbour.

"At least stay long enough to permit an introduction, else how will you ever speak to her publicly?"

Having forced the lady to converse on an intimate level while they brushed knees in a hackney cab, he would have found a way.

His mother rang for Jenkins and informed the butler to usher Miss Kendall into the drawing room as soon as she knocked on the door. The dull thud of the brass knocker hitting the plate echoed through the hall. The sweet timbre of her voice reached Valentine's ears. The clip of her boots on the tiled floor sent his heart thudding against his ribs.

Damnation—this was downright ridiculous.

Following Jenkins' introduction, Miss Kendall stepped into the room, wearing the knowing smile that gave a man no clue what she was thinking. Her composure faltered for a second when her gaze swept over him. Excellent.

"Honora, please forgive the intrusion." Miss Kendall stepped forward with outstretched hands, and his mother stood and gripped them affectionately. One might call the matron a hypocrite. Who embraces a suspected thief? But Honora Valentine condemned no one until proven guilty.

"An apology is unnecessary, my dear." Honora wore a beaming smile as she gestured to Valentine. "You have heard me speak about my son. Allow me to present Lord Valentine. He has recently returned from a lengthy visit overseas." The last sentence bore a hint of disapproval regarding his absence.

Valentine inclined his head, and Miss Kendall offered her hand. For the second time in a matter of hours, he captured her fingers and pressed his lips to her glove.

"Ah, my lord. I did not expect our paths to cross again quite so soon." Brown eyes, as dark and delicious as liquid chocolate, glowed with amusement.

Honora frowned as her gaze moved back and forth between them. "What? You know Miss Kendall?"

"We met briefly this morning." Even when Valentine released his grip of Miss Kendall's hand, his fingers still tingled. "In the park."

He despised lies and untruths.

On the rare occasion, they were necessary.

"In the park?" His mother looked bemused.

The corners of Miss Kendall's lips twitched. Surely the minx was not about to confess they had met on the duelling field.

"Lord Valentine kindly warned me how unsafe it is for a woman out alone at dawn." The lady offered his mother a reassuring smile. "I informed him I carried a pistol and would shoot any scoundrel who dared to overstep the mark."

His mother chuckled. "Miss Kendall is an expert shot. Hamilton taught her when she was but a girl. A man would not want to rouse her ire on a cold autumn morning."

"No." Valentine groaned inwardly. "I am aware of her skill

with a pistol. Indeed, when I noted her butler loading luggage into a hackney, I feared she may have accidentally shot a vagrant and had consequently booked passage on the next ship to sail from Dover."

Miss Kendall raised her chin. "You should not jump to conclusions, my lord, else one might mistake you for a gossip. Let me put your mind at ease. My brother has been staying with me temporarily and has now moved on."

Curiosity forced him to ignore her teasing. A host of questions burned in Valentine's mind. Had her brother lashed out in rage? Had she grown tired of the pup's foolish antics?

"Do I look like a man who thrives on tittle-tattle, Miss Kendall?"

Their gazes locked. Sparks flew. The air thrummed with excitable energy.

Valentine felt the heat of his mother's stare and decided he had already revealed too much.

"Well, I shall leave you to your business." Valentine offered a graceful bow.

"Oh, wait," his mother said. "Did you not tell me that your friend Mr Drake wishes to hire Mr Cassiel for a dinner party?" She turned to Miss Kendall. "Do you happen to have the man's card to hand, my dear?"

Miss Kendall stiffened. A look akin to panic flashed in her eyes. After a brief pause, she cleared her throat. "No. I'm afraid I do not. Mr Cassiel works on recommendation only."

Valentine observed her odd reaction. "Then you know how to contact him?"

She pursed her quivering lips. "I—I can enquire on your behalf." A faint blush stained her cheeks. "The nature of his business means that he must be cautious when selecting clients. Persecuting those with unconventional ideologies is a pastime for some."

Valentine supposed it was a plausible explanation. "Please

reassure him that my interest is genuine. That I fall into the category of the spiritually curious."

"Really? You strike me as the logical sort." Miss Kendall narrowed her gaze. "Mr Cassiel will wish for a private meeting before agreeing to provide a service for your friend."

"I understand." After the meeting, Valentine would stalk the mystic to discover more about his background. "Please tell him it is a matter of urgency."

"Mr Cassiel determines whom he sees and when, but I will explain that your quest for enlightenment is pressing."

Yes, perhaps those clients with expensive jewels on display took priority.

Honora cleared her throat and eyed them both suspiciously. "Are you certain you only met this morning?"

God's teeth. Valentine had stayed far too long. A blind fool would notice his interest in his mother's neighbour.

Miss Kendall offered Honora a reassuring smile. "Most certain. Though we seem to lock horns over the simplest things."

"That's because my son is unused to dealing with enlightened ladies." His mother chortled. "Well, you cannot stand here exchanging quips all day. Is there not somewhere you need to be, Lucius?"

"Indeed. No doubt you're eager to hear what prompted Miss Kendall's visit." No one was as eager as he.

"I am on my way into town and came merely for advice regarding a dress for this evening." Miss Kendall screwed up her dainty nose. "I'm to attend the Rockford ball and haven't the first clue what to wear."

The Rockford ball? The place was a hive for those keen to gamble away their fortunes. There would be more than a few scoundrels in attendance, more than a few eager to find some other means of entertainment once their coffers ran dry.

"May I suggest something conservative, Miss Kendall?" Lord, he sounded like a doddery matron not a virile man in his late twenties. "Rockford's gaming tables attract a rather wild crowd."

Miss Kendall offered one of her beguiling smiles. "Rest assured, my lord. I am accustomed to dealing with challenging situations. But in case you're in any doubt, know that I am never without my pocket pistol."

CHAPTER FIVE

"All I can say is thank heavens you're both alive." Portia Durrant's seductive gaze drifted over Jonathan Kendall before coming to rest on Valentine. She kept her hungry eyes trained on him as she sipped champagne. "Fighting a silly duel, and all because of me."

Valentine firmed his jaw. Neither the golden glow of the chandelier nor the soothing music of the orchestra could settle the writhing frustration in his stomach. He wanted to correct the misconception—had fought the duel merely because honour demanded he act—but he could not risk Kendall revealing the truth about his sister's involvement.

"The least said about it the better." Valentine scanned Lord Rockford's ballroom, searching for Aveline Kendall. Oddly, her brother knew nothing of her desire to attend and had scoffed at the suggestion.

So what had prompted the lady to accept the invitation?

"When it came to skill on the field, we were evenly matched," Kendall boasted whilst salivating over the exposed swell of Portia's breasts. "Is that not correct, Valentine?"

Valentine seethed at the suggestion they were somehow equal.

One derogatory remark from Mr Kendall and Valentine was liable to lash out and rid the pup of his arrogant grin. The fool should be grateful he wasn't stretched out cold and bare on a mortuary slab.

"Being an expert marksman, I would say we were far from evenly matched when it came to skill," Valentine corrected in a tone sharp enough to draw blood. "But I suppose we both employed an element of logic in a life-threatening situation."

The lie slipped easily from his lips. He did not give a damn about Kendall. But his conscience would not permit the dullard to ruin Miss Kendall's reputation. The lady was quite capable of doing that on her own.

Valentine cast daggers of disdain Kendall's way. One wrong word and he would rip the man to shreds. Being the considerate, rational one in his group of friends did not mean men shouldn't fear him. Though why he held his tongue to protect a woman he hardly knew proved baffling.

"When a man faces the prospect of death, it must make him consider what is important." Portia ran her tongue across the seam of her lips, lips stained almost as red as her fiery hair. "No one wants to live a sad, lonely existence." She turned to Valentine, placed a gloved hand on his arm and whispered, "No one wants to sleep in a cold, empty bed."

Valentine considered Lady Durrant. As a debutante, she had been vibrant and exciting. And yet it had not been enough to satisfy him. Now, he found an ugly bitterness hiding behind the lavish exterior.

He could not keep his vow.

He could not marry Portia Durrant.

But the widow was right about one thing. "When a man stares down the barrel of a pistol, it certainly makes him evaluate his life."

"Oh, and what were your findings?" Portia's arched brow gave an air of arrogance to her countenance.

He had discovered that the calm, ordered existence he craved was only possible when a man had detached from his emotions. He had discovered that he was fallible when dealing with an intelligent woman out to prove a point.

"A man may think he knows his mind," Valentine said, "but he is often mistaken." Fearing Lady Durrant might misunderstand his meaning, he added, "Yesterday's dreams and desires no longer seem so appealing today."

The comment drew his thoughts back to the lady who had taken permanent residency in a cosy corner of his mind—the lady responsible for his attendance at the ball this evening.

Impatience burned.

Would Miss Kendall make an appearance?

Excitement flared.

Would he feel the same lack of control in her presence?

"Well, *my* mind is resolute," Jonathan Kendall said, desperate for attention. He captured Portia's hand and brought it to his lips. "I am unwavering in my devotion and beg that you mark me down for every waltz."

Portia stared down her nose at Valentine. She turned away from him and bestowed a coy smile on the doe-eyed Mr Kendall. "You know I never use dance cards. You know I make it a rule only to dance with the most captivating man in the room."

Valentine had heard enough.

What the hell made him think he could marry this woman? He needed a woman he admired more for her heart and mind than her body. Despite trying to convince himself otherwise, Valentine could not overlook Portia's coquettish ways or devious manner simply to ease his mother's anxiety regarding his marital status. Moreover, he had to question his mother's judgement for encouraging the match.

Once again, Valentine scanned the room looking for Miss Kendall. Was she dancing with one of the many gentlemen clambering to offer? Would the gaiety of the evening awaken a need for pleasure? Would she grow more flirtatious after the umpteenth glass of champagne?

The notion that another gentleman might claim the privilege of holding her close caused knots in his stomach. Knots! Devil take him. He was not a boy fresh out of the schoolroom.

The lady might well be a thief, he told himself hoping to eradicate this mild infatuation.

"Then perhaps you might like to take a stroll in the garden," Mr Kendall said, his devotion to Portia Durrant evident in his slippery tone. "Once there, you might find that my gift will prove captivating enough to tempt you to dance."

"A gift? For me?" Portia laughed and batted Kendall on the arm with her closed fan.

Valentine turned away for fear of casting up his accounts on Rockford's polished oak floor. Had Portia not beckoned him over he would have avoided her company tonight. Then again, he had not planned to attend at all.

"Then let us slip away from here, Mr Kendall," Portia continued, raising her voice loud enough for Valentine to hear, but he turned his attention to the host of people filling the ballroom.

The thrum of anticipation in the air drew his gaze beyond the dancers taking their places for the quadrille, to the row of marble pillars running parallel to the far wall. Like a tiger on the hunt, he studied the revellers, hoping to glimpse the lady who was as annoying as she was arousing.

Aveline Kendall was in the room.

He knew it like he knew his own name.

Convinced he could smell the stimulating tones of her Floris perfume, Valentine's gaze flicked back and forth. Blood raced through his veins. His breath came a little quicker. Like the earth's magnetic pull, the tug in his gut drew him away from Portia Durrant, and he slipped stealthily through the crowd searching for his prey.

How odd that he knew exactly where to find her.

The first glimpse of those tantalising curls caressing Aveline Kendall's jaw caused untold havoc with his insides. She stood hidden behind a marble pillar, her slender fingers gripping the structure as she peered at the crowd. As if aware of his approach, she turned her head and their gazes locked.

The pounding of his heartbeat in his ears drowned out the lively hum of music and conversation. It was as if no one else in the room existed. Pure carnal lust shot through Valentine's body like a lightning bolt. Never had he experienced such powerful tremors.

As he drew closer, he imagined pulling her into an embrace and kissing those bewitching lips. In reality, he could do nothing but stare.

"Lord Valentine. I did not expect to find you here this evening." Miss Kendall inhaled deeply to catch her breath. "Honora seemed convinced you were otherwise engaged."

For a moment it was as if Valentine had entered an ulterior world. The calm, emotionless man had vanished, replaced by a blithering idiot who struggled to form a word. It wasn't the exposed curve of her breast encased in grey silk that captivated him—though the urge to see her naked drummed a potent rhythm in his loins. It wasn't that she looked every bit the Grecian beauty from a mythical land—regal, mysterious. It was the intelligence in her eyes, coupled with a hint of vulnerability, that held him spellbound.

"After receiving your note this morning, I thought it best to keep a watchful eye on your brother."

He could hardly tell the truth, could hardly confess that his desire to see her was too great to keep him away. She had commanded a permanent place in his mind ever since she aimed the muzzle of her pistol at his chest and threatened to fire.

"I presume you're here for the same reason," he added.

Why else was she hiding behind a pillar, spying on the guests? A blush touched her cheeks. "My brother is the bane of my existence. He will not be content until I have to drag his blood-soaked body off the duelling field."

"And now that he no longer lives in your house, you must resort to traipsing around town to keep him from challenging another poor soul to a dawn appointment."

The lady arched a brow. "One would hardly consider you a poor soul, my lord."

"No? Then how would you describe me, Miss Kendall?"

Clearly, the question unnerved her. Her chin trembled, and he could almost hear the war raging in her mind as she fought the urge to lie. She would tell the truth, of course. He knew it the moment she straightened her shoulders.

"A man as rich as Croesus cannot be considered poor. I cannot pity a man possessed of a handsome countenance and an intelligent mind. And with your rigid sense of honour, I can find nothing deficient in your moral character."

When assessing the worth of anyone's good opinion, one must examine the motive behind the compliment. Was Miss Kendall merely expressing facts, or had he heard a hint of admiration? He could not tell. Would she think of him tonight during those moments before sleep? Or was this strange obsession playing tricks with his mind?

The first strains of a waltz drifted through the room, giving him a perfect opportunity to test a theory, to gauge her body's reaction to him.

"Then as you appear to hold me in such high esteem, Miss Kendall, perhaps you might like to join me on the floor."

She drew her head back in shock. "You're asking me to dance?" Biting down on her lip, she glanced back over her shoulder, towards the door. "Forgive me, but I fear I lack the skill necessary to keep up with you."

Valentine chuckled. "Is this where I pander to your inexperience only to discover you dance with the poise of an angel?"

Miss Kendall stared into his eyes and gave a coy shrug. "My

father taught me to dance when I was a girl, though I have never graced a ballroom floor."

"Then I imagine you're an expert." Valentine offered his hand. "Allow me to apologise in advance for my careless footwork."

"You, careless? You are toying with me again, my lord, just as you were this morning."

Oh, he was most definitely toying with her, but not in the mocking sense. When in the company of Miss Kendall, he slipped into the role of an amorous flirt.

"I am asking you to dance," he said, "not elope to Gretna Green. There is no need to look nervous."

"Under present circumstances, the prospect of running away sounds rather appealing." The lady placed her gloved hand into his, and he led her onto the floor.

Valentine's fingers throbbed with the need to touch her, to run his hands over every soft curve. His mind ached to hear her stimulating conversation. Possessed of a ravaging hunger, he longed to devour every aspect of this woman until thoroughly sated.

The first twirl drew a breathless gasp from her lips. As they glided around the floor, it was clear neither had anything to fear. Their steps were smooth, in perfect unison. A wild, vibrant passion for the dance took them to another place, one where every musical note, where every sleek movement satisfied on a level deeper than anything he had experienced before.

He could not tear his gaze away from her parted lips, from the way her chest heaved as she tried to catch her breath, from the look of wonder swimming in her eyes. In his mind he was making love to her, thrusting deep, pouring everything of himself into her willing body.

For a moment he felt free. Free from the nightmares of the past. Free from the fear that a monster lurked within him, too. Free from the constraints of his position.

The dance ended all too soon, and he resisted the impulse to drop to his knees and beg for another. Instead of using the opportunity to study the workings of the lady's mind, to determine the language of her body, he had only succeeded in understanding himself a little more.

This lady had a power over him even he could not comprehend. She might be a thief, and it didn't seem to matter. She wanted nothing from him, and he liked that, too.

Valentine took a moment to glance around the ballroom. All eyes were upon them. Whispers breezed through the crowd, passing from one person to the next like crisp leaves in the wind. And while Portia Durrant and Jonathan Kendall glared at them with the devil's own eyes, the wolves were gathering. Every rakish lord of the *ton* edged closer to the dance floor, ready to sink their bared fangs into Miss Kendall's milky-white flesh.

Panic crushed the air from Valentine's chest. A primal urge took hold. The urge to mark his territory, stake his claim. For a man usually so composed, so disengaged, such disturbing emotions were new to him.

"I shall return you to your chaperone," Valentine said, hoping she had the sense to command the companionship of a matron or friend. Her brother lacked the ability to care for himself let alone a woman as alluring as Aveline Kendall.

"Chaperone? I came alone, my lord."

"Alone!" Had she lost her mind? Clearly, intelligence and wisdom were not the same things. He supposed he should take comfort from the fact most people would assume she came with her brother. As he escorted her from the floor, Valentine leant closer and whispered, "Every rogue in here will be vying for your attention."

"Surely not." She looked puzzled. "Few people know me here in town."

"Some men do not care for introductions."

Perhaps Miss Kendall was unaware of the threat.

Perhaps she thought herself capable of dealing with devils.

The lady cast him a reassuring smile. "Once I have attended to a personal matter, I have no intention of staying, no intention of ever setting foot in a ballroom again." She placed a gloved hand on his arm. "Thank you. You really are a remarkable dancer. It brings to mind my favourite Epictetus quote."

Hungry to hear anything that fell from her mouth, Valentine said, "Oh, and which one is that?"

Her eyes were still alight with excitement from their dance. "The key is to keep company only with people who uplift you, whose presence calls forth your best."

"And do I call forth your best, Miss Kendall?"

"Certainly, when it comes to duelling and dancing."

The compliment touched him.

Valentine lowered his voice to a more intimate level. "Perhaps the same might be said for other vigorous activities." His gaze dipped to the impressive swell of her breasts. Good God! With Aveline Kendall, he wanted to be the worst kind of scoundrel.

She raised a mocking brow. "If you're referring to your vice for amorous activities, I shall have to trust your word. Alas, your bedchamber is one place I shall never venture."

Had she thrown down the gauntlet?

Never had the prospect of seducing a woman into bed seemed so appealing.

"I imagine you never thought to duel or dance with me, either."

A rosy glow touched her cheeks. The lady confounded him on every level. On the one hand, she appeared confident, in command of her mind and emotions. On the other, she looked as vulnerable and naive as a debutante making her first appearance. She danced like a courtesan—with a sensual sway that promised skill in other areas, too. She blushed like a virgin—embarrassed at the mere prospect of his lewd suggestions.

"While I find your playful banter somewhat amusing," she said, focusing on a point beyond his shoulder, "my quarry is on the move."

Valentine glanced behind to see Jonathan Kendall and Portia Durrant slip out through the terrace doors. The sudden pang in his chest had nothing to do with jealousy and everything to do with the fact Miss Kendall was about to follow them out into the garden.

He should offer to accompany her.

What? And have every person in the room believe she's his mistress?

"If you have come to berate your brother, I assure you, the matter is best dealt with away from here, away from prying eyes." Devil take it. He could not even offer her a safe escort home in his carriage. Valentine scanned the room, caught sight of Lady Cartwright's garish orange turban. "Allow me to arrange for your friend Lady Cartwright to see you home."

A smile formed on Miss Kendall's luscious lips and she looked at him as if he were a puppy—adorable and laughably inexperienced. "As a spinster, I am afforded a certain degree of recklessness, my lord."

"As a young, desirable woman, you are mistaken." The words left his lips without thought.

The lady sucked in a breath. "As always your chivalrous nature informs your judgement."

Anger flared at the remark. His overzealous need for gallantry was not the problem here.

Valentine gripped her elbow. "Don't be a fool. One day you may wish to marry. If there is one thing I know about those in Society, it's that they never forget." It was why his mother had fought so hard to hide the family secret.

"You don't understand," she whispered through gritted teeth. She tugged her arm free from his grasp. "My brother took something from me, something that matters more than reputation, something I would risk my life to see returned."

The intensity in her voice shocked him. "Then, as a woman

with an abundance of intelligence, I strongly advise you apply a degree of logic."

She jerked her head back and blinked rapidly. Heat swam in her eyes, but it was not anger he saw there. "So you think me desirable and intelligent. Are you trying to seduce me, Lord Valentine?"

Valentine scoffed. Was she trying to unnerve him with her direct approach? Oh, she was playing with a master.

"Trust me, Miss Kendall," he drawled. "Were I intent on seduction, you would be in no doubt."

Miss Kendall raised a coy brow. "That is fortunate, as it saves me having to rebuke your advances."

The need to prove her wrong took hold. In three moves, Valentine could have her panting in his arms. One firm, masculine hand gripping her hip would unsettle her steely composure. But they were in a ballroom full of vultures looking for a fleshy morsel of gossip, and some were already circling.

Valentine stepped aside and made a sweeping gesture. "Your reputation is your own affair." All attempts of chivalry had fallen on deaf ears. If titles were given for determination, this lady would be a duchess. "Keep to the path," he advised. Wolves prowled the perimeter. "Stray at your peril."

She moved to place a gloved hand on his arm but drew it back. "I do not mean to appear ungrateful. Your concerns are welcome and duly noted. But I cannot let the matter rest. I am a victim of the worst kind of betrayal and cannot leave here without answers."

Water welled in the corners of her eyes. The sight tugged at an unfamiliar place deep in his gut. The urge to force his fist down Jonathan Kendall's throat surfaced.

"Would you care for a handkerchief?"

Miss Kendall shook her head and inhaled deeply to gather her composure. "I refuse to shed another tear over that fool."

"Your brother has lost sight of what is important," he agreed.

"Only the worst kind of man steals from his family."

The comment did more than pique Valentine's interest.

Did Jonathan Kendall have prior knowledge of the unusual ruby his father had sold? Had he stolen into his neighbour's house in the dead of night and swopped the precious stone for a paste replica? If one could steal from one's family, then why not from a stranger?

"What must you think of me?" she suddenly said, giving him another rare glimpse of her vulnerability. "I make my brother sound like a common criminal."

"All families have their struggles," he managed to say as she backed away. He knew first-hand what it was like to love a devil. "All families have their secrets."

"Yes, I believe they do." She cocked her head to one side. "May I say that your mother's appraisal of your character is wholly accurate? You are every bit a gentleman. Thank you again for the dance. Good evening, my lord." With that, she moved past him and headed for the terrace doors.

If only she knew of the raging desire lingering beneath his cool facade. Had he not already warned her? He was a gentleman in every regard but one. Valentine sighed inwardly. While he had partaken in liaisons with women, he was far from a licentious rake. And yet with Miss Kendall, he wanted to be both the best and the worst version of himself. He wanted to comfort and protect, ravage her mind, pump so hard into her willing body he no longer cared about being a dutiful son.

A hard lump formed in Valentine's throat as he watched Aveline Kendall slip out into the night. There was but one option open to a chivalrous gentleman.

Destiny forced him to follow.

CHAPTER SIX

Thank heavens there were only three steps leading down from Lord Rockford's terrace to the manicured lawn. Ava's pulse raced so fast she feared her trembling legs might buckle under the strain. The nervous energy thrumming through her veins had nothing to do with the thought of confronting Jonathan, or of meeting the dashing widow who possessed the innate ability to capture every man's interest.

No. Her attraction to Lord Valentine was the cause.

The man had a magnetic charm, could seduce a woman with a single glance. The powerful pull drew her dangerously close no matter how hard she tried to keep her distance. She should have refused his offer to dance, but her hand had slipped into his large palm long before logic intervened.

Oh, but the waltz had been spectacular.

He danced with panther-like grace—sleek, confident, every solid muscle working in unison. There were moments where she glimpsed a voracious hunger in his eyes, moments when the heat radiating from those blue gems ignited a fire deep in her chest. Their fluid movements on the floor conveyed a natural ease that one hardly ever experienced with a stranger.

And yet she no longer regarded Lucius Valentine as a stranger. Despite knowing him for less than a day, she regarded him as a friend. He seemed to be of a similar mindset. Why else would he show concern for her reputation? Why else would he seek her out in a ballroom full of desirable ladies?

A playful squeal to Ava's left drew her attention beyond the path to the tall topiary shrouded in darkness. There was merriment to be had amid the shrubbery if one was so inclined. Lord Valentine's warning to stay on the path was not unfounded. And while he no doubt thought her reckless—the exact opposite of what he desired in a woman—and far too stubborn for her own good, she would heed his advice.

Besides, from what she had witnessed, the rakish gentlemen congregated in the card room and were not apt to go hunting for virgins to ruin.

Ava scanned the garden looking for Jonathan. Rows of lanterns and braziers illuminated the walkways, and she spotted him strolling arm in arm with the fiery-haired temptress. It had to be the widow. Since Ava's arrival, Jonathan had followed the woman around like a pet dog in desperate need of stroking.

The couple stopped near an ornamental stone temple with Corinthian pillars and a dome roof. From this distance, it was impossible to identify the statue taking pride of place in the centre, but Jonathan had led the widow behind the sculpture and Ava knew it was time to act.

Taking a deep breath, she marched towards them. Every purposeful stride roused her ire. The sharp November chill in the air nipped at her bare forearms. A restless wind whipped at her hair, forcing her to walk in the middle of the path for the flames flickered wildly in the open braziers.

Ava received a few strange looks as she pushed past the ambling couples. A woman walking alone in the garden must be a harlot or a dimwit. One lady made a snide remark about hurrying to a lovers' tryst. Had Ava not been in a hurry, she might have corrected the judgemental old hen.

As Ava drew closer to the Grecian inspired temple, she caught sight of Jonathan clutching the widow's hand. He pressed something shiny into her gloved palm.

Lady Durrant gasped. She gripped the sparkling object between her fingers and stared in awe. "Oh, it is more beautiful than I imagined." A pleasurable sigh left the widow's lips. "More beautiful than you described. Your father was a talented craftsman."

Ha! Would Lady Durrant feel differently about its quality if she knew Ava's mother was the creative genius behind the designs?

"You have slender fingers," her Judas brother said. "The ring will be a perfect fit."

Ava stopped breathing. A sharp pain pierced her chest. Nausea swept through her in a sickening wave to weaken her defences.

How could he?

How could he give away her most prized possession?

While her heart ached with disappointment, and her thoughts were lost in a hazy cloud of confusion, Ava crept closer. Lady Durrant was so engrossed in the ring she failed to notice Ava's approach.

"And you have more jewellery as beautiful as this?" Lady Durrant asked.

"Indeed."

"Thief." The word tumbled from Ava's lips in a croaked whisper. "Thief," she repeated with more vehemence.

Jonathan swung around. The lines of irritation etched into his brow faded. "Ava?" Shock rendered him frozen. He cleared his throat. "What the hell are you doing out here?"

Panic flashed in his grey eyes. Was he worried she would reveal the truth about the duel? Was he worried she would make him look foolish in front of his beloved Lady Durrant?

"I might ask you the same question," Ava said, stepping behind the large marble statue of a bathing goddess. "Are you so keen to impress *this* lady that you would steal from your family?"

Lady Durrant smirked. "Oh dear. Someone is a trifle upset."

"A trifle upset?" Ava's curt tone rang with the contempt born from her brother's betrayal. It carried the disdain she held for women who used their feminine wiles to manipulate men. "Clearly I have failed to convey the true depth of my feelings. Allow me to correct any misconception for I am outraged."

Distraught.

Heartbroken.

Jonathan's eyes bulged in their sockets. He would never forgive her for embarrassing him, for ruining his chances of marrying such a distinguished lady.

"You're overreacting," Jonathan whispered through gritted teeth. He turned to the widow whose hair carried the same fiery glow as the flames dancing in the braziers. "Lady Durrant, allow me to present my sister Miss Kendall. I'm afraid she possesses the annoying habit of prying into other people's affairs."

Lady Durrant's snort spoke of both amusement and arrogance. Her green gaze slithered over Ava's outdated dress, and a smile touched her thin lips. Jonathan managed a weak smile, too.

"Well, Miss Kendall," Lady Durrant began, "I must praise your skill on the dance floor. One might say that fortune favours you this evening. Lord Valentine is an accomplished dancer though he rarely takes to the floor."

"Then I am pleased I did not disappoint him." Ava glanced at the lady's hand clenched as tight as a clam. She would have her mother's ring back even if she had to prise open the harlot's fingers.

Lady Durrant raised her powdered chin. "Either way, Lord Valentine achieved the desired result. The dance will quash any rumours regarding the disagreement with your brother."

Was that the reason the lord sought her out?

Was she a fool to believe he might enjoy her company?

"And the dance gave *me* an opportunity to test a theory." Ava paused. The last thing she wanted was to hurt Jonathan, but he needed to hear the truth. "You're toying with my brother to make Lord Valentine jealous. I saw the way you looked at him while we danced."

Lady Durrant laughed. "Oh, you really are a prim little darling." Her amusement faded, and she shot Ava a look cold enough to freeze the Thames. "Keep to your books and leave the ballroom etiquette to those with more experience."

Ava bit her tongue. She wanted to say that she would rather be wise than wanton, but only the weak and insecure needed to have the last say.

Ava gripped the sleeve of Jonathan's evening coat. "I have no control or influence over what you do, but I will have my ring returned else there will be hell to pay."

"*Your* ring?" Two deep furrows appeared between Jonathan's brows. "What the hell are you rambling on about now?" He shrugged out of her grasp. "I do not know which one of your *enlightened* friends brought you here this evening, but I suggest they take you home before you have a fit of the vapours."

The stress and tension of the day's events brought a bulging lump to her throat. Frustration sat like a dead weight in her chest. Enlightened ladies rose above petty squabbles, and so she sucked in a breath and gathered her composure.

"You gave Lady Durrant a ring," she said calmly. "I wish to see it."

There was a moment's hesitation before her brother answered. "Why? It is of no consequence to you."

Of no consequence?

Ava refused to leave before glimpsing the jewel. She stepped forward.

Jonathan thrust out his arm to prevent her from moving closer to the coquette who seemingly took pleasure from their petty trials. When Ava failed to retreat, her brother wrapped his fingers around her upper arm.

"Stopping meddling in things that do not concern you." Jonathan firmed his grip. "Go home where—"

"Remove your hand from the lady's arm, Kendall, unless you wish to meet at dawn tomorrow." A tall, athletic figure moved in the shadows.

Ava recognised the relaxed sophistication of Lord Valentine's voice. He appeared from behind a Corinthian column. While his countenance spoke of calm self-assurance, the determined look in his eyes said he was not a man one provoked.

"This is a family matter, Valentine."

"Indeed." The viscount glared at Jonathan. Raw masculine energy emanated from every fibre of his being. "And Miss Kendall is my mother's closest friend. Consequently, I will not permit her mistreatment."

Ava swallowed. A tiny part of her wanted to inform Lord Valentine that she did not need his help. A larger part wanted to wrap her arms around his neck and rest her weary head on his broad shoulder.

"I want to see the ring, that is all," Ava said, finding her voice. "The ring Lady Durrant holds securely in her palm."

Lady Durrant scoffed. "I don't have time for these childish games."

"Then show Miss Kendall the ring," Lord Valentine countered. "She would not ask without good reason."

Jonathan shook his head. "I'll not pander to her irrational demands."

A soft sigh breezed from the viscount's lips. "A logical man might question who is the irrational one here. The one asking a simple question or the one being deliberately unreasonable."

A warm glow filled Ava's chest. Not since her parents' deaths had anyone jumped to her defence. She looked up into Lord

Valentine's bright blue eyes, a little in awe of his strength and tenacity.

"For all the saints," Lady Durrant said, thrusting out her open hand to reveal the sparkling gold band sitting in her palm. "By all means look, but it belongs to me now."

Ava stared at the sapphire stone edged with diamonds. Disappointment crept like a vine around her heart to strangle any hope. While it was not the ring given by her mother as a birthday gift, it was a family heirloom left to Jonathan to present to his bride.

Tears choked the back of Ava's throat. "You have proposed marriage to Lady Durrant, and she has accepted?"

Ava would rather he married a market hawker as long as she had a good heart. She glanced at Lord Valentine to gauge his reaction to the shocking question though he appeared indifferent.

"Marriage?" Lady Durrant mocked. She gave a hapless shrug as her arrogant gaze swept over Lord Valentine. "The possibility is open to discussion, but no, I have purchased this ring from your brother."

Jonathan groaned as he dragged his hand down his face and rubbed his jaw.

"You have sold Mother's most prized possession?" As hard as it was to tear her attention away from Lord Valentine, Ava focused on her brother. "Does Lady Durrant speak the truth? Has she purchased Mother's ring?"

A tense silence ensued.

"It belongs to me now," Lady Durrant interjected, pushing the ring down into the valley between her breasts. "I shall leave you to argue about the details." She craned her elegant neck. "Do I hear the strains of a waltz? Come, Valentine. We should return to the ballroom and leave the Kendalls to their business. If we're quick, you may accompany me in this dance."

Ava held her breath while she waited for Lord Valentine's answer. When she dared to raise her eyes in his direction, she found him watching her intently.

"I am sure there are other men willing to lead you about the floor," Lord Valentine replied though he kept his gaze trained on Ava. "Nevertheless, I shall leave if Miss Kendall wishes it so."

Ava's pulse raced.

She wanted an end to her troubles, wanted one more dance with the gallant lord who made her head spin and heart flutter. She wanted him at her side to offer support and comfort. But it was best to put an end to this hopeless infatuation.

"Thank you, my lord, but this is a private matter. You came for an evening's entertainment not to be embroiled in my family's affairs."

The viscount's penetrating blue eyes flashed with disappointment. "As you wish." He inclined his head and then turned to Jonathan. "The warning stands. Lay a hand on your sister, and we *will* meet at dawn." With that, he offered Lady Durrant his arm and the couple withdrew to the path leading back to the house.

Every crunch of the gravel stones beneath the lord's evening shoes only served to enhance the pain of regret. But there were more important things to deal with than a fleeting attraction.

She stared at Jonathan. "How could you?" Frustration returned with a vengeance. "You know what that ring meant to Mother. You know she wanted you to present it to your bride."

"It is too late for sentiment." Jonathan pushed a hand through his mop of dark hair. "I needed the money. Portia offered almost double what I might expect elsewhere."

Ava resisted the urge to punch him in the arm. "Elsewhere? You mean the pawnbrokers." Was that where he had taken the other items he had stolen from the house? Or was Lady Durrant starting a collection of Kendall trinkets? "Do you need money to pay another gambling debt?"

She peered deeply into his empty grey eyes, searching for a redeeming quality, searching for a faint flicker that reminded her of her father. How could a son fail to inherit at least one of his father's traits, be it intellect, honour or an irresistible charm?

The thought roused the image of Lord Valentine. Ava glanced out across the manicured lawn to see him ascending the stone steps. Lady Durrant clung to his arm as if to let go would see her swept out to sea by a powerful wave.

"I owe money to the Maguires," Jonathan suddenly confessed, his tone as solemn as his expression.

"The Maguires?" Ava had overheard Lord Sterling mention the name numerous times while he lounged in her drawing room drinking port with her brother. "Not those rogues who run the blood-sport arena?"

Lord, it was said the brothers were as ruthless as the beasts they trained to fight.

"The odds were in my favour. Can you believe a monkey beat a Bull and Terrier?"

The Maguires knew how to lure simple-minded men into their gambling trap. No doubt the dog snarled on cue while slobber dripped from its sharp fangs. The monkey knew to run and hide from the terrifying sight.

"How much?" Ava said bluntly. "How much did you lose?"

"What? Only a thousand."

"Only a thousand!" Ava almost choked. It was more than most people earned in a lifetime. Thank heavens her parents' will stipulated that he could only draw the interest from his inheritance and could not touch the capital until his twenty-fifth birthday. "Even so, your allowance covers such a ludicrous expense."

Ava predicted Jonathan's reply before he opened his mouth. This was not his only debt.

Jonathan threw his hands in the air. "Not when the Maguires charge a daily interest of ten per cent," he complained, forgetting the men were crooks and that he was a victim of his own stupidity.

While anger still thrummed through her body, her soft heart ached with the need to offer comfort. But then another thought struck her.

"What about Father's watch, his seal ring, the diamond and onyx signet, the sapphire tiepin?" Panic fluttered in her throat.

Jonathan bowed his head. "They are no longer in my possession."

A solitary tear slipped down her cheek. "You fool."

The soft words roused his ire.

"Oh, you may preach from your pedestal, but a man must behave like other gentlemen if he is to make his way in Society."

Ava clasped a hand to her heart. From his Bohemian upbringing, had Jonathan not witnessed the value of individuality? Had he not witnessed the power of true love and learnt that money and reputation were no replacement?

She stared at the brother she hardly knew.

"I want the names of those who purchased Father's belongings," Ava said, her raging emotions absent from her tone. She had a focus now. Something to keep her busy, to make her life appear fulfilling.

"A gentleman cannot sell his worldly goods privately," Jonathan retorted. He cupped her elbow and drew her farther away from the gravel path. "What would people think?"

"That did not stop you selling Mother's ring to Lady Durrant."

"Portia understands me. She understands my dilemma."

"Of course she does."

No doubt Jonathan's troubles provided endless hours of entertainment.

"I trust her."

Good Lord, he was a hopeless cause.

"She is in love with Lord Valentine," Ava said, and who could blame her? "Anyone can see that."

Jonathan shrugged. "And when she realises he has no intention of offering for her, she will turn her attention to me."

Talk of Lord Valentine sent Ava's stomach pitching and rolling.

"You cannot be certain of anything," Ava said. "Lord Valentine is a private man who guards his emotions." He behaved with dignity and decorum—except when teasing her about his after-dark activities. "There is no telling what he may be thinking."

"Valentine is bored in her company. Despite every attempt, Portia cannot make him jealous."

Ava frowned. So Jonathan was willing to enter into a relationship with a woman who loved another? Did he not have an ounce of self-respect?

"And yet Lord Valentine escorted her back to the ballroom." Indeed, while Ava was worried about Jonathan owing money to the worst kind of scoundrels—and her heart and head were abound with hopeless notions of romance—Lord Valentine was dancing. "No doubt they are waltzing about the floor without a care in the world."

"He left with Portia because you told him to go," Jonathan reminded her. "When she realises Valentine doesn't want her, I shall be waiting in the wings."

But Lord Valentine had to marry someone. A man of his integrity did not break a vow. Images of him courting a host of beauties played havoc with her mind. Oh, the least time spent thinking about Valentine the better.

"Then if you did not sell our father's jewellery privately," she snapped, returning to the reason they stood shivering in the garden, "whom did you sell it to?"

A sigh left her brother's lips. It should have been the sound of shame, but it sang of frustration. "To various pawnbrokers."

"Pawnbrokers!" Hell's bells, she had no hope of recovering the items now. "Which ones?"

"I was in my cups and cannot remember."

"You cannot remember?" In an effort to remain calm, she imagined the moment Jonathan kicked open the door of Mr Fairfax's room, punched the deceitful rogue in the stomach and gathered Ava into his arms. "Then I shall have to search each one."

A heavy silence loomed.

In the distance, the orchestra played a Baroque tune, Vivaldi perhaps. Laughter drifted out into the garden. Gaiety permeated the air.

"Take me home," Ava said. An air of melancholy had settled in her chest. While she would traipse from one pawnbroker to the next searching for her family's treasured possessions, she had no hope of persuading Lady Durrant to return her mother's ring. "I trust you are staying with Lord Sterling for the time being."

"You gave me little choice in the matter."

"It is not my fault, Jonathan. You have given me every reason not to trust you." Ava suddenly recalled the reason for visiting the Rockford ball. "You took the pink diamond ring from my box. No doubt you were too intoxicated to remember that, too. No doubt it graces another lady's finger. A lucky find in some tatty old pawn-broker's shop."

Jonathan's jaw slackened as his brows drew downward. "Ava, I swear I have not touched your things. I know what that ring means to you. It is probably caught up in a string of pearls."

Oh, he was full of lies, brimming with excuses.

But she wouldn't rest until the ring was back in her possession.

"So you did not enter my room this morning?"

He hesitated. "I may have. I thought to reclaim my pistols."

"I suppose you know nothing about Mother's vanity box or Rosewood writing slope. Both have miraculously vanished, too."

"Vanished?" All colour drained from Jonathan's face. "Are you sure you have not misplaced them?" The anxious look marring his features sent her nerves scattering. "Perhaps Mrs Stagg moved them."

"Are you saying you did not take them to pay your debts?"

"Of course not. My debts are my own affair." He bowed his head, tapped his lips for a moment while deep in thought. "Have your neighbours reported any suspicious activity? What of your friend Lady Valentine? She does live opposite."

This inquisitive line of questioning suggested Jonathan was innocent of the thefts from her house. But good liars knew how to avoid suspicion. Ava was wasting time trying to get any sense from her brother. As always, she would deal with the matter herself, carry out her own investigation.

"Well?" he pressed. "Has Lady Valentine mentioned anything untoward?"

"No. Honora would have told me had she seen unsavoury characters loitering about the place." Perhaps the Maguires had stolen into Ava's house merely to frighten her brother. Perhaps she had been a little hasty in packing Jonathan's belongings.

Jonathan glanced back over his shoulder as if expecting to find a hideous figure lurking in the shrubbery. "Then I shall escort you home. And I insist on remaining with you in Park Street this evening."

Ava snorted inwardly. So that was his game.

"You may escort me home. You may even check the house if you must. But I would rather be alone tonight."

That was a lie. Who wanted to lie in a cold bed with nothing to do but replay the night's events?

Jonathan nodded. He escorted her along the gravel path, back to the house. Ava was so absorbed in plotting where she might begin her search for her father's treasured possessions, she failed to notice Lord Valentine standing on the terrace until she reached the top step.

Ava's heart pounded as their eyes met. Lord Valentine stood alone, his back pressed against the wall as he smoked a cheroot. From his elevated position, he had a perfect view of the garden.

Had he been watching her?

Had the gallant gentleman been waiting for an opportunity to come to her aid?

Lord Valentine blew a stream of smoke into the cold night air. There was something masterful about him, something wickedly dangerous lingering just beneath his smooth countenance.

"Good night, Miss Kendall," he said as she moved to walk past.

"Good night, my lord," Ava replied, though she knew her night would be a restless one. One fraught with fantasies. One fraught with dreams of a dashing lord being anything but chivalrous.

CHAPTER SEVEN

For two days, Valentine stalked Miss Kendall along the streets of London while she visited every pawnbroker between Mayfair and Covent Garden. There had been no time to slip inside shops and enquire as to the nature of her visit.

What misfortune had driven her to seek temporary relief?

Was she desperate to raise funds to cover her brother's mounting debts? From what Valentine had heard, there were more than a few.

Regardless of the reason, the task caused the lady distress. She wore her sadness like an oversized coat. It swallowed her vivacious charm. The weight drowned the elegance of her bearing, leaving her shoulders slumped, her clumsy gait lacking the grace that conveyed confidence and good breeding.

Twice, she stepped out into the road as if oblivious to the oncoming traffic.

Twice, Valentine had come crashing to a halt, only to clasp his hand to his heart in relief to find her unhurt.

Just when he decided to stop hiding in the shadows and offer assistance, he noticed he was not the only gentleman interested in monitoring the lady's movements. Dressed in a fine demi-surtout with a fitted waist, and gripping a silver-topped walking cane as if ready to bat away beggars, the fellow was not a pickpocket from the rookeries. Still, he was eager to hide his identity for he had raised the collar of his coat to obscure the line of his jaw, and had pulled the brim of his top hat down over his brow.

Miss Kendall stopped abruptly in the middle of the footpath. She withdrew a note from her reticule and read it before glancing up at the Grafton Street sign as if she had lost her way. Her pursuer stopped, too, feigned interest in a ream of fabric in the draper's window though he continually looked over his shoulder, waiting for Miss Kendall to move.

Valentine considered grabbing the man by his fancy lapels and throttling him until he explained precisely what business he had with the lady. Instead, he merely studied the scene, knowing he would learn more from his observations than he would from a lying scoundrel's mouth.

Thrusting the paper back into her reticule, Miss Kendall continued her journey along Grafton Street—and the gentleman continued his pursuit. Soon, the lady would arrive at the Seven Dials, and then all manner of criminals would mark her as prey.

Panic flared.

Daylight was failing. Fog descended. Both brought unease. Shopkeepers lit their window lamps, the soft yellow lights like a scattering of stars in a cloudy sky. The grey mist crept through the street, rising, thickening, swallowing everything in its wake. All movements proved dangerous. Soon it would be impossible to tell where the pavement ended and the road began.

Fear gripped him.

The gentleman had crossed the busy street, perhaps to avoid detection, perhaps because he thought to corner the lady once she reached the crossroads. Valentine was so desperate to keep his gaze trained on the suspicious scoundrel, he lost sight of Miss Kendall. He squinted, searching for the burgundy silk that decorated the lady's bonnet.

He entered the bookshop, scanned the numerous patrons struggling to peruse the books beneath the dim candlelight, ignored the offer of assistance. There was little point entering the tobacconist. He raced to the next shop, peered through the dirty glass panes in the bow window and spotted the lady standing before the wooden counter.

Valentine had no choice but to enter.

The overhead bell tinkled as he pushed at the swollen door. The shop was dark and dingy, made more welcoming by the array of silver items sparkling in a display case behind the counter. The place smelt musty, damp, of old leather, polish and the clawing scent of desperation.

The pawnbroker raised his chin by way of a greeting, but Miss Kendall did not turn around.

"As I've explained, miss, I've nothing of that description. Can't say there's much call for seal rings," the lean man with crooked spectacles said, practically ignoring the lady to focus his attention on Valentine. "Good day to you, miss. I've other people to serve."

"But you have not even looked at the design." Miss Kendall pushed a piece of paper across the battered counter and stabbed her finger at a pencil sketch. "The ring is unique. Hexagonal in shape. The inscription around the head is in Greek."

"Greek, you say? Then the answer is no." He shook his head. "The fancies prefer Latin."

"Will you not at least do me the respect of examining your books?"

With his grubby hand—the middle finger sporting an expensive gold sovereign ring—the man grabbed the cover of the old tome situated on the counter and slammed it shut. Dust particles flew from the board. The broker coughed. "There's nothing I can do without the receipts. Come back with the papers."

Miss Kendall huffed. "I have already told you. I don't have the papers."

"And I can't return an item without them."

Miss Kendall sighed. "Trust me. I doubt my brother even remembers where they are."

"Then it will be nigh on impossible for him to claim an item without proof of ownership."

In a sudden and uncharacteristic fit of temper, Miss Kendall thumped her fist on the counter. "Why won't you help me?"

Feeling her obvious distress, Valentine cleared his throat and stepped forward. "Perhaps I may be of some assistance, Miss Kendall."

She swung around at the sound of his voice. Her watery eyes widened with shock. "Lord Valentine! What are you doing here? You seem to make a habit of creeping up on me when I least expect it."

"Fate often delivers the unexpected," he replied, reciting his friend Dariell's words. Valentine cast the broker a hard stare. "And it seems I have arrived just in time."

Miss Kendall inhaled deeply. "Even a gentleman with your grace and charm will have no luck persuading this man of my cause. Apparently, there is nothing he can do without the original chitty."

The urge to offer her physical comfort took hold, but all he could do was place a gentle hand on her back. Even the smallest contact sent heat shooting up his arm. Miss Kendall shuddered beneath his touch.

"Allow me to try." Valentine's hand slipped from her back before his whole body went up in a blazing inferno. He turned to the fellow who looked like he'd not felt a splash of water on his face for weeks. "The journey across town can be treacherous for a lady alone." Valentine removed his calling card from the inside pocket of his coat and placed it on top of the tome. "Do me the respect of checking your ledger. I would not wish her to have another wasted journey."

Valentine raised an arrogant brow and glared at the pawn-broker while he waited for a reply.

The man peered at the card over the rim of his lopsided spectacles. "Give me a moment, milord."

Miss Kendall's eyes widened. "So, just like that, you decide to be helpful. What part of his lordship's argument did you find most persuasive? The fact he is a gentleman or the fact he is a member of the aristocracy?"

This time, Valentine placed his hand on her arm. "I suggest we give the fellow a chance to observe the entries before he changes his mind."

Miss Kendall looked at his hand, then at the broker who had opened his tome. She nodded, turned away and walked over to the window. Wrapping her arms tightly across her chest, she stared out at the fog-drenched street. With her slender fingers encased in blue kid-gloves, she rubbed her upper arms in comforting strokes while she waited.

The cold chill of loneliness filled the room.

It breezed over the random curiosities strewn about the floor —portraits of people long since departed, a viola with a broken string, a leather valise embossed with someone's faded initials.

The fresh crispness in the air came to settle around Valentine's shoulders, a reminder that a part of him was numb inside, was just as cold and lonely. Disappointment cut deep when delivered by the hands of a loved one.

Needing to draw comfort, too, Valentine imagined coming up behind her, pulling her close to his chest, letting his mouth come to rest on the perfect skin at her throat. She would turn to him, twine her arms around his neck, kiss him so deeply the ice around his heart would melt and trickle away.

That was the way with fantasies. They were perfect. Devoid of pain and problems.

"Here it is." The broker's voice disturbed Valentine's reverie.

"I took the ring, along with two silk waistcoats, a silver letter opener and snuff box."

Miss Kendall gasped as she hurried to the counter. She gripped the edge of the wooden surface. "Did my brother deposit anything else? A watch? A diamond and onyx signet ring?" She paused and gulped. "A rare pink diamond ring?"

The broker shook his head. "That's the lot. Come back with the papers and—"

"Can I see the ring?" Hope swam in Miss Kendall's bewitching brown eyes.

Valentine would have offered her the world rather than see the look of longing fade.

"Wait a moment." The broker scurried off through the door to the left of the counter. Keys rattled. Another door opened, the loud clunk upon closing indicating a heavier metal door.

A tense silence hung in the air while they awaited the broker's return.

"You're certain it is the ring I mentioned?" Miss Kendall's hungry eyes observed the broker keenly as he returned to the room. She stared at the red velvet pouch in his hand. "I shall know the moment I see the markings."

"Don't ask me what it says." The broker handed Miss Kendall the pouch.

Trembling fingers made it impossible for her to remove her gloves.

"Permit me." Valentine took the pouch, tugged at the strings and removed the shiny gold ring with Greek engraving around the hexagonal head.

Miss Kendall froze for a few seconds. "That is my father's ring," she said, gazing in awe. "I wish to repay any money advanced to my brother and reclaim this item."

The broker offered a weak smile. "I paid the gent twenty-three pounds and four shillings for all items deposited, but without the receipt, you'll need to pay the purchase price."

Miss Kendall frowned. "I have no need for silk waistcoats. How much do you require for the ring?"

"Forty pounds for all items deposited," the broker said in a monotone voice.

"Forty pounds!" Muttering to herself, she reached into her reticule while Valentine placed the ring back inside the velvet pouch. "I have thirty." Miss Kendall slapped the folded notes onto the counter. "And you may keep the apparel and silverware."

The broker flashed his crooked teeth. "I'll need forty for the trouble."

Valentine reached into his pocket, withdrew a note and placed it on top of Miss Kendall's pile. "That makes fifty. I think you'll agree it is more than ample for a gold ring engraved in Greek as opposed to Latin."

With an eager hand, the broker snatched the notes across the counter and checked their value. "A pleasure doing business," he said, clutching his bounty and scurrying off to his back room.

Left alone in the musty old shop, Valentine offered Miss Kendall the ring. "Allow me to escort you back to Park Street, Miss Kendall." His thoughts flew to the scoundrel waiting out on the street. "As a man preoccupied with chivalry, I must insist."

Miss Kendall smiled. "You may escort me home, my lord, as I must repay your twenty pounds as a matter of urgency. Hold on to the ring until I am back on familiar territory."

"Please, Miss Kendall, do not insult me by offering to repay a gift." Valentine placed the pouch into the inside pocket of his coat. "And I shall return the ring once I have seen you safely to your door."

"No!" With a hint of panic, she shook her head. "Keep it safe for me. Just for a little while. I cannot risk losing it again."

The mere fact she trusted him with a personal treasure touched him in a way nothing else ever had. Pride, coupled with a desire to live up to her expectations, settled in his chest. Did her request have something to do with her brother's sleight of hand?

"Your father's ring will be perfectly safe in my care."

She smiled again, although the heavy sense of loneliness still lingered behind the softness of her features.

"I hope you remember where your coachman parked your carriage," she said, glancing at the window where passing shadows slipped like spectres through the blanket of fog. "Though you don't have a hope of finding it in this weather."

Valentine hesitated. "I am without my carriage today. I walked across town."

Would she draw the wrong conclusion? A man of his breeding ventured to these parts merely to partake in scandalous activities —be it gambling, drinking or whoring. And she had not asked why he needed the services of a pawnbroker.

"Come," he said before her mind processed the information. "It will take the best part of an hour to walk home, and the streets are treacherous." On a foggy night, carts and carriages were known to mount the pavement.

The shop bell tinkled, and another patron entered—a thin woman with a pale, weary face. A small child with sad eyes clutched her hand. The broker hurried from his hideaway to examine the treasure she had placed on the counter—a gold cross and chain.

Miss Kendall sidled next to Valentine. She touched his arm, and his world tilted. "Please, my lord, I would offer her assistance had I not emptied my reticule."

Valentine met her gaze. It occurred to him that this spell she had cast over him meant he would do anything she asked. And so, he retrieved another note from his pocket, strode up to the woman, took her hand and thrust it into her palm.

The woman looked up at him with the same air of wonder, the same look of admiration currently swimming in Miss Kendall's eyes.

Valentine accepted her heartfelt thanks and then moved to open the door for Miss Kendall.

As they left the shop, Miss Kendall thrust her hand into the crook of his arm. She held on to him with the familiarity of a lover, not a woman who had come close to shooting him mere days ago. Of course, the intimate gesture had more to do with the hazardous conditions outside than with any romantic feelings.

Navigating the fog-drenched streets proved more dangerous than expected. One wrong turn might be disastrous. Dark shadows appeared through the mist, barging into them, banging shoulders. Miss Kendall hugged Valentine's arm with both hands and pressed her body close. The damp air carried the acrid smell of sulphur that choked the throat. When she dropped her hand to cough, Valentine slid his arm around her waist and held her in a vice-like grip.

Shouts, cries and the anxious neighs of horses echoed all around them.

A terrified gasp left Miss Kendall's lips.

"What's wrong?" Valentine's heart skipped a beat.

"I heard someone call my name." She peered into the blanket of nothingness.

"Who?" His thoughts turned to the mysterious stalker. "A voice you recognise?"

"I-I'm not sure. A voice from the past."

Valentine felt her body shudder as he kept her in a secure hold. A large shadow appeared through the grey cloud to block their path. The figure did not dart out of the way in shock but forced them to come to an abrupt halt. In the seconds it took to recognise the upturned collar of the surtout, the man pulled a blade from his walking cane, dropped the shaft and attempted to cut the drawstrings on Miss Kendall's reticule.

"What? No! Valentine!"

Valentine wasted no time coming to the lady's aid. He let go of Miss Kendall, grabbed the scoundrel's arm and twisted until the blade tumbled to the ground. He kneed the rogue in the groin and, with a punch worthy of his friend Devlin Drake, smacked his fist into the man's cheek.

Miss Kendall shrieked.

A vitriolic curse burst from the blackguard's mouth as he stumbled back.

Valentine kicked him to the ground, grabbed Miss Kendall's hand and took flight.

"Ow!" someone shouted as Valentine barged into a crowd of people as he hurried past them. "Mind where you're going."

"Valentine, wait." Miss Kendall puffed and panted. "I cannot keep up with you."

"Just hold on to me." It took one skilled swipe with a blade to kill a man or woman for that matter. Fear held him in a stranglehold. But he kept moving. The blackguard might be three steps behind, and Valentine would not know. "Whatever you do, don't let go."

The hazy glow of a gaslight drew his attention. The familiar sign of Collier's bookshop sent a wave of relief washing over him. At least they were heading in the right direction and were but one street from Golden Square.

"Valentine, wait," Miss Kendall repeated, once again addressing him as an intimate friend. "Can we not stop for a moment?"

From his recollection, they were near the mews on Rupert Street. Perhaps it would serve them well to hide for a time. The likelihood that the rogue was still stalking after them was slim. Still, he would not take a chance. He slowed to a walking pace and looked for where the pavement met the cobblestones.

He drew Miss Kendall through the entrance to the mews and pulled her behind the stone archway. It was dark, the faint glow of lanterns hanging from the stalls beyond, and the chink of a hammer hitting metal confirmed they were not entirely alone.

"Thieves are bountiful on a night such as this," he whispered as he pressed her back against the stone column and shrouded her with his body. "If you must rest, then let it be away from the main thoroughfare."

The tops of their boots touched. They were so close the smell of her perfume—iris, rose and jasmine—filled his head. The heat from her body warmed every fibre of his being.

"The rogue tried to cut the drawstring on my reticule," she said between laboured breaths.

"Perhaps he followed you to the pawnbroker. Knew you would have something valuable."

"No doubt." Miss Kendall looked up into his eyes. "I'm glad you were there. The fog descended so quickly." The words were tinged with mild panic. "I don't know what I would have done had—"

"Hush." Valentine placed his finger on her lips. "There is no need to worry." Their bodies were so close he felt the rapid rise and fall of her chest. "You're safe now. That is all that matters."

Slowly, he drew his finger down over her lips to her chin, and then cupped her cheek in a gesture of reassurance—well, that was what he told himself.

"Fear is somewhat exhilarating," she whispered in a hushed tone he found highly sensual. "My blood is pumping so fast I can hardly catch my breath."

His breath came quick, too, though it had nothing to do with almost losing one's life to a knife-wielding scoundrel.

"Perhaps we are both lacking a little excitement in our lives, Miss Kendall." This was not the calm, sedate life he envisioned for himself when he returned from his travels abroad, and yet he had never felt more alive.

"Excitement often leads to recklessness," she replied.

He stared at her parted lips. "In such a case, one might lose sight of Society's rigid rules. One might be inclined to ignore the consequences of one's actions."

Her mouth curled into a half smile. "And what would tempt a man of your experience to behave so rashly?"

Valentine moistened his lips. "Oh, I think you know."

A vibrant energy sparked in the air between them.

"Kissing a lady in a dark corner of the mews might be considered reckless."

"Reckless and irresponsible," he agreed. "And would a lady with worldly experience be willing to pander to my whims?"

Miss Kendall blinked rapidly. "Once won't hurt."

"Once will not be enough," Valentine said, his voice low and husky as his mouth came crushing down on hers.

The touch of her lips set his body aflame.

She did not wait for him to set the pace but moved her mouth frantically over his as if desperate to drain every drop of pleasure. Their breathing grew urgent, ragged. A low moan resonated in her throat, the sound as erotic as anything he had imagined while fantasising about her in bed last night.

Aveline Kendall tasted like no other woman before. She tasted of wild, forbidden fruit warmed from the heat of the sun. She tasted as rich and as intoxicating as the finest wine, a combination that made him dizzy. She tasted exotic—strangely unique though highly addictive. The urge to delve into her mouth took hold. With one hand, he cupped her neck, his thumb coming to rest on her cheek as he traced the seam of her lips with his tongue. Then he pushed inside the warm, wet den of iniquity that was sure to rid him of every noble intention.

The intrusion startled her for a second, no more, and then she matched the desperate sweeps of his tongue. He thrust deeper. Took command. Plunged into her mouth to sate the hunger writhing in his veins. But there was only one way to bring this mating of mouths to a climax and anything more than a passionate kiss was a step too far considering their current location.

Valentine tore his lips away. "Perhaps that is enough excitement for one evening. The gentleman in me is aware that I have already overstepped the mark."

Miss Kendall's dark eyes devoured him as she moistened her lips. He almost caved beneath the look of longing he witnessed there.

"You certainly don't kiss like a gentleman," she said, struggling to catch her breath.

"When one loosens the strings of restraint, gallant gentlemen are often the most sinful."

He felt like a stag in rutting season. He wanted to tilt his head back, roar and bark, clash antlers with any other male who had designs on mating with this female.

"You certainly have great depth of passion, my lord."

"And as a woman brimming with worldly experience, I'm sure you know that is not the barrel of your pocket pistol pressing into your abdomen."

Miss Kendall's eyes widened in shock, but one shake of the head and she soon recovered. A smile touched her lips, and Valentine knew she had thought of a witty retort.

"Thank you for informing me," she said. "Now I am in no danger of whipping it out to blow dust from the barrel."

CHAPTER EIGHT

"I know we consider our meetings all-lady affairs," Honora said, gesturing for them to help themselves to the finger sandwiches laid out in the centre of the round table in her sitting room, "but my son has a particular interest in the topic today, and I hope you don't mind if he makes a brief appearance."

Ava's stomach skipped up to her throat.

How could she sit across from the viscount without blushing?

Memories of the heated kiss she shared with Lord Valentine last night still burned in her mind. Never had she been so consumed with fanciful thoughts or romantic inclinations. And yet her fingers itched to caress his bare chest. Her lips longed to ravage his expert mouth. Indeed, when he insisted on escorting her home, and they lingered on the corner of Mount Street, there was a moment when he stared at her mouth and she imagined he might kiss her again.

"I have known Lucius since he was a boy," Mrs Madeley said, bestowing the other ladies seated around the table with her usual nothing-fazes-me grin. Today, she wore the same drab blue dress and artisan cap she always wore when discussing topics of a literary nature. "I have never found him to be one of those condescending gentlemen who constantly criticise. Perhaps we may even teach him something."

Lady Cartwright's red ringlets—which everyone knew to be a wig for the matron was approaching sixty—bobbed beneath her white cap as she nodded. "I think it will be the perfect test," she said whilst piling her plate high with sandwiches. "If we can speak openly in front of a viscount, then it might give those reserved ladies amongst us a little more confidence."

All heads turned to the hunched figure of Matilda Faversham. With a heart-shaped face and porcelain skin, Society might consider the lady a beauty if she did not tremble every time she spoke.

"Well?" Honora asked. "Are you in agreement, Matilda?"

Miss Faversham opened her mouth and snapped it shut.

Ava sat next to the girl and so tapped her affectionately on the arm. "It will do you a power of good, as Lady Cartwright said."

Miss Faversham's eyes brightened with a look of admiration. "Very well. If you think it is all right, Miss Kendall, Lord Valentine m-may attend the meeting."

Honora breathed a relieved sigh. "Excellent. Once we've eaten, we shall join him in the drawing room."

Heat rose to Ava's cheeks. "Lord Valentine is already here?"

"Yes, he spent the night."

"The night?" Ava's pulse raced.

After a leisurely morning in bed, was he dressing in the room above them? She pictured him in nothing but a pair of breeches slung low on the hips. In her mind's eye, she saw mussed golden hair, a rakish lock hanging over his brow. She saw the ripple of muscles in his abdomen as he shrugged into his shirt.

"Though I am not sure he got any sleep. Jenkins found him in the drawing room at three in the morning, cradling a glass of brandy."

The drawing room gave one a perfect view of Ava's house. After the incident on the way home from the pawnbroker's shop,

Valentine had seemed agitated. Did he fear the rogue had followed them home? Had he kept watch on her house all night?

"Men." Lady Cartwright chuckled. "We use sleep to forget about our problems, and they are quite the opposite."

There was some truth to the lady's statement. Sleep had been the only thing to ease the strange ache that commanded Ava's body whenever she thought about the handsome lord. Sleep banished the heartache that accompanied thoughts of her missing ring, too.

Matilda cleared her throat, but it was a moment before she spoke. "M-my father once drank a whole decanter of brandy upon receiving the bill from my mother's milliner. She does so love her hats."

Everyone gave a nervous laugh for they all knew of the major's temper and could imagine the scene playing out quite differently.

A tense silence ensued, the sound broken by the clink of a china teacup on the saucer. The conversation soon turned to more topical subjects—Ecuador declaring independence, a poem in the *Gentleman's Magazine*, of all places, that explained the correct nosegay one might send as a love token. Violets for faithfulness. Marigolds for marriage. Ava wondered what token one sent when consumed by raging lust.

They finished their repast, and the footmen cleared away the plates and platters.

"Let us remove to the drawing room where my son is waiting."

Honora stood and led the way.

Ava joined the back of the queue as she tried to gather her composure. Heavens above, her legs trembled so violently anyone would think she was being presented to the king. How had one kiss—one remarkable kiss—turned her into such a wreck?

After a minute's pause in the hall, Ava entered and found Lord Valentine paying court to his mother's friends. Mrs Madeley, being an advocate of equality, was not fawning over him as Lady Cartwright was wont to do. And poor Miss Faversham shook visibly under the weight of the gentleman's stare.

"Ah, and Miss Kendall is here, of course." Honora shooed the other ladies away leaving a direct path to the handsome lord.

Heavens, he looked spectacular in dark blue. The colour brought out the vibrant hue of his eyes.

A sinful smile touched Lord Valentine's lips as his gaze settled on Ava. "Miss Kendall. What a pleasure it is to see you again. Let us hope we may find common ground regarding our assessment of *The Modern Prometheus*."

"My lord." Ava inclined her head. She was hot. Her stays were too tight. It took immense concentration to reply. "Disagreements can be healthy if one is willing to embrace other people's opinions."

The tip of his tongue swept over his full lips. For all the saints! It occurred to her that Lord Valentine was right. One kiss was not enough. The need for another grew inside like an opium addiction. One taste would ease the writhing hunger. One taste would leave her desperate for more.

"I can accept anyone's opinion if made with a degree of intelligence and logic." He gestured to the gold damask sofa and chairs set out in a circle, though his penetrating blue eyes remained fixed on Ava. "Shall we take our seats? I am interested to hear your opinions regarding the title and what relevance it bears on the novel as a whole."

"That is simple," she said as the rich tone of his voice seduced her from across the room. The coil of desire unwound slowly deep in her core. Who would have thought an intelligent conversation could be so arousing? "In referring to Prometheus, the author hints that sin is a major theme. Does the novel not examine the quest for knowledge waged against moral implications?"

A pleasurable sigh left the lord's lips. "Is it knowledge Victor Frankenstein seeks or power, Miss Kendall?"

Oh, it was an excellent question. The urge to probe his mind whilst running her hands over his bare chest proved distracting.

"I trust you have each read all three volumes," Honora said, breaking the spell.

The other ladies nodded.

"But you must excuse my memory," Lady Cartwright said, taking a seat on the sofa, "what with me being the first to accept guardianship of your treasured volumes, my recollection might be hazy."

Miss Faversham scurried to share the sofa with Lady Cartwright while Ava sat directly opposite Lord Valentine. Try as she might, she could not ignore the way the viscount's muscular thighs filled his breeches.

A discussion regarding the anonymous author was to be the first topic for debate. Some felt the novel must have been written by a gentleman of prominence who wished to distance himself from other authors of gothic novels. How strange that in a group of ladies seeking equality for their sex they did not consider *Frankenstein* the work of a woman.

Something about the way Lord Valentine watched them during their analysis spoke of more than an interest in literature. He was studying them, observing, making mental notes. The fact Matilda Faversham continued to stare at the goblet in Honora's glass display cabinet captured his attention.

While they discussed the relevance of the monster's appearance on Victor's wedding night, Lord Valentine scanned Lady Cartwright's clothing. Did he know that Lord Cartwright had restricted her allowance? Did he know that the lady's ostentatious dress was merely a means to disguise a lack of funds?

"I think the moral of the story is that all men are beasts," Lady Cartwright said with a chuckle. She glanced at Valentine and smiled. "Present company excluded, my lord."

"Of course." Lord Valentine inclined his head. "And what is your opinion, Miss Faversham?"

"M-me?" The poor girl nearly slipped off the sofa. "Well, is it that men c-commit atrocities as a means to control? Is it that life is dreadfully unfair?"

No doubt her experience at home formed the basis of her opinion.

"Do you not think it leans more to the fact that man is a product of his environment?" Ava said. "Perhaps when we judge people we cast them in a role they feel compelled to portray."

Lord Valentine hummed. "There is merit in your interpretation, Miss Kendall."

"And what are your thoughts, my lord? I understand the novel is a particular favourite of yours."

He straightened as if rising to the challenge. "But for a little kindness and compassion, we might have read an entirely different story. All men, even those Society deem hideous, want to be loved, Miss Kendall. All men seek that one person who brings meaning to their lives."

The room fell silent.

There was sadness behind his words, a deep sorrow she had never heard expressed. It roused a need to offer comfort. It roused a warm affection in her chest that had been slowly simmering since their first meeting.

She wanted to kiss him.

She wanted to hear the passion in his voice when he told her one kiss was not enough.

Ava cleared her throat. "Then it is the one thing upon which we all agree. Be it, man or woman, we are all seeking the same."

After another period of silence, Honora came to her feet and rang for refreshments.

Lord Valentine remained lost in thoughtful contemplation while a conversation about Madame Roscoe's operatic performance as Almirena in *Rinaldo* took place around him.

While tea was served, Lord Valentine stood and moved to

stare out of the window. Numerous times, an apprehensive Honora glanced at her son and sighed.

Ava poured Valentine a cup of tea and carried it over to him. "You should drink this if only to please your mother. She does worry."

Valentine accepted the offer of refreshment with good grace. "She has no need to worry about me."

"Does she not?" Ava observed his slightly slumped shoulders and the doleful expression still marring his handsome features. "I know we have not known each other long, but I consider us friends."

"I should hope extremely good friends after what happened between us last night."

Her cheeks burned at the memory, but she did not avert her gaze. "Then as we are accustomed to a certain intimacy, let me say that you may speak to me regarding any matter you find troubling."

Valentine glanced briefly at his mother who instantly turned away from whatever interesting titbit had given Lady Cartwright a fit of the giggles, to smile affectionately at her son.

"Likewise," the viscount stated, "you may call upon me as your confidant, day or night."

The last word sent Ava's stomach roiling again.

"I know that your brother's problems rob you of sleep," he added.

Was he making a logical assumption, or had he witnessed her pace the landing with her candle at three in the morning? And if it was the latter why did he care?

"I'm sure a gentleman of your intellect can piece together the facts," she said, deciding that anyone who had her interests at heart was worth trusting. "My brother has a problem saying no to those intent on fleecing him of everything he owns. Some of the items pawned to pay his gambling debts are sentimental. Hence the reason you found me at a broker's in Grafton Street."

"Hence the reason he sold your mother's ring to Lady Durrant."

"Indeed." Though why the widow wanted such an item when she might purchase anything her heart desired from a jeweller proved a mystery. "I will not rest until I have recovered my father's watch and signet ring."

She had more pressing problems than that.

A note meant for Jonathan, delivered to the house by a boy in ragged trousers and a beaten top hat, confirmed there was to be another monkey-baiting spectacle at the Westminster Pit tonight. One did not need Socrates' insight to know he would attend. Until Ava knew what had happened to the birthday gift from her mother, she would hound her brother to the ends of the earth.

Then another thought struck her.

Was Lord Valentine in similar dire straits? Yesterday, he had walked across town instead of taking his carriage. He, too, had been visiting a pawnbroker though now she came to think about it, he neither deposited nor reclaimed a thing. No. Lord Valentine's estate was amongst the wealthiest in the land. And he had happily paid the twenty pounds at the broker's and refused repeated offers of repayment.

"May I ask you something?" Ava said after noting the other ladies were still deep in conversation.

"Have I not just expressed my desire to act as your confidant?"

"Then please consider my line of questioning more inquisitive than intrusive."

"Line of questioning?" Lord Valentine arched a brow. His gaze dropped to her mouth. "You may probe me all you wish, Miss Kendall. You may use any method necessary to tease the answers from my lips." He took a sip of tea and continued to study her over the china rim.

Ava blinked to dismiss the image of her straddling him on a chair while she kissed him to distraction. "What were you doing in Grafton Street yesterday? What need does a man of your wealth have for visiting a pawnbroker?"

After a moment's hesitation, the lord lowered his cup. He glanced once at his mother who failed to meet his gaze this time.

"An item of considerable value was stolen from my mother's home, and I am charged with the responsibility of finding it," he said in a hushed voice. "A pawnbroker's shop is the obvious place to look."

It took a few seconds for the information to penetrate. Thoughts of her missing ring, of her mother's writing slope and vanity box entered her mind.

"What? A thief has broken into this house, too?" she whispered.

Had Jonathan been telling the truth when he proclaimed his innocence?

Had a mysterious blackguard carried out a spate of thefts?

A crippling unease settled in Ava's chest. Jonathan had asked if Lady Valentine had mentioned thefts in the area. Suspicion flared. Was Jonathan so desperate for funds *he* had committed the unthinkable act?

"What do you mean broken into this house, too?" Lord Valentine frowned.

"I have also had precious objects vanish from my home."

"Recently?"

She nodded. "Within the last two weeks."

"I see."

A wall of silence stood between them though Ava knew his mind worked as frantically as hers and no doubt considered the same damning questions.

"You think Jonathan might be responsible." There, she had put a voice to their misgivings. She considered the honourable gentleman standing before her, decided she would take his advice and confide her secrets. If she had any hope of saving her brother, she could not do so on her own. "Jonathan owes money to the Maguires."

"The Maguires?"

"Two brothers responsible for dog-fighting and bear-baiting at the Westminster Pit."

Lord Valentine jerked his head back. "Then he is in more trouble than you suspected."

"He assures me he did not take my mother's writing slope or her vanity box." Ava swallowed deeply. She coughed to clear the croak in her throat. "He ... he assures me he did not take the pink diamond ring my mother gave me for my twenty-first birthday."

The muscle in the viscount's jaw twitched. "Damnation."

The room fell silent. Ava turned to find *they* were now the topic of interest.

Ava forced a chuckle. "We are discussing the probability that true villains are not as hideous as the monster but hide behind a more agreeable facade. You are welcome to join the debate."

"Ah, no, no." Lady Cartwright raised her hand and waved for them to continue. "In truth, that book gave me nightmares for nigh on two weeks."

"Oh," Matilda Faversham said. "I assumed I was the only one who found it terrifying."

Ava waited for the ladies to resume their conversation before turning back to Lord Valentine.

"You should not be living in that house alone," the lord whispered.

"I am perfectly capable of taking care of myself."

"No, you're not."

"Yes, I am."

Lord Valentine shook his head. "What about Mr Cassiel?" he suddenly asked.

A nervous shiver ran the length of her spine upon hearing the mystic's name. For a moment, she could not breathe. "Mr Cassiel?" The man knew things, things he had never heard nor witnessed. The man had a way with words that robbed the mind of rational thought. "What of him?"

"He had unrestricted access to this house." The lord looked briefly out of the window at her house across the street. "You are acquainted with him on a personal level."

"If that is a polite way of asking if we are lovers then the answer is no," she muttered through gritted teeth. "I hired him in a professional capacity, nothing more." If anything, he made her skin crawl. She didn't like that he could read her mind, delve into her soul.

"Good."

"Good?"

A wicked glint flashed in his eyes, eyes as enticing as the ocean on a scorching hot day. He bent his head and whispered, "If I'm to kiss you again, I want to know I am the only man you desire."

Heat flooded her chest, crept up her neck. She cast a furtive glance about the room before replying. "What makes you think I desire you?"

Arrogance radiated, and he gave a confident smile in response. "I tasted the hunger on your lips, Miss Kendall. I felt your eager hands roam over my chest, heard the breathless pants that said you want me."

Good Lord!

How had they gone from talk of that vile man, Cassiel, to this?

For a second, she floundered beneath his stare. While she wanted to unsettle his composure by denying his claim, she knew honesty was perhaps the best policy.

"Lust is a powerful thing, my lord, and you're an extremely handsome man." Her attraction to him went beyond the physical. Her attraction to him went beyond anything she could explain.

"I am?"

"Yes, but in answer to your concerns regarding Mr Cassiel,

the man has never set foot in my home and could not have taken my precious belongings."

The change in topic did nothing to dampen her ardour. The sudden need to feel his hard body pushing her back against the stone wall played havoc with her insides.

"I shall reserve judgement until I have met him. Have you forgotten you promised to recommend me? My friend Mr Drake is keen to test the mystic's abilities."

She *had* forgotten—deliberately so.

In truth, she had no desire to approach Mr Cassiel again. She had no desire to hear the terrifying words that had plagued her since that night. "The man possesses a talent beyond this world. But let me tell you, hearing from the deceased brought no comfort."

It brought nothing but pain.

Lord Valentine straightened. "You're convinced you—"

"Ah, Miss Kendall." Perhaps feeling that Ava had spent far too much time conversing alone with the viscount, Honora approached. "Come, we must go through to the library and decide on the next novel."

"Of course." Ava inclined her head in agreement. She turned to Lord Valentine. "I thank you, my lord, for an interesting conversation."

"As my son prefers to listen to you, Miss Kendall, might you discuss the merits of marriage with him?" Honora said with some amusement. "Lady Durrant will not wait forever."

Jealousy woke from its slumber to hiss and writhe in Ava's chest at the mere mention of the widow's name. "I am not sure I am qualified to speak on the subject."

"Nonsense. Your parents' marriage was Society's greatest love affair. I'm told they were devoted their whole lives."

"Yes. My parents shared a deep and abiding connection until they drew their last breaths."

Honora shook her head and sighed. "Such a terrible tragedy."

The words echoed Mr Cassiel's whispered comments when Ava was alone with him in this room, when her mind had somehow been lost in a whirl of confusion.

Mr Cassiel had said things no loving daughter wanted to hear.

Mr Cassiel had said that her parents were murdered.

CHAPTER NINE

A deep sense of foreboding left a hollow space in Valentine's chest. Hours had passed since he parted ways with Miss Kendall, but he could still picture the harried look in her eyes when she spoke of her brother's debts.

Rogues who ran organised dog-baiting events were the sort who made an example of weak-minded fools. A lost finger. A broken kneecap. A healthy tooth extracted merely to make a point. Jonathan Kendall deserved his fate. His sister deserved an end to her troubles.

A knock on the study door drew Valentine from his musings.

Hastings entered. "There's a ragamuffin at the servant's door demanding to see you, my lord. Apparently, it concerns a job in Park Street which you hired him to oversee earlier today."

"Damnation." Valentine jumped out of his seat behind the desk. He had paid the boy to watch Miss Kendall's house and to report any suspicious activity. "Show him in."

Hastings frowned. "Into the kitchen?"

"Into the study. And have Sprocket prepare my carriage." Valentine would be ready regardless what news the boy had to depart. "And hurry."

With a skip in his step, the butler hastened from the room.

Valentine paced the floor while he waited, his mind plagued by a host of hideous scenarios. His heart pounded against his ribs. Had Jonathan Kendall's failure to pay brought the Maguires knocking on his sister's door?

Hastings returned with the boy.

"There's no need to hold me arm. I ain't gonna steal nuffin'." He shirked out of Hastings' grip and came to stand before Valentine. "Evenin', governor." The boy doffed his dirty cap to reveal a mop of unkempt black hair.

"Good evening," Valentine said, ignoring the vile stench of the streets that clung to the boy's clothes. "You have news regarding the house in Park Street?"

"Aye, but I swear you ain't gonna believe a word. I promise I'll let the crows eat me eyes if I'm tellin' a lie."

Valentine inhaled a sharp breath. Nothing surprised him when it came to Aveline Kendall. "Is the lady unharmed? Is her house secure?"

"Aye. No one's visited the whole time I was there."

Relief settled in Valentine's chest, though it only eased his fears temporarily. Something was amiss else the boy would not be here. "You're going to tell me the lady has left the house, aren't you?"

The boy nodded. "She left wearin' gentlemen's clothes."

Bloody hell!

Panic charged through Valentine's body like a mad bull at the fair. "Was she alone?"

"She was with an old man dressed all fancy like. I swear on me mother's grave the man's her butler."

Valentine exhaled pent-up stress. At least Miss Kendall had the sense not to go out alone. "Did you follow her? Do you know where she went?"

"She gave me a half crown and patted me head," the boy said, "and told me to wish her luck before climbin' into a hackney. I ran as far as Green Park but couldn't go no more." The boy looked at his feet and wiggled filthy toes visible through holes in shoes that looked two sizes too small. "But I heard her tell the driver to head to Westminster. Orchard Street."

"Westminster?" What business had she there? Valentine glanced at the mantel clock. "What time was this?"

The boy shrugged. "I came straight here. But there's a fight on tonight at the Pit 'tween Samson and Raja. They reckon every swell in London will cram into the stalls."

Every swell looking to fritter away their legacy.

Valentine turned his attention to Hastings. "Take the boy to the kitchen and feed him. If he so wishes, he may have a bed in the coach house for the time being. And send a footman out first thing in the morning to purchase new shoes." Valentine retrieved a handful of sovereigns from his desk and thrust them into the boy's grubby hand. "I'll have another job for you tomorrow so get a good night's sleep."

Tomorrow, the hunt was on for Mr Cassiel.

The boy gave a wide-mouthed grin. "Aye, governor."

"My lord," Hastings corrected. "If you are to work here, you will address Lord Valentine with the respect befitting his station."

"Right you are, milord."

"Tell Sprocket to meet me outside with the carriage in five minutes." If Miss Kendall had gone to the Westminster Pit, there was no telling what he might find. Amid the hustle and bustle of drunken aristocrats, Valentine would take comfort knowing his coachman was nearby.

While Hastings escorted the boy to the kitchen, Valentine dressed quickly and raced out of the front door. With his mind so distracted, he almost barged into the hulking figure of his friend Devlin Drake.

"Stone the crows, Drake." Valentine clutched his hand to his heart and stepped back. "You scared me half to death."

"I scared you?" Drake did not look at all pleased. "God's

teeth, Valentine. Have you no thought for your friends? I have not heard from you for days. I had every intention of returning to Blackwater, but your odd behaviour keeps me in town. Three times, I have called around and left a note. Either something is dreadfully amiss, or you need to dismiss your butler."

"I haven't time to talk now. I am needed across town."

Drake frowned. "Now I know something is wrong. Never, in all the time I've known you, have I heard a thread of panic in your voice." Drake glanced back over his shoulder at Valentine's carriage. "I am coming with you. During the journey, you can explain what the hell is going on."

"This is not your fight."

It wasn't Valentine's fight, either. Yet he felt responsible for Miss Kendall. Perhaps it stemmed from a need to prove himself worthy. To give him a cause, a purpose. While he supported his friends in their quests for vengeance, it was too late to do anything about the devil haunting Valentine's dreams. His father was dead.

"Your fight is my fight. Are we not as close as brothers?"

Valentine considered his friend's broad shoulders and dark, devilish features. Only a fool would reject Drake's offer of assistance. And if Miss Kendall had entered the Pit, heaven knows what trouble awaited them.

"Very well," Valentine agreed. "I shall tell you everything on the way."

They settled into the carriage and were soon rattling through town. After enquiring after Drake's wife, Juliet, and giving a brief outline of events since the duel near Chalk Farm, Valentine said, "And so, I suspect Miss Kendall has dressed in gentlemen's clothes with the intention of visiting the Pit. I can only assume she plans to accost her brother to prevent him from squandering his inheritance."

"The Pit?" Drake's tone conveyed shock and a hint of admiration. "The lady has courage in abundance."

"Courage? She is oblivious to the dangers." Indeed, one might consider her actions reckless if they did not stem from love and a sense of duty.

Drake folded his arms across his chest and relaxed back in the seat. "You seem to have spent an awful lot of time with Miss Kendall these last few days."

"The lady is a close friend of my mother's, and you know I will do anything to bring Honora peace."

"Not quite anything." Drake smirked. "Your mother wants you to marry the widow and yet you have had ample opportunity to make Lady Durrant an offer. One might believe you're stalling."

Valentine was about to construct a suitable reply, but Drake knew him better than anyone, and he was tired of pretending. "I have no desire to propose to Lady Durrant."

The truth brought a sudden sense of calm.

"But did you not come home to prove to Lady Durrant that you are a man capable of commitment?"

"Partly." He came home when he realised the nightmares of the past lived within him and no amount of miles could change that. "I also came home to assist you in your need for vengeance."

Drake pursed his lips. "But you said you were determined to marry the widow."

"Devil take it, Drake. I know what I said. But I spoke out of duty and certainly not from a place of love."

This time Drake could not suppress a chuckle. "You don't know how relieved I am to know you have abandoned all designs on Lady Durrant. The widow is no good for you. You need a woman who teases your mind as well as your—"

"Then wait until you meet Miss Kendall. The lady drives me to distraction in every regard."

"Good. Someone had to bring chaos to your ordered life."

"Even so, a man would have to think long and hard before attaching himself to a lady who acts so impulsively. Miss Kendall is a little wild and far too unconventional." She was exciting and bewitching, too. He grew hard listening to her intelligent conversation. And her hot mouth made him forget the past ever existed.

"Then I can hardly wait to meet her."

The queue to enter the small brick building, home to the dog-fighting arena known as the Westminster Pit, stretched half the length of Duck Lane. With the absence of gaslights, the narrow lane lay in darkness. A sea of shadows moved and swayed as each man in turn either gained or was refused entrance.

A single lantern hung over the shabby wooden doors where two men, whose necks were as wide as their heads, took receipt of the ten shillings entrance fee.

"For the same price I could purchase a ticket to Almack's," Valentine muttered to Drake as they joined the queue. "Though at least here a man has no need to worry about manners or etiquette."

"The crowd is renowned for being boisterous."

"At Almack's?"

Drake snorted in amusement. "Well, an argument over a place on a dance card can be a rather gruesome affair. I heard it was carnage when someone added brandy to the ratafia."

"No doubt it will be carnage in the Pit tonight." Valentine estimated there must be fifty men waiting in line and the arena held two hundred at most. "Every light-fingered cove in the district will look to gain entrance."

"When one stands amongst thieves and gamblers, there is always a fight." Drake sounded almost pleased at the prospect.

"Speaking of fights." Valentine lowered his voice. "Have you any news from Lockhart? Dariell went to join him after the duel, and I've not heard a word since."

Drake nodded. "Our friend is still in hiding. Dariell has found an actress to play the role of Lockhart's wife."

"Does she realise what is involved? Does she know she is risking her life? Proving one is innocent of murder is no easy feat."

They shuffled along a few paces.

"With Dariell's level of perception and insight, I am sure he will choose a lady more than capable of the job."

"Then I shall be ready to support them in any way I can." The pact they had made—Greystone, Drake, Valentine and Lockhart —bound them together. The bond went beyond an offer of assistance. Valentine would risk his life to save his friends.

"As will I." A weary sigh breezed from Drake's lips. "If the plan should go wrong, Lockhart might find himself swinging from the gallows."

"Dariell would not encourage Lockhart to act were he not assured of success."

A sudden commotion at the front of the queue captured their attention. A group of drunken ne'er-do-wells who clearly lacked the funds to pay the entrance fee let alone gamble away a fortune were trying to push past the giants on guard duty.

A high-pitched screech preceded gasps and cries. The group scattered, held on to their top hats as they took flight and scampered along Duck Lane. The thought that Miss Kendall had made it past the thugs on watch was like an icy hand squeezing Valentine's heart.

"From what I can tell, the guard with the squashed face drew a blade from a swordstick and swiped the tip over one man's face," Drake said, having the advantage of being a head taller than most men. "It serves our purpose. They've chased at least ten men out of the queue."

Indeed, another minute or so and Valentine found himself paying the fee.

One look at Devlin Drake and the rogue on the door said, "There'll be no trouble tonight."

Drake inclined his head. "I come merely to watch the gruesome spectacle."

Another brutish guard ushered them through a narrow hall into a red-bricked room no more than twenty feet square. In the centre stood a wooden platform with aisles around all sides—space for the owners to mentor their savage pets. Spectators were squashed into the gallery above, more crammed behind a low wall on the ground floor separating them from the vicious animals waiting to tear each other apart. From a glance, most were from the upper echelons, men with more than a few sovereigns to spare. Or maybe not in Jonathan Kendall's case.

"Do you not find the whole scene somewhat barbaric?" Valentine asked.

"Barbaric?"

"The room is packed with men waiting to watch two dogs fight to the death."

"And one woman," Drake said as they barged their way into the lower gallery. "You suspect Miss Kendall is somewhere amongst the crowd. How the hell do you hope to find her?"

A loud cheer rent the air as two men approached the arena. One was dressed in fine clothes—a mustard coat and buckskin breeches. With thick auburn hair and excessive side whiskers, he looked like any other fashionable well-to-do gent. In comparison, the stout fellow's long blue coat looked equally expensive though his stance and bearing bore the uncouth signs of a man brought up on the streets.

The stout man dragged a Bull and Terrier behind him on a rope lead. The animal snarled and snapped at anyone who dared come within a foot of its master. The room erupted into a cacophony of jeers. Hands shot into the air, men waving their crumpled notes calling out their bets to the boys paid to run and exchange them for dockets.

No sooner had the din settled than the man in the mustard coat led his contender into the arena. This time, hushed mutterings breezed from one spectator to another.

"Tell me my eyes do not deceive me," Drake said, gaping at the creature who had climbed up into his owner's arms.

"No," Valentine replied, equally surprised. "That is most definitely a monkey."

The low-pitched whispers grew louder until one nabob shouted, "Twenty pounds on Maguire's monkey to win."

So the well-dressed gent was one of the Maguire brothers. He looked too timid to dabble in blood sports. Not at all the sort who left men quaking in their boots. Then again, Dariell might be small and slender, but he could kill a man with a single blow.

The monkey responded with an odd squeak as it raised its fist and punched the air.

"Thirty, here."

"Take my bet!"

"Forty!"

"There is no way the monkey can beat the dog," Drake said as the room exploded into uproar once again.

"That is what they want you to think. The organisers stage the event to fleece young bucks of their parents' hard-earned coffers." Valentine scoured the sea of excited faces in the crowd. "Never mind the distractions. Help me look for Miss Kendall."

"A description might prove useful," Drake mocked.

Valentine formed a mental picture. Miss Kendall was intelligent and witty, sometimes vulnerable and naive. Often a little shy, yet wildly passionate. Miss Kendall was a delightful package of contradictions. She had beauty and brains in abundance, the latter being somewhat questionable tonight.

"She has silky brown hair and eyes the colour of melted chocolate. She has a proud chin and determined countenance." And the only kissable lips and plump breasts ever to tempt him.

Drake smiled. "And will she be able to watch this disgusting fight without averting her gaze?"

Valentine shook his head. "I imagine she'll find the gruesome display abhorrent."

"Then we have an advantage. We shall look for a pretty fellow with his head bowed. Of course, the urchin may have been mistaken."

"No, she is here," Valentine said without hesitation. The nervous rolling in his stomach told him so.

The raucous jeering quietened until the room echoed with nothing but the murmurs of hushed conversation. The dog, lovingly named Samson, snapped and snarled as his owner led him into the ring. The monkey, Raja, clung on to Maguire, resulting in a few last-minute bets from those hoping Samson would bring an answer to their prayers.

The animals were washed and weighed in front of the multitude of witnesses. Silence descended when the referee gripped hold of his bell. Three loud clangs and the bout began.

Valentine studied the crowd of two hundred as the animals darted about the arena. Someone had to do something to stop the vicious sport. Perhaps he should rouse support for a petition. What was the point of sitting in the House of Lords if not to bring about change?

"Having spent two minutes evading the dog, the monkey has now jumped on its back," Drake informed him.

A sudden movement to their left drew Valentine's attention. Men moaned and complained at the interruption. People jostled back and forth as a slender man pushed through the crowd. He was the only one not watching the fight.

Valentine tapped Drake on the arm. "I think I've spotted our target."

"Thank the Lord. That monkey is liable to jump out of the arena and savage the spectators."

With Drake in tow, they pushed through the crowd in pursuit.

Anyone who dared think of complaining took one look at the giant with eyes as dark as the devil's and turned quickly back to watch the gory match.

Valentine tried to see what had captured her attention, but the monkey pulled the dog's tail, and the crowd threw their hands in the air, some to cheer, some to boo in protest. An argument started between two patrons. These sorts of events were rife with disagreements. The losers often looked to take their frustrations out on those more fortunate. It would not surprise him if the whole room erupted into a mass brawl.

The thought sent Valentine's pulse racing.

The sooner he got Miss Kendall out of the rogues' den, the better.

Miss Kendall—well, he hoped it was the woman who drove him to distraction and not some foppish dandy—had practically made a full loop of the lower gallery. Losing patience, Valentine prodded men in the back to move them out of the way.

He was but three feet from her when another scuffle broke out. This time, one of the burly guards who had been taking payment at the door, grabbed an unsuspecting fellow from the crowd and dragged him past the arena.

Miss Kendall gasped. "Jonathan," she cried, but the word was barely audible above the din.

An old man with a white cavalier-style beard cupped her elbow, but she tried to shake free of his grasp.

"Excuse me." Valentine barged into one man and almost trampled over another in a bid to reach the lady. "Kendall?" he called. "Kendall!" he cried, louder this time.

Miss Kendall swung around. Stone-cold fear flashed in her eyes. Her cheeks were pallid, her lips drawn thin in despair.

Every chivalrous bone in his body throbbed with the need to ease her woes.

"Valentine?" she said, struggling to catch her breath. "Is it really you?"

The old man beside her gulped in surprise, but then his shoulders sagged as if he was suddenly pleased someone else might accept responsibility for this reckless creature.

Miss Kendall stepped closer and placed a trembling hand on Valentine's chest. "I'm so glad to see you." Hope washed away all sign of pain in her eyes. The lady threw herself into his arms as a sob burst from her throat. "Oh, Valentine. I need your help."

CHAPTER TEN

T he sight of Lord Valentine's handsome face brought suppressed emotions rushing to the fore. Ava was a fool to think she could come to the arena and persuade Jonathan to keep his purse strings knotted. Being in the first group of gentlemen admitted, Ava had found him with ease. They had argued. More people piled into the Pit, and he had stormed off into the crowd.

"Oh, Valentine." The viscount's coat was warm, comforting. The spicy scent of his cologne clung to the garment. Every time she inhaled, her shoulders relaxed a little more. "It is all my fault."

Lord Valentine rubbed her back in soothing strokes. He took a gentle hold of her arms and forced her to look at him. "Did you come here hoping to drag your wayward brother home?"

"Yes, and I thought I might speak to Mr Maguire," she said, stepping closer when the cheering in the arena grew so loud it became hard to hear. "To see if he will freeze the interest payments, see if he will accept a repayment plan."

A look of horror marred the viscount's face as his protective hands slipped from her arms. "Please tell me you have not approached Mr Maguire."

"No. Not yet."

A relieved sigh escaped him. "You're a beautiful woman, Miss Kendall. I'm sure I do not need to tell you what Maguire might suggest in order to comply with your request."

The compliment distracted her momentarily.

But then the memory of Mr Fairfax tugging at her bodice flashed into her mind. Those icy fingers had mauled and clawed at her clothing. His actions had taught her that some men saw women as a commodity. Some men would stop at nothing to advance their careers.

"When it comes to prudence, I have most definitely lost my way." Ava drew her coat across her chest and shivered. "I have been such a fool, Valentine. A blind fool who lacks the strength to deal with her own family."

The lord pursed his lips. He muttered something, but a rowdy jeer from the crowd swallowed his words. The viscount leant forward, his mouth but an inch from her ear.

"Let me help you. It has nothing to do with the fact you're a woman." His hot breath teased the sensitive skin on her neck. "This is too much for one person to deal with alone."

Ava pulled back and looked at him.

Her heart swelled to twice its size until there was hardly any room left in her chest.

She was a little in love with Lord Valentine.

"Yes," she said, knowing that the pain she would invariably feel when they parted would be worse than the assault by Mr Fairfax, worse than the worries she had for her brother. But tonight, Valentine was here at her side, willing to provide a strong arm of support. And he appeared to be the only one with any sense, for she had most definitely lost use of her mental faculties.

"Yes?" the viscount clarified. "You agree I may act in your stead?"

Ava nodded. "I would be most grateful if you could help to ease this burden."

Lord Valentine smiled and slapped his hand to his chest, covering his heart. "At last, an opportunity to play the gallant knight."

The comment drew a weak chuckle from her lips. "Like everything else, I am confident you will excel in this matter, too." Ava's gaze moved past the viscount's shoulder to the hulking figure standing behind.

Noting her interest, Lord Valentine said, "Allow me to present Mr Drake. We will concern ourselves with more in-depth introductions once I have spoken to Mr Maguire." He glanced at Twitchett. "Am I right in thinking you are in Miss Kendall's employ?"

Twitchett bowed. "Indeed, my lord. As well as butler, I fulfil many roles in the Kendall household. Know that I will assist you in any way I can."

Lord Valentine gave a curt nod and then turned his attention back to Ava. "I suppose it is too much to ask that your butler might escort you home."

"Home? I cannot abandon my brother in his time of need."

Valentine sighed. "Then there is little point insisting. You're to stand with Mr Drake while I make the negotiations." He craned his neck and looked at a point beyond her shoulder. "Do you know where the lout took your brother?"

Ava gestured to the door to the left of the arena. "They went through there."

"Then follow me." Lord Valentine sidled slowly past, his body brushing against her as he manoeuvred through the cramped space.

For a heartbeat, he paused. A look passed between them that spoke of various emotions—respect, compassion, a tenderness that went beyond anything she had ever known.

Ava gulped as she resisted the urge to touch him.

When he continued through the crowd, she followed. Mr Drake slipped in behind, his menacing countenance acting as a shield. Together, they made their way to the wooden door with the opaque window. Lord Valentine turned the brass knob and seemed surprised to find the door unlocked.

The dingy corridor led to another door, one far sturdier. Raised voices echoed. The thud of a fist hitting hollow wood gave them pause. The scrape of a chair on the boards reached Ava's ears, too. A dog growled. A man whimpered.

They crept to a halt outside the door.

"What are you going to do?" she whispered, touching the back of Valentine's coat.

"The only thing I can do. I shall knock and pray someone answers."

"Please be careful." Those three words carried the weight of her affection.

The corners of his mouth curled into a weak smile. "Should anything untoward happen, Drake will hurl you over his shoulder and bolt to the exit." He glanced at his friend. "Is that understood?"

"Indeed," Mr Drake replied.

Ava was in no mind to argue, and so she nodded in agreement.

Sucking in a deep breath, Valentine rapped twice on the door. The sound was met with silence. He knocked once again, harder this time. The clump of heavy footsteps preceded the sudden jerk of the door opening. The burly fellow who had grabbed hold of Jonathan and dragged him from the arena held it ajar to block their view.

"Lord Valentine to see Mr Maguire," the viscount said with an air of confidence expected from a man of his station. "And I do not have an appointment."

The man whose face bore a striking likeness to the dog in the arena—flat and ugly with a squashed nose—narrowed his gaze. "Mr Maguire is busy."

"Yes, busy throttling the life out of my brother." The comment burst from Ava's lips, but it was too late to reclaim it.

Lord Valentine firmed his jaw but did not say a word about her sudden outburst. "I'm certain a man of Maguire's prominence does not permit the hired help to make his decisions."

"I speak on behalf of Mr Maguire."

"Speaking on your master's behalf is vastly different from speaking *for* him. Will you not allow Maguire to decide for himself?"

"Show them in, Milligan." The stern voice sliced through the air from the room beyond.

Milligan's top lip twitched. He looked ready to bite as he stepped back and opened the door fully.

They entered with some caution.

It was a small room, painted entirely in moss green smudged with soot from the open fire. A strange scoreboard filled the far wall—slate boards with lists of numbers and names, brass dials and sliders used to track bets and odds. The place smelt of wet dogs and stale sweat. A thin man with spectacles and wiry copper hair sat behind a battered oak desk. Jonathan sat hunched in the chair opposite. He looked at Ava, and his cheeks flamed red with shame.

"Mr Maguire?" Lord Valentine asked.

"Connor Maguire," the scrawny man replied in a cockney accent tinged with a Southern Irish intonation. He did not stand but twirled the handle of a small pocket knife around his bony fingers as he spoke. Not once did the blade cut or mark his skin. "Martin is in the arena with that savage beast he calls a pet."

"You speak of the monkey?" Lord Valentine said.

Mr Maguire nodded. "If you've bet on the dog, then you'll leave with an empty purse."

"Thankfully, I am not a gambling man."

Mr Maguire studied the viscount for a moment before his sharp gaze moved to Mr Drake. Ava defied any man not to shiver when looking into those black eyes, but clearly, Mr Maguire had seen enough brutality to remain indifferent. One sweeping glance at Ava's attire brought a smirk to his lips.

"If you've come to save Kendall here," Mr Maguire began, "then you'll need more than a pouch filled with sovereigns."

A brief silence ensued before Lord Valentine asked, "How much would it take to clear Mr Kendall's debts and render the matter closed?"

Jonathan squirmed in his chair. "I do not need you to act as—"

"Oh, do be quiet." Ava bristled to Lord Valentine's defence. She was tired of listening to the nonsense that came out of her brother's mouth. "Can you not see that people are trying to help you?"

"I do not need *his* help," Jonathan countered.

"I beg to differ. You should be grateful such an honourable gentleman is willing to take the time and trouble to act on your behalf."

"Valentine is acting on your behalf, not mine. Any fool can see that."

Ava supposed there was some truth to the comment. She couldn't look at Lord Valentine for fear of blushing, but oddly she noted Mr Drake's mouth widening into a satisfied grin.

Mr Maguire threw the blade in the air. He caught it by the handle and stabbed the point into the desk with enough force to penetrate a man's chest. The candle flickered in the lamp casting eerie shadows over his skeletal features.

Everyone froze.

"Then you've got the money to pay me, Kendall," Mr Maguire said in a tone filled with menace and mockery. "Why didn't you say so? I'd not have had Milligan drag you away from the entertainment."

Entertainment? The sport was merciless and barbaric.

"Well, I do not have the money at the moment." Jonathan's meek voice grated. "But perhaps my luck might change tonight."

"You championed the monkey to win?" Lord Valentine sounded hopeful.

Jonathan cast the viscount a sidelong glance. "Don't tell me you bet on the dog."

"As I said, I am not a gambling man. One has a responsibility when one inherits."

Ava would wager the lord had never made a foolish decision in his life. What was it that made the two men so vastly different? Jonathan had been afforded a childhood filled with love and excitement and adventure. But what about the viscount? While love for his mother radiated from him like a blazing beacon, neither he nor Honora ever mentioned his father.

"You have the advantage," Jonathan sniped. "You were born a gentleman. Some of us have to earn our place."

Lord Valentine snorted. "And you think by causing your sister distress that makes you an honourable man? With that mentality, you will never rise to the ranks."

"Enough!" Connor Maguire cried.

The black dog—who looked more terrifying than the one in the fighting ring—sat up from his fireside basket and barked.

Ava's blood ran cold. Her heart skipped two beats. The animal looked ready to attack and rip the jugular out of anyone who stood in its way.

"This ain't some fancy gentleman's club," Mr Maguire continued. "You can squabble like children in your own time."

A tense silence ensued before Lord Valentine repeated his earlier question. "How much to settle Mr Kendall's account?"

Mr Maguire's top lip curled in amusement. "Kendall here is two days late with his payment and owes twelve hundred."

"Pounds?" Twitchett's eyes widened in shock.

"We ain't talking brass buttons," Mr Maguire retorted.

"Twelve hundred pounds," Valentine muttered.

"Thirteen if he fails to pay by the stroke of midnight."

Valentine rubbed his hand over his chin and then said, "Will you accept a note from me?" Slowly, and showing Maguire every exaggerated move, Valentine reached into his coat, removed a calling card and placed it on the desk.

Mr Maguire yanked the knife from the desk and used the tip of the blade to drag the card closer. He scanned the script and after a moment nodded. "I'll take your note, but the interest remains until the full debt is paid."

"And the rate?"

"Ten per cent of the original debt charged daily."

"Bloody hell," Mr Drake whispered. He glanced at Ava and inclined his head by way of an apology for his coarse language.

"You will have full payment tomorrow." Valentine cast Jonathan a look as deadly as any swipe with a blade. "All thirteen hundred pounds."

With the growling dog watching them, Ava moved cautiously to Valentine's side. "I cannot let you pay my brother's debts. If I thought he might change, then I would find a way to repay you, but sadly I fear you will be as good as throwing your money on the bonfire."

Valentine's blue gaze softened as he searched her face. She saw compassion there, and something else, something that made her stomach grow hot, that made her heart leap about in her chest.

"I know the strength it took to ask for my help." He spoke in an intimate tone as if they were the only people in the room. "Your brother speaks the truth. I do not give a damn about him."

Valentine added nothing further. He did not need to.

He turned his attention to Connor Maguire. "Failure to make the payment will result in Mr Kendall losing the use of a limb. Am I correct?"

Mr Maguire nodded. "The place is old, the floors uneven. Many a gentleman has tripped on his way out and broken an arm."

A desperate whimper escaped Jonathan's lips.

"Brute," Ava whispered but hoped Maguire heard.

He did.

The rogue chuckled as his beady gaze raked over her, though the sound in no way expressed amusement. With a firm grip of the knife, he pointed it at Jonathan. "Maybe I'll cut off a finger tonight. If your friend here doesn't pay tomorrow, it will be an ear and then a limb."

Devlin Drake craned his neck and cracked his knuckles. Anger radiated. He looked ready to unleash the devil's wrath.

Mr Maguire narrowed his gaze. "Ah, you want to fight. The lady and the old man might disagree." He looked briefly at Ava. "Such a pretty face. Such a shame to leave an ugly scar."

A growl resonated in the back of Lord Valentine's throat. Those perfect blue eyes turned almost steely silver. Never had a man looked so terrifying and so irresistible at the same time.

Valentine stepped forward and straightened to his full height. "I swear if you harm a hair on her head I will raze this place to rubble and see you buried beneath it."

A deep adoration burst to life in Ava's chest, pushing panic aside. It flowed through her body until every part thrummed with need for this man. The emotion may have overwhelmed her, had the other Maguire brother not entered the room with Raja in tow.

The dog snarled and snapped in his basket.

Connor Maguire jumped up from his seat and brandished his knife.

Martin Maguire took one look at the threatening scene and sent Raja to attack Lord Valentine. The monkey flew across the room with lightning speed, bounced up onto the desk and lunged at the shocked lord, knocking off his top hat.

A tirade of violent curses left Mr Drake's mouth.

Valentine was forced to swipe the monkey to the floor, but the creature proved relentless.

"Get that thing off him," Ava yelled.

Twitchett removed his hat and batted Raja away while Mr

Drake tried to catch the primate by the back of its red velvet collar.

The dog barked, and Connor Maguire sent the vicious animal racing over to nip and snap.

Ava had no choice but to act.

Pulling her trusty pistol from the inside pocket of her coat, she cocked the small weapon and aimed at Connor Maguire. "Get that monkey off Lord Valentine before I shoot. And let me tell you I have already fought one duel this week and have no qualms pulling the trigger."

It took the Maguire brothers all of two seconds to command their savage pets to heel.

"You," she said, pointing at Martin Maguire. "Take these animals and wait outside."

A tense silence ensued.

"Leave, Martin," Connor instructed, "and take Raja and Caesar with you."

Ava waited for them to vacate the room.

"Now," she said, catching her breath. Her legs were shaking, but she had to at least attempt to look composed. "I think we can all agree that was unnecessary. Let us go back to the moment before you foolishly threatened me."

Connor Maguire stared down his pointed nose. "Let me tell you, anyone who pulls a pistol on a Maguire rarely lives to make the same mistake."

"Then I may as well shoot you." Ava firmed her jaw to stop her teeth chattering. "That way I only have one brother to contend with."

She glanced at Valentine. All colour had drained from his face. Blood trickled from a scratch on his cheek. For the first time since making his acquaintance, she saw fear flash in his eyes.

The scoundrel raised his hands and grinned. "I said rarely. Seems I can't punish a lady for my own mistake." He turned to his crony. "Since when did we stop searching the patrons?"

Milligan hung his head.

Ava got the distinct impression that, at some point later in the evening, the man would feel more than the sharp edge of his master's tongue.

"We were at the point where you accepted Lord Valentine's offer," she said. "Let me tell you that there is no man more trustworthy." Ava realised that she had to show Maguire respect if they hoped to escape without being assaulted by the monkey. "I have a ring on my finger that you may keep as a sign of my respect and good faith."

"No!" Valentine interjected. He delved into his waistcoat pocket, then unfastened the chain and placed his watch on the desk. "Take this instead. It is yours to keep, a token of my word as a gentleman."

"No!" It was Ava's turn to protest. "I cannot let you do that."

"I already have." There was a hardness to his tone that told her not to oppose him. Somehow, she would find a way to repay him.

Mr Maguire stabbed his knife back into the desk. He picked up the watch and examined the gold casing. "I'll accept the watch as a token of respect. And I'll expect thirteen hundred pounds on my desk come tomorrow afternoon."

"Agreed." With eyes brimming with contempt, Valentine cast Jonathan a sidelong glance before saying, "I want your word that Mr Kendall will not be permitted to gamble here again."

Mr Maguire grinned. "I can't be held responsible for another man's weaknesses. But if Milligan here should see him in the Pit, he will boot his backside all the way back to Mayfair."

Jonathan dragged his hand down his face but did not protest.

Connor Maguire stood and called for his brother to enter.

Martin Maguire came marching into the room. He held Raja in his arms as if the primate were a child in need of coddling. Caesar growled and bounded over to its master.

Connor Maguire raised his hand to quieten the animal. "Milligan will show you all out. In future, keep the lady on a leash."

Ava might have protested, but she knew to bite her tongue.

They sidled past the monkey, taking care not to startle the creature, and were shown out through the arena where men were wagering on the next bout. Milligan waited until they had exited onto Duck Lane and then he slammed the wooden doors behind them.

Ava placed her pistol back in her coat pocket and exhaled deeply to release the tense breath she'd been holding for hours.

"My carriage is waiting on Orchard Street." Valentine's voice was thick with barely contained anger.

"I shall walk," Jonathan said, no doubt wishing to avoid another lecture.

"Like hell you will." Lord Valentine gritted his teeth. "I'll not rest until I have seen you to your damn door."

Ava blinked in shock at his sudden outburst.

Anger no longer radiated from Mr Drake's countenance. Indeed, he seemed to find the current situation somewhat amusing.

Lord Valentine cupped Ava's elbow and propelled her forward. Mr Drake shadowed her brother, and they all marched to the end of Duck Lane.

"Thank you," Ava whispered in the hope it might help to lighten the lord's mood. "I shall visit the bank in the morning and withdraw the necessary funds."

"I shall pay the debt, Miss Kendall." He did not look at her but kept his gaze focused on the carriage parked a little further along Orchard Street. "I gave my word as a gentleman."

Now was not the time to argue. She would wait until Valentine's mood settled.

"The watch—was it very valuable?" she asked as she jogged to keep up with his long strides. She wondered if losing the watch was the cause of his discontent.

"The watch belonged to my father, given to me on the day he died."

Oh, heavens! No wonder he was so angry.

Ava came to an abrupt halt, forcing him to stop, too. "Then we must go back. I cannot let you give away something so valuable." It hurt her heart to think of him parted from such a prized possession.

Lord Valentine's eyes flashed icy blue. "I don't give a damn about the watch. But you, my dear Miss Kendall, will stop this nonsense once and for all. You, Miss Kendall, will explain what the hell you think you were doing dressed in gentlemen's clothes whilst visiting the Westminster Pit."

CHAPTER ELEVEN

A burning rage flowed through Valentine's veins, so hot he struggled to fill his lungs no matter how many times he drew breath. Miss Kendall remained quiet at his side until they reached his carriage.

"Is there room for us all?" she asked, her tone conveying nerves mingled with mild irritation.

"Mr Kendall will sit with Sprocket." Valentine refused to gaze into the fool's pitiful face. "Else I fear I might wrap my hands around his scrawny neck and throttle the damn life out of him."

"Must you curse?" Miss Kendall countered. "It is unlike you to deviate from your usual moral stance."

"Moral stance?" Valentine mocked. "Madam, you pulled a pistol on a notorious rogue. Your brother almost got us all killed tonight. Forgive me if I appear somewhat unsettled." Valentine yanked open the carriage door. He could not recall the last time his blood boiled, the last time he lost complete control. "Please, get inside before the Maguires change their minds."

Miss Kendall huffed, but she obeyed his command and climbed into the conveyance.

"I shall sit atop, too, my lord," the white-haired butler said. "If there's room."

"As you wish. Someone must keep an eye on Mr Kendall though I doubt he can cause mischief from up there."

"Look, Valentine," Jonathan Kendall began, "I didn't know my sister would come to the Pit tonight. I didn't—"

"Save your excuses for someone foolish enough to listen." In his present volatile mood, Valentine could not be held accountable for his actions. The farther away he was from Jonathan Kendall, the better. "We will discuss this some other time. For now, just do as I damn well ask."

Kendall bowed his head and climbed atop the box to squash next to the butler.

Valentine turned to Drake, who grinned back in amusement. "What is so funny?"

"You," Drake replied, steering him away from the carriage's open door. "For a man who prides himself on his calm composure, you really are struggling tonight."

Valentine exhaled a weary breath. He did not need to hear he lacked restraint. "And I doubt you will ever let me forget it."

"What is even more astounding is that you are completely oblivious to what is going on here."

Valentine folded his arms across his chest, curious to hear his friend's opinion. "And what is going on? Please, feel free to enlighten me."

Drake gripped him firmly by the shoulder. "If you don't know, I am certain all will be revealed in due course."

The sound of Miss Kendall clearing her throat drew Valentine's gaze back to the carriage. The lady sat forward on the plush seat and peered at them. "What happened to hurrying before the Maguires change their minds?"

"That woman will be the death of me," Valentine muttered. Were he an oafish brute he would tan her backside for her reckless behaviour tonight, though he was more inclined to caress the plump cheeks and rain sensual kisses the full length of her spine.

"And what a wonderful death it would be," Drake replied.

Ignoring Drake's teasing, Valentine instructed Sprocket to head for Newman Street and then to Drake's abode.

They climbed into the carriage. Valentine squashed next to Drake. He wanted to study Miss Kendall's expression and could not take the chance of sitting next to her without berating her for her stupidity, without dragging her into his arms and ravaging her mouth.

He loved that she had risked her life to save him from the damn monkey.

He feared what that meant.

They sat in silence as the carriage rumbled along the streets.

Once at Newman Street, Jonathan Kendall alighted. Valentine waited until the buffoon entered the house—only to ease Miss Kendall's anxiety—and then rapped on the roof.

"Well?" Drake said after a few moments. Clearly he had grown tired of feigning interest in the passing shadows. "Did you not promise a more thorough introduction?"

Valentine sighed. It was unlike him to be so lapse.

"Miss Kendall, allow me to present my trusted friend Mr Drake. We spent the last five years together in India and the Far East." He turned to Drake. "Miss Kendall is my mother's dear friend and close neighbour."

Miss Kendall smiled. The power of it pierced through the chink in Valentine's armour to hit him squarely in the chest.

"Ah, Lord Valentine tells me you have an interest in the macabre, Mr Drake."

Damnation!

Why could she not simply nod and discuss the inclement weather like most ladies? Then again, Miss Kendall was unlike any other woman of his acquaintance.

"The macabre?" Thankfully, Drake's blank expression masked his surprise.

"You are keen to hold a seance," Valentine said in a tone that suggested Drake was absent-minded. "Keen to meet the mystic, Mr Cassiel, who possesses an ability to talk to those who have crossed to the next plane."

"I am?" The corners of Drake's mouth curled up in amusement. "I am," he said more convincingly. "My brother passed away some years ago while I was abroad. Guilt can be a crippling thing, Miss Kendall."

"I understand," she said in a solemn voice. "My brother and I were to help my parents in the mine on the morning the accident occurred, but they were up at sunrise and went ahead without us. There is not a day goes by when I do not wonder if I may have helped in some way had I been there."

An empty feeling, accompanied by a crippling nausea, roiled in Valentine's stomach. Bile bubbled up to his throat. He shared Miss Kendall's deep sense of regret. Perhaps if he had stayed awake, he might have noticed his father leave the house in just his shirtsleeves on a cold winter's night. He might have followed him from their clifftop estate and prevented a terrible tragedy. But when one's parent had an illness of the mind, actions were often erratic, unpredictable.

"Our friend Dariell believes everyone's destiny is already written," Drake said, his voice thick with compassion. "We cannot begin to understand why these things happen but must accept that they happened as they should."

"How insightful," Miss Kendall replied. "I shall try to remember that on those dark days when the heavy cloud of grief descends. But I am not sure Mr Cassiel will bring you the answers you seek."

"I have come to terms with my loss," Drake said, and Valentine felt the heat of his friend's stare boring into his temple. "Some friends still struggle."

Valentine felt Miss Kendall's stare, too, though he did not meet her gaze lest she note the truth of it in his eyes.

"And was there anything in particular that helped you to accept your brother's passing?" Miss Kendall sounded hopeful. "I only ask as I have a personal interest in the answer."

Valentine was just as curious, though he knew there was but one significant change in Drake this last month.

"The answer is love, Miss Kendall. I fell in love and recently married." He gave an amused snort. "Actually, it happened the other way around, but I am madly in love with my wife all the same."

A tense silence filled the small space. A space made infinitely smaller by Drake's large frame.

The silence gave Valentine a moment to reflect on the mixed emotions fighting for supremacy in his chest. Anger raged for the risk Miss Kendall had taken this evening. Fear held him rigid when he considered that he might have lost her tonight. Lust fought to override all else, for he wanted to pleasure her until she forgot about her sad memories, forgot that her brother was an imbecile. And hope emerged, hope that in doing so he might help himself, too.

"I see," she said as if love were unobtainable. As if she had more chance of slipping through time to wake with her parents on that ill-fated morning.

"Do not sound so downhearted, Miss Kendall." Drake straightened as the carriage rolled to a stop outside his house on Wimpole Street. "A woman with your intellect and beauty will have no problem finding a husband who adores you to distraction."

As if Valentine hadn't enough to deal with, jealousy slithered through his veins. Miss Kendall was his. No other man would care for her as he did. No other man could converse with her on her favourite topics. Could he not quote Epictetus? Did they not share an understanding of the themes in modern literature?

"You are very kind, sir. But as Lord Valentine will tell you, few men are willing to take a wife who behaves so unconventionally."

Valentine saw Drake's huge grin through the reflection in the glass.

"You do not need a few men," Drake said. "You only need one."

Miss Kendall chuckled. After the trauma of the night's events, it was music to Valentine's ears.

"Good night, Miss Kendall." Drake shifted to the edge of his seat, and the carriage swayed. "Few women would risk their lives for those they love. I believe your unconventional behaviour should be celebrated not mocked."

"Thank you, Mr Drake. I shall treasure the compliment. Far too often I am made to feel like a fool. Rest assured, I shall send word to Mr Cassiel so he may attend your upcoming dinner party."

"My dinner party? Oh, my dinner party."

"Good night, Drake," Valentine said, keen to get rid of him for there were a few things he wanted to say to Miss Kendall. "Give Juliet my warmest regards."

Drake patted Valentine on the back. "Dariell was right. You have had a few surprises these last few days, and I suspect there are more to come."

Drake alighted. He had barely reached the front door when it swung open, and Juliet rushed into his arms. They kissed on the doorstep—the doorstep of all places!

"They seem very much in love." Miss Kendall's soft voice drifted across the carriage.

"They are."

Valentine opened the window and instructed Sprocket to head to Mount Street.

The carriage lurched forward.

Silence ensued.

Valentine struggled to think—there was a novelty.

The gruesome image of Aveline Kendall lying in a burgundy pool of blood entered his mind.

"You should have come to me before charging off to the Pit," he said, his tone more subdued than when he had confronted her in Duck Lane. "My life flashed before my eyes when you pulled out the pocket pistol."

Miss Kendall's tight expression relaxed. "I could not trouble you with my brother's affairs. You have assisted me more times than I can count. And what did you expect me to do, stand there and watch that maniac monkey scratch out your eyes?"

"Maguire could have hurled the blade at your heart before you had time to fire." The thought froze the blood in his veins. "What would I do then?"

Her bottom lip trembled. "I don't know what you would do. I only know that I could not stand back and see you hurt. In a few short days, you have become my dearest friend." A sob caught in her throat. "The only person I trust."

Perhaps her distress stemmed from the sudden realisation that she could have died tonight. Perhaps her revelation about her parents had brought painful memories to the fore.

Valentine crossed the carriage to sit beside her. All traces of fear and anger dissipated, leaving nothing but an abiding affection for this woman.

She shuffled around to face him. "I am so sorry, Valentine. I did not mean to embroil you in this whole sordid affair."

"Sordid?" He cupped her cheek and wiped away a tear with his thumb. "There is nothing shameful or immoral about the way we feel. Lust is a perfectly natural emotion when two people are as close as we are."

It was more than lust, and he damn well knew it.

She gave a weak smile. "I wasn't talking about us."

"No, you were talking about the fact I was attacked by a monkey and will be the talk of the *ton* should anyone discover what occurred. You're talking about the fact I must pay Maguire thirteen hundred pounds if we want rid of him for good."

With trembling fingers, she touched the scratch on his cheek. "And what of your handsome face? What of the precious watch left by your father? The watch you gave away to save me the pain of losing another family treasure."

"I witnessed the distress in your eyes when Lady Durrant showed you the ring. I couldn't bear to see it again." He would come to her aid in a heartbeat should another opportunity arise.

"Oh, Valentine." Her tears fell more rapidly. "Never have I met a man more honourable."

"Honourable? Miss Kendall, currently my thoughts might be considered disreputable."

"They are?"

"Most definitely."

Her luscious lips curled up in amusement as she blinked away the water droplets clinging to her lashes. "Are you in need of excitement, my lord? Do you wish to behave as recklessly as you did that night in the mews?"

"You know damn well I do."

Her breathing grew shallow as she gazed at his mouth. "Then know you're the only man I desire."

"Then you have no objection if I kiss you?" He removed her top hat, gloried in the way the silky locks tumbled down around her shoulders.

"No, no objection."

A raging desire for her flared. Blood flowed too quickly through his veins. He was in danger of ruining the moment, acting like a green boy fresh from the schoolroom. Drawing on the discipline that had kept him sane for most of his adult life, he inhaled deeply.

With gentle hands, he cupped her cheeks and pressed a chaste kiss to her warm lips. The briefest contact sent a rush of euphoria from his head to his toes. Her potent scent stimulated every nerve.

God, he wanted this woman in every way possible. He wanted to feel the heat from her bare skin. He wanted to watch her face as he entered her body to fill her full. He wanted to hunt for her lost treasures, see the glow of happiness in her eyes upon their safe return.

Valentine drew back and then kissed her again, just as soft, just as tender.

"I have never felt desire like this." Her words breezed across his cheek.

He could not lie. He had felt the thrum of desire many times, although never as potent. Never as powerful. And so he searched the once cold and lonely organ beating in his chest.

"You're the only woman ever to find a way into my heart, the only woman I want to cherish and protect."

She leant forward and kissed him, once, twice. The third time it was as if a dam inside had burst and she could no longer contain the flood of emotion.

"Kiss me as you did in the mews," she panted, threading her arms around his neck. "Kiss me in the frantic way that made me dizzy."

Needing no further inducement to ravage her senseless, Valentine captured her mouth, teased her lips apart and plunged deep.

Their tongues tangled, hot, wet, needy. Their breathless groans permeated the air. They fought the duel neither had wanted on that cold November morning near Chalk Farm. But there was nothing calm and ordered about their need for satisfaction. Her fingers slipped into his hair, tugging, urging him to give more, to delve deeper.

"Valentine," she hummed when his hand slid up over her waistcoat to cup her breast. For once, he was glad she wore gentlemen's clothes. Unconfined by stays, her nipple hardened beneath his touch. The urge to rip open the waistcoat and lavish the sensitive peak took hold.

But then the carriage jerked and rolled to a sudden halt.

It took a moment to drag his head from the clouds, to realise that the two people atop the box expected Miss Kendall to alight. But he would rather be damned than let her go now.

"Perhaps you should wait here while you send your butler in to warm the house." His voice was thick and husky.

"Twitchett."

"I beg your pardon?"

"My butler's name is Twitchett."

"And he's called Twitchett because …" Such an unusual name must come with an amusing story.

"Because that's his name."

"Of course." Frustration, coupled with a burning passion to strip Miss Kendall naked, forced him to say, "Send Twitchett inside. I have not finished with you yet."

Ava's eyes brightened. "Believe it or not, I like it when you're masterful." She pulled down the window, instructed Twitchett to return to the house and slip a warming pan between her bedsheets.

Valentine dismissed all notions of him fulfilling the role of body heater. He could not enter Miss Kendall's house at night, not with his mother a hundred yards across the street. And he had to try to protect this lady's reputation—despite working against the odds. Hence the reason they had parked on Mount Street.

"I shall follow along in a few minutes," she informed Twitchett with some embarrassment.

Valentine considered the soft curves squashed into her brother's breeches. "A few minutes will not be enough," he growled. "Tell him you will be an hour."

Miss Kendall did as he asked—there was another novelty.

"Inform Sprocket he is to circle Green Park twice before returning to Mount Street," Valentine added. That should give them time to explore their growing relationship.

Miss Kendall pulled her head back in through the window. "But will he not find that a rather odd request?"

"Sprocket doesn't care." He considered the fact she might

have changed her mind. That matters might be progressing at far too rapid a pace. "Unless you're having second thoughts. In which case, if you wish to accompany Twitchett, I shall not be offended."

She studied him for a moment. He recognised the glazed look of longing swimming in her eyes. "You always consider my needs before your own." She leant forward and kissed him, a quick and rampant mating involving open mouths and eager tongues.

"Well, I think that answers my question," he said, licking his lips to capture the essence of this beguiling woman.

She thrust her head out of the window, gave Sprocket instructions as if she were the coachman's mistress. The prospect of her filling the role had crossed Valentine's mind more than once tonight.

Closing the window, she settled into the seat opposite.

The conveyance bounced on its springs as Twitchett alighted. It lurched forward, but Miss Kendall gripped the edge of her seat rather than use it as an excuse to tumble into his lap.

She stared at him in the dark confines of the carriage. The heat of her gaze scorched his skin. Whilst he was a man of some experience, he wasn't sure how to approach the current situation.

But then Miss Kendall spoke. "Take off your clothes."

Whilst his peers considered him a man of intellect, he would never have predicted that comment would fall from her mouth.

"I beg your pardon?" he teased as he wanted to hear her repeat the words.

Miss Kendall swallowed. "Take off your coat, your cravat and waistcoat. Drag your shirt over your head."

Valentine smiled. "I like it when you're masterful."

Despite the cold November chill in the air, he wasted no time doing as she asked. Stripping while she watched proved highly arousing. During the process, she devoured him with her bewitching brown eyes. Numerous times she glanced at the bulge in his breeches. Damn. His cock throbbed with the need to enter her tight body.

"Hmm." She moistened her lips as she scanned every inch of him. "May I touch you?"

Bloody hell!

Was this a test?

Did she not know he was about to burst from his breeches?

"Madam, I am yours to command. Do with me what you wish."

Miss Kendall bit down on her bottom lip as she crossed the carriage. In another move that pleased him as much as it surprised him, she came up on her knees and straddled his thighs. She reached out and placed her palms flat against the hard planes of his chest.

"Your heartbeat is pounding hard against my hand."

Hell, his heart was not the only organ desperate to pound long and hard.

Valentine's hands settled on her waist as he drew her further onto his lap until his swollen cock pressed against her most intimate place. "And can you feel that, Ava? My heart and my body are both keen to further our acquaintance."

With a firm grip of her hips, he ground against her, watched in awe as her lips parted and her eyes glazed. The sweetest moan he had ever heard resonated in her throat.

Her hands moved to caress his chest. "You're so hot, so hard."

Valentine hummed. "Are you talking about my chest or the other part of my anatomy?"

Her cheeks flushed scarlet. "The muscles in your shoulders are as solid as marble."

"During my time abroad, I learnt to protect myself in more ways than one. I might be the best shot amongst my peers, but I can fight just as well with my fists."

"Unless your opponent is a monkey," she countered as she

bent her head and pressed kisses along his jaw. "Then a moral dilemma makes combat more difficult."

Valentine closed his eyes and savoured the feel of her mouth as she moved to the sensitive skin on his neck. The tips of her fingers brushed over his nipples. Devil take him. If he was not mistaken, he was the one being seduced. And she was doing a remarkable job. Then again, she had boasted about being a woman with worldly experience.

"Speaking of moral dilemmas," he said, sensing the restlessness inside her building. When she found her release, the sight would be spectacular. "I'll not make love to you in a carriage, Ava."

She sat up and looked at him. Doubt flashed in her eyes. "You won't?"

"An hour is not long enough to pleasure you as you deserve." And with the added jerking of the carriage, a man might miss the moment to withdraw. "And I'll not have you walk the length of Park Street in a state of dishabille."

He could have said that it was a sacred act, saved for their wedding night, but enlightened ladies of fortune did not marry, and he was not strong enough to resist this temptress. If they continued their friendship, it was only a matter of time before it reached the inevitable conclusion.

And yet he wanted more than a passionate liaison.

He wanted her.

That was all.

He wanted her in his life.

Permanently.

So why was he making it more complicated?

"I understand," she said, reaching down to move her mouth across his in a kiss that spoke of abiding affection. "As a gentleman, you prefer that we were in bed."

Hell no!

Well, yes. In bed, he could lavish her body from head to toe.

"I have no qualms making love to you here." He was not a prude. "I am merely thinking of you." He could be wild and rampant like the best of rakes. He could bend her over the seat and thrust until dawn. The thought sent another rush of blood to his cock.

"I understand," she reiterated. "The first time can be unpleasant I'm told."

"Unpleasant?" Valentine snorted. "For you, love, I would make everything perfect."

It took a moment to absorb what she had said. He had been so focused on the latter part of the sentence that he had missed the crucial part. Clearly, lust played havoc with a man's mind.

"The first time?" he said, repeating her words.

A nervous smile touched her lips. "Yes. Enlightened ladies often embrace such things as part of being progressive. But surely it is not wrong to treasure one's virginity." She sounded defensive.

Valentine scoured his mind, trying to find the reasons why he thought she had already taken a lover. "But you said you were in love once." That thought stabbed at his heart. "You said you knew the difference between the moans of pleasure and pain. From the way you kissed me, I assumed—"

"I said I thought I knew love. I did not say I had partaken in sexual relations with a man."

"And so I would be your first?" he clarified. His heart swelled at the prospect.

"Most definitely," she snapped. "You're the only man who has ever roused a deep passion. You're the only man I could take as a lover."

As a lover?

Not a husband then?

"Then permit me to seduce you properly. Perhaps you might join me at home tomorrow evening for dinner." He would explore her mind, and later her body. He would pleasure her until she could not live without him. "I have a huge bed with more than ample room for two."

She hesitated. "If you wish to entertain me at home, you will have to think of a way I may enter unnoticed."

"Trust me. I will think of something."

CHAPTER TWELVE

"I could always wear gentlemen's clothes tomorrow evening," Ava suggested. Excitement tickled her stomach as she imagined entering his private domain. There was something to be said for recklessness. "I know you cringe whenever you find me wearing them, but you seemed to like the feel of my silk waistcoat tonight."

Valentine dragged his shirt over his head, and Ava almost groaned in protest. "Madam, I am still trying to come to terms with the fact I cannot have you right now. Must you remind me that there is nothing but two fine layers of material covering your modesty?"

Ava smiled. The flames of passion still danced in his eyes. The look held her spellbound. As did the knowledge that she cared so much for this man, she would permit him anything.

The air in the carriage was still charged with excitable energy. Numerous times, she imagined kissing him and letting events take their natural course. When two people shared such a powerful attraction, nothing could keep them apart.

"I could sit and watch you dress and undress all night," she said. Desire still thrummed through her veins, too.

He wrapped his cravat around his neck and tied it into a simple knot. "Trust me. Tomorrow we shall have plenty of time to fulfil our fantasies."

As she watched him button up his waistcoat and shrug into his coat, it occurred to her that Lucius Valentine was not the sort of man to bed an innocent—not without making a declaration. In a moment of insecurity, she might have concocted a story in her head, one that made her feel inadequate, inferior. The tale would spin out of control, fed by her one and only experience with an evil man determined to have his wicked way.

But it was not that way with Valentine.

A man did not give away a prized heirloom to save a lady the pain of parting with hers if he didn't care. And so she would embrace the passion they shared in the hope it would blossom into something lasting.

She loved him.

Perhaps one day he might learn to love her, too. If not, she would have to be thankful that she had experienced a glimmer of the love her parents shared.

"We're approaching Mount Street," Valentine said, dragging her from her musings. "I cannot let you walk the length of Park Street alone."

"Twitchett will be watching at the window. Between the two of you, I am sure you will keep me in your sights until I am safely through the front door."

The carriage slowed to a stop.

Silence ensued.

Ava didn't want to leave him. She reached out and took hold of his hand. "Thank you for coming to my aid this evening. Thank you for assisting me with the pawnbroker yesterday. Clearly I was wrong when I said I could take care of myself."

"Everyone needs help at some point in their lives." He caressed the back of her hand with his thumb. "Not everyone finds the strength to ask."

Their gazes locked. She felt the essence of his soul stretch across the carriage to soothe her senses. Until a sudden and violent rap on the window sent her heart shooting up to her mouth.

"What the hell?" Valentine blurted, equally surprised by the aggressive nature of the caller. He peered through the glass at the figure beyond. "It's your butler."

"Twitchett? But he is always so calm and rational."

Valentine glanced at her and raised a brow. "Most people would say the same about me, and yet in your company, I appear to have lost all grasp of logic." He leant forward and opened the door.

"Forgive me, my lord," Twitchett panted in a stream of white mist. "But you must come quickly. There has been an incident at the house."

"An incident?" Ava shifted to the edge of the seat. "Is it Mrs Stagg? Is she hurt?"

"No, but she is shaken. I've given her brandy to settle her nerves."

Without further comment, Valentine moved to the door and vaulted down to the pavement. He turned and offered Ava his hand. His other hand settled on her waist, and he assisted her descent.

"Thank you." She was about to suggest he return home, but a firm hand settled on her back and propelled her along the street.

"But you cannot enter my house, Valentine." She looked to Honora's house, noted the soft glow of candlelight spilling out from an upstairs window. "What about your mother? What if she sees you?"

"I think we have passed the point of worrying about my mother. Besides, she is far more astute than I."

"And my reputation?"

Valentine smiled. "Is in utter ruins after this evening's debacle at the Pit. We will have to see what can be done about it, but presently we have other matters that require our attention."

Ava swallowed past the lump in her throat and cast him a sidelong glance. She wondered what she had done to deserve the friendship of such a wonderful man.

"The drawing room and your bedchamber are in a dreadful state," Twitchett said.

Panic sprung to life in Ava's chest.

What of her treasures hidden under the boards?

They entered the house, and Twitchett closed the door. He led them into the kitchen where Mrs Stagg and Bernice were seated on wooden chairs, sipping brandy from chipped china teacups. Tears trickled down the maid's face.

"What happened?" Ava rushed to comfort them.

"Oh, miss, there was nothing I could do to stop him!" Mrs Stagg pulled a handkerchief from her apron pocket and blew her nose.

"Him? Do you speak of my brother?" Surely not. Ava had spent most of the evening with Jonathan.

"No, the brute I found rummaging around in your desk."

Valentine stepped forward and placed a reassuring hand on Ava's back. "Can you describe the fiend you caught?"

Ava expected the housekeeper to say he had copper hair, tiny spectacles and a vicious dog called Caesar. But then Mr Maguire would have had to ride like the wind considering the fact they had only recently left him at the Pit.

"He was a tall gent with black hair and thick side whiskers. Don't ask me how he got into the house for he never made a peep." Mrs Stagg sniffed and took another sip of brandy. "It's only by chance I sent Bernice in to draw the curtains."

"Did this man speak to you?" Valentine said in the compassionate tone of a constable questioning a victim. "Did you notice an accent? Was he a gentleman or a man from a poorer part of town?"

"He said he was waiting for Miss Kendall." Bernice spoke in her usual timid tone. The girl tugged on her white cap—an action that seemed to settle her nerves. "I called for Mrs Stagg, and that's when … that's when—" Bernice whimpered.

"That's when he drew his sword from his walking stick and chased us into the broom cupboard. He told us if he saw us again he'd cut out our tongues and eat them for dinner."

Valentine's eyes grew wide. He covered his mouth with his hand for a moment. "Did the cane have a silver top? Was he dressed in a brown fitted coat with a raised collar?"

Ava frowned. He spoke as if he knew the man. Equally, something about the description resonated with her, too.

Mrs Stagg blinked rapidly. "Yes, he had beady black eyes and bushy black brows. When he looked at you, it was as if he could reach right into your chest and rip out your heart."

Bernice's shoulders shook with a silent sob. "Rip your heart right out," she repeated.

"I swear he made me feel giddy just by looking at him," Mrs Stagg added.

The icy hand of fear settled on Ava's shoulders. She shuddered as a bitter chill swept through her body. Every hair at her nape stood to attention. She opened her mouth to speak, but it was as if the devil knew what she was about to ask and had stolen her voice.

"Did he speak with an accent?" Valentine said, repeating his earlier question.

Bernice shook her head. "None that you'd recognise."

"Even when he threatened to end our lives," Mrs Stagg added, "he spoke in that soft, slow way that made my head spin."

Good Lord!

They spoke of Mr Cassiel. Ava was convinced of it.

What need did the mystic have for entering her home?

"Except when he spoke to the lady," Bernice said. "Then he barked orders as if his life depended on her doing as he asked."

"The lady?" Valentine frowned. "There were two of them?"

Mrs Stagg handed Twitchett her empty cup as if seeking a refill. "We never saw the lady. The fiend locked us in the broom cupboard before she arrived. Then they went rummaging through the house."

The last comment dragged Ava out of a state of shock. Twitchett's words echoed in her head. He had mentioned her bedchamber. Heavens. She had all night to question Mrs Stagg.

Without comment or further thought, she hurried from the room. Somehow, she made it to the top of the stairs though her legs trembled so violently she had no idea how she remained on her feet.

Ava burst into her bedchamber.

The sight hit her like a hard punch to the gut.

Part of her wished that Twitchett hadn't lit the lamp. She stumbled back and gripped the doorframe. She heard the heavy thud of someone mounting the stairs. Valentine came behind her. His strong hands settled on her upper arms, and she leant back against him for support.

The room lay in utter disarray.

It looked like a fierce storm had blown through the place and whipped up a frenzy. Every item she owned lay strewn about the floor—dresses, undergarments, the entire contents of the armoire. The drawers on her dressing table had been emptied and discarded with equal negligence. There wasn't a sheet or blanket left on the bed. A trail of white feathers led to the slashed pillows in the corner.

It was all Ava could do to breathe.

Valentine's arm came around her shoulders and across her chest so that she remained locked in his embrace. Not since her parents' deaths had she felt so secure, so protected. With Valentine, there was a closeness that went far deeper than friendship or adoration, deeper than a lust for carnal pleasures.

"I know how distressing this is," he said in the tender voice that made her want to kiss him until her troubles melted away. "Clothes and furniture can be replaced." He paused. "But what about your jewellery?"

Ava closed her eyes for a moment, imagined lifting the boards to find the space beneath empty. "I pray the intruder did not discover my hidden treasure trove." She took hold of Valentine's arm. "Come, help me clear the mess so I may examine the boards."

As always, he obliged.

They stepped over her belongings and crossed to the opposite side of the bed. Valentine picked up a drawer and slid it back into the table. Gathering her hairbrush and the ornate silver hand mirror that had once belonged to her mother, he set them down on top.

"Be careful, there is broken glass to the left," he said, placing a guiding hand at her elbow. He inhaled deeply. "From the overwhelming scent of White Rose, I suspect it's a perfume bottle."

Ava peered at the shards of green glass on the floor. "Oh, hell's bells." She couldn't help but groan with frustration. "You do realise how much it costs to shop at Floris. Well, the damage is done. I shall just have to purchase another."

"It is your one and only indulgence," he reminded her, the beginnings of a sinful smile touching his lips. "I hope you will allow me to purchase a replacement as a gift."

"A gift?" She raised a coy brow. "And have everyone think I'm your mistress?"

His smile faded. "You know there is more to our relationship than that."

"In what other capacity does a gentleman buy a lady perfume?"

Valentine stared at her. He opened his mouth to speak but hesitated. Eventually, he said, "I wish to buy you perfume regardless of how it looks. Now, is this the place you want to examine?"

He stamped on the Turkish rug, seemed surprised at the hollow echo beneath his feet.

Ava knew she had been stalling. Part of her preferred to live in ignorance. She bent down, gestured for Valentine to step back while she moved the rug and raised the board. Relief flooded through her when she saw the jewelled boxes.

Lifting one out of the dusty narrow space, she handed it to Valentine. "Open it. Tell me it is full to the brim with minute gems."

Dipping his fingers into the box, he withdrew a handful of tiny but vibrant stones. "They may be small but kept together in a box like this they look remarkable."

"Most are worthless though they are priceless to me."

"Then they belonged to your parents," he said.

"My father mined every gem and crystal in that box."

"Have you ever thought of making something with them?"

"I have many pieces of jewellery that far surpass anything one could make with those."

"Singularly, they are too small to be of any use. But together the stones make a rather bold statement. You could set them into the back of a hand mirror. They would work equally well in a hair comb."

Could he read her mind?

Did this marvellous man know her innermost desires, her secrets?

"I have various designs sketched. I take after my mother in that regard." Ava had not mentioned her aspirations to another living soul. "She was the creative genius, my father the expert when it came to geology. He worked tirelessly to help her see her dreams realised, and she worshipped him for it."

"And yet people showered him with praise for his beautiful creations."

"My mother had no need for fame or notoriety. She loved her work and her family. That was enough."

It would be more than enough for Ava, too.

Valentine's gaze turned curious. "You say you have sketched designs, yet I sense you have not taken the next step to develop the craft."

"I may attend a meeting of ladies who crave enlightenment, but it is still very much a man's world. Before one might begin, there are questions regarding premises and tools. I would need contacts abroad, need to learn about the importing of goods, perhaps charter a ship."

He shrugged. "All of which are feasible for a woman with your intelligence."

From a kneeling position, Ava looked up at him. Love filled her heart. The need to tell him came in a euphoric rush. Lord knows how she kept it at bay.

"I would happily assist you in your endeavour," he added.

"You have always been kind and complimentary, even when I have acted like a complete buffoon."

"Tonight, your recklessness almost got you killed," he agreed. "But your intentions are always honourable. They come from a place of goodness, and no one can condemn you for that."

"No," she breathed.

After a brief pause, she focused her attention on the other jewel-encrusted box beneath the boards. With care, she lifted it out of its hiding place and opened the lid.

"Is there anything missing?" Valentine asked with some hesitation.

Ava examined the contents. "Not that I can tell."

A sudden flicker in the corner of her eye drew her gaze back to the hollow space. Curious, she reached down and ferreted around amid the dust and cobwebs. A gasp caught in her throat when her hand settled on a ring.

"Blessed saints!" She retrieved the pink diamond ring and stared at the rectangular-shaped stone, a burst of elation stealing her breath. "I—I don't understand. It must have fallen out of the box."

Valentine crouched beside her. "Is that the ring you thought your brother had given to Lady Durrant?"

"It is," she replied with an air of wonder. "It is the only reason I went to Lord Rockford's ball."

"Then I am glad it was missing for a time."

Ava met his gaze. "You are?"

"Else, when would we ever have danced the waltz?"

The memory of the first time he held her in his arms brought a flush of heat to her cheeks. "And what a wonderful dance it was." How could she be angry at her brother when his wild antics had brought them together?

A sudden pang of guilt hit her squarely in the chest. Jonathan had protested his innocence and yet she had found it impossible to believe him. He might be reckless with his own funds, but he had not stolen into her room and helped himself to her treasures.

And neither had the intruder.

Which begged the question—what was the rogue searching for?

And if it was Mr Cassiel, who was his female accomplice?

"Earlier, when Mrs Stagg described the intruder," Ava began as she returned the ring to the box, closed the lid and placed it back beneath the board, "it was as though you recognised him."

Valentine handed her the box of coloured stones and then came to his feet. "There are things we need to discuss." His weary sigh spoke of a burden. "About my mother's missing ruby, about the fact I witnessed the same man who broke into this house follow you to the pawnbroker."

Ava's heart lurched. "Mr Cassiel followed me to Grafton Street?"

"What?" Valentine frowned. "The man your housekeeper described is the mystic?"

"Yes. I am certain of it." Doubt crept into her mind. She had been certain Jonathan had stolen her ring, too. "But what purpose would he have for committing such a terrible act?"

Valentine dragged his hand down his face and rubbed his jaw. "That is what we must ascertain." He reached out to her. "Come. I am not leaving you here. You're coming home with me."

"What? Tonight?" Heavens, this man was full of surprises.

"Yes, tonight."

"But—"

"Do you not want to stay with me, Ava?"

A nervous tickle fluttered up from her stomach to her throat. When he spoke in such a sensual tone how could a woman resist? "Yes, of course. But I cannot leave the servants, not after what happened here this evening."

"Then we will lock the house and take them with us."

"Oh."

"Any more objections?"

There was one.

"What about Honora?" It suddenly occurred to Ava that his mother might present some opposition to their blossoming friendship. After all, had he not vowed to marry Lady Durrant? "She hopes you will make Lady Durrant an offer."

An incredulous gape marred his fine features. "We all know there is no chance of that happening. What amazes me is that you think I would plan to pleasure you in my bedchamber while having designs on marrying someone else." Disappointment rang loud.

"That was not what I said." Ava scrambled to form a defence. Her voice sounded jittery, a result of what he planned to do with her once alone in his home rather than nerves. "Yet I do not wish to cause Honora distress."

"My mother's judgement is a little lapse at the moment."

"Honora's judgement is never lapse." Though Ava struggled to see why the matron would want her son to marry a woman so shallow and deceitful. Indeed, the more Honora pressed her son, the more he backed away.

Interesting.

"Let me worry about my mother. Besides, in her eyes, the daughter of Hamilton Kendall can do no wrong."

To hear her father's name uttered aloud filled Ava's chest with a warm glow. "I shall remind you of that the next time you find me in gentlemen's clothes at the Westminster Pit."

CHAPTER THIRTEEN

"And so you were to investigate all the ladies who attend your mother's meetings?" Ava said from her seat at the opposite end of the dining table.

The dim lighting, the roaring fire and his best bottle of claret might have set the scene for seduction had they not been discussing the fact she was on the list of those suspected of stealing his mother's ruby.

Bringing her to his home in Hanover Square had affected Valentine in ways he had not thought possible. A flurry of emotions had plagued his senses since she stepped over the threshold. A deep feeling of satisfaction settled in his chest. Aveline Kendall belonged in his house, in his life, in his bed. The urge to protect her surfaced.

Here, she was safe.

Here, he might pretend she was his.

"Honora wished me to discover if any of her friends had motive enough to steal her precious gem," he replied, feeling somewhat ashamed that he had not broached the subject earlier.

"You speak of the ruby you said my father sold on his last visit to England?" Ava clarified.

She had not touched her supper since he explained the nature of the theft that occurred at his mother's house. Thankfully, the selection of meats and pastries were served cold.

"I do."

"Then I do not need to tell you that the stone is rare and consequently worth a king's ransom."

"The paste replica is impressive in itself," he agreed.

"Neither my brother nor I knew anything of the sale. There was no record amongst my father's accounts. Mr F-Fairfax perished along with my parents in the mine, and so we presumed the ruby was either lost or stolen."

"Mr Fairfax?" A pang of jealousy stabbed Valentine's chest. He wasn't sure how he knew, but he sensed she was once fond of the gentleman.

"My father's man of business. He may have known why my father neglected to mention he had sold the gem to your mother."

"I cannot speak for your father's motives for failing to disclose the sale." Valentine sipped his wine as he studied her expression. She seemed irritated. Her down-turned mouth spoke of frustration and a heavy sadness. "And if it is any consolation, my mother has faith that you are in no way involved in the deception."

"I should hope so." She stared at the wine in her glass, lost in thoughtful contemplation. "Perhaps my father used the funds to purchase the house. Perhaps it suited his purpose to have me live opposite a woman he clearly held in high regard."

"Perhaps."

She glanced at the slices of ham on her plate but pushed the china away.

"And have you had any success during your investigation?"

Guilt weighed heavily in his chest. "Your brother's problems have monopolised my time. I have yet to focus my attention on prying into the suspects' private affairs."

"I see." Her tone carried a hint of shame. Out of thirst or some other need, she took a large gulp of wine. "I doubt any of the ladies who meet at your mother's house had anything to do with the theft."

"Someone had prior knowledge of the stone. Else how would they have made a replica?" The more the questions and answers were batted back and forth, the more he felt her withdrawing from him. This was not how he envisioned a night spent sharing an intimate supper. "Which brings me back to my suspicions about Mr Cassiel."

The mere mention of the man's name wiped the colour from her cheeks.

What was it about the mystic that unnerved her so?

Valentine recalled the first time he enquired after Cassiel whilst in his mother's drawing room, recalled the way Ava's dark eyes flashed with fear. That was before she suspected him of ransacking her home. Had something happened during the seance that night? If so, there was every chance it was relevant to current events.

"Must we speak of him?"

Valentine's heart wrenched. What the hell had the blackguard done to her?

"You said you first noticed various items missing from your home two weeks ago," he reminded her. "That was when Mr Cassiel came to my mother's house. Since then, a man matching his description has trailed you across town, tried to steal your reticule and has since broken into your house regardless of the fact there were witnesses."

A shiver ran through him.

Angelo Cassiel grew more desperate, more dangerous, by the day.

"What if I am wrong, and it is not him at all, but merely someone with the same dark hair and penetrating gaze? I cannot condemn a man on a whim no matter how much he terrifies me."

Valentine downed a mouthful of wine to calm the sudden

anger that pushed to the surface. No wonder men turned to drink when plagued by volatile emotions.

"Then we will hire him for Drake's dinner party and use the opportunity to examine the man further."

Ava jerked her head back in shock. "We? But you cannot expect me to attend. I couldn't. I couldn't sit with him alone in a room again, Valentine. Do not ask it of me."

Taking his wine glass, Valentine pushed out of his chair. He came to sit in the chair to her right. While he had purposely kept his distance for fear of ravaging her mouth like a madman, he could not comfort her from the opposite end of the table.

"I will be there with you," he said, placing his hand on hers. Any contact always sent his stomach somersaulting. "Together, we will discover if he is the rogue we seek, and what he wants with you. If we are wrong, then we must seek professional assistance."

"Professional assistance?"

"Hire a runner or an enquiry agent."

She dragged her hand out from under his and gripped his fingers. "He told me things, things he could not have known." Her eyes misted. "He told me something that plays over and over in my mind, and it scares me, Valentine."

Regardless whether the mystic was guilty of theft or not, Valentine would throttle him for causing the lady distress.

"Remember that they're the words of a fraud, and should be discarded without thought."

"You don't understand. He spoke the truth. Mr Cassiel knew what my parents wore on the day they died." She squeezed his hand harder as the first tear trickled down her cheek. "He knew of their plans to return to England."

Men like Cassiel knew how to extract information from their unsuspecting prey. They had a certain way of speaking that made a person divulge snippets of their life, enough for them to form a mental picture, enough for them to make predictions.

"Did he say anything else?"

More tears fell. He wanted to take her in his arms, but then he might never learn what the rogue had said to cause her so much pain.

"He said—" A sob choked her throat. She coughed. "He said that my parents did not die in the mining accident. He said they were murdered."

Murdered?

A blinding fury forced Valentine to his feet. "Then he will pay dearly for his lies. The man has taken his theatrical farce too far." Upon witnessing the signs of her distress, he drew her to her feet and embraced her while she sobbed until there were no more tears left to shed.

"I miss them, Valentine," she blurted into his waistcoat. "It is hard enough to know they met their end in such a tragic way, crushed by the sudden rockfall, but to think someone may have robbed them of their happiness. It is too much to bear."

That bastard, Cassiel, had no right to prey on the defenceless with his wicked tales. What the hell did he hope to gain?

"When we meet with Cassiel, we will determine the truth if I have to strangle the man to within an inch of his life."

"If he is the … the intruder, I doubt he will agree to another meeting." She wrapped her arms around his waist and laid her head on his chest.

"Of course he will." Valentine stroked her hair as the wracking sobs subsided. "If Mr Cassiel is innocent, he will want our business. If he is guilty, the desperation of his actions tonight suggests he needs something more from you. The opportunity will be too tempting to resist."

Ava looked up at him, tears still glistening in her eyes. "How would I have ever managed without you? I thought I was stronger than this but—"

"Hush, love." He placed his finger on her lips. "You're one of the strongest women I know." In that respect, she reminded him of his mother. Honora's tireless efforts to protect her family made her a force to be reckoned. "No doubt you would have found a way to deal with this, even if it meant shooting every blackguard who dared cross your path."

"I would never pull the trigger. I could never take a person's life."

"What about a monkey's life?"

A faint smile brightened her countenance. "I could not hurt an animal, either, but I would wrestle the creature to the ground if need be."

It was his turn to laugh though the action aggravated the scratch on his cheek.

He wiped her tears away with his thumbs and pressed a soft kiss to her lips. "You should eat something. Trauma can make a person ill, and you need to bolster your strength for what lies ahead."

"But I'm not hungry."

"Won't you at least try?"

She stared at him as her sadness lifted. He wondered if it was his own desire he saw reflected back at him. But her breathing grew shallow, and she moistened her lips. He knew then that she wanted him.

"I do not want to think about Mr Cassiel tonight, Valentine. I do not want him to occupy my thoughts when I go to sleep." She placed her hand on his chest. "Help me find a distraction."

"A distraction?"

"Help me feel pleasure, not pain."

A hard lump formed in his throat. Ava's honesty proved highly arousing.

This was the moment to ask of her expectations. Did she want more than a wild ride in bed? Was she aware of the consequences, of the risks?

"You're certain this is the course you wish to take?"

"I do not ask you to make promises." She came up on her

tiptoes and kissed him tenderly on the lips.

No? Well, she damn well should.

"I ask only that you follow your heart," she added.

Valentine stared into her hazy brown eyes and realised he had been following his heart since the day she approached him in the field near Chalk Farm. Indeed, logic told him that it was wrong to take an innocent woman to bed—not at all the actions of a respected peer of the realm. And yet the thought of making love to this woman consumed him.

He wanted her.

For once in his life, consequences be damned.

Besides, he was a man known for embracing responsibility and would do what was required should unforeseen problems arise.

"And are you following your heart, Ava?" He was certain she cared something for him.

"My heart has craved a union since you pushed me up against the stone wall and kissed me in the rampant way one expects of a rake."

The muscles in his abdomen clenched at the memory. "Did I not warn you? The gentleman in me will be mindful of your comfort. The licentious libertine will plunge into your body with only pleasure in mind."

"I have always avoided libertines, until now." Desire flashed hot in her eyes.

Lust pounded in his blood.

Valentine captured her hand and led her from the dining room. They never spoke as they ascended the stairs. He drew her into his bedchamber and locked the door.

The fire in the hearth roared.

Candles burned in the candelabra to cast a warm glow over the red walls.

The room was set for seduction.

"How will this work?" she asked as she stood in the middle of his bedchamber.

Valentine smiled as he slipped out of his coat and draped it over the chair. He moved to the four-poster bed, parted the gold curtains and sat on the end.

"As a man who embraces equality," he said, watching her intently as he relaxed back and propped himself up on his elbows, "I believe it is your turn to remove your clothes."

Her eyes widened. A nervous laugh escaped her. "Surely you're not serious."

"A libertine never jests in the bedchamber." He was somewhat thankful she wore gentlemen's clothes. It meant he wouldn't have to assist her with stays. "Take off your coat, your cravat and waistcoat. Drag your shirt over your head. Let me see you as I have longed to do from the moment we met."

She stared at him, appeared rooted to the spot.

"You're safe here," he added as he tugged at his boots and discarded them. It was a lot to ask of an innocent, and he did not want her to feel uncomfortable. "We need to undress, Ava. But if you would rather go behind the screen, rather I assisted you—"

"No. I want to undress for you. I am just a little nervous that is all."

"As was I when I stripped to my waist while hurtling along in a carriage in November." And his heart was beating just as fast. His cock throbbed with the same compelling need. "Is it wrong that I wish to worship your body as well as your mind?"

"No, it's not wrong." She breathed a sigh as she shrugged out of the coat and it landed on the floor. "Actually, it's quite flattering."

With their eyes locked, she unbuttoned the waistcoat and untied the simple knot in the cravat. Both garments slipped to the floor. Valentine's fingers itched as he watched. His mouth was dry. His heart pounded against his ribs.

Ava tugged the loose shirt from the breeches and then ran her fingers through her hair until the luxurious brown curls fell over her shoulders. He saw the outline of her hard nipples pressing against the fine lawn as she moved, and decided he was too impatient to wait.

"Help me undress." He came to his feet, was already unbuttoning his waistcoat as he closed the gap between them. Urgency almost made him rip the damn thing off his shoulders.

Ava fiddled with his cravat, and he helped her untie the knot. When they both stood in their shirts, she looked at him and arched a brow. "Who will go first?"

Valentine slid his arm around her waist and pulled her close until he felt the heat from her body. He kissed her, softly at first, until the raging fire within demanded more. One hand settled on her left buttock and squeezed, the other fisted into her hair, angling her head for a more in-depth exploration of her wicked mouth.

Their tongues danced in unison to the drumming beat of their passion.

Their ragged moans and pants filled the room, the sound sending another surge of blood to his cock.

"Tell me you want me, Ava," he said as he gripped her shirt and dragged it over her head.

The sight of her soft round breasts almost rendered him speechless. The pinkest nipples he had ever seen demanded his attention.

"God help me, you're so beautiful."

Without another word, he scooped her up into his arms and lowered her down onto the coverlet. In her embarrassment, she drew her arms across her chest, and so he climbed on top of her, pressed the full length of his body against hers and held her hands above her head as he reclaimed her mouth in another searing kiss.

Uncontrollable lust saw him grind his hips against her despite the fact they still wore breeches. Ava writhed beneath him, her legs instinctively wrapping around his hips as if her body ached for the pleasure he had promised.

He was in danger of being swept away by his passion. The urge to mate, to pound hard came upon him. But his pledge to bring her satisfaction was one vow he was determined to keep.

"Don't move," he said, releasing her hands. "We need out of these damn breeches."

She unhooked her legs, and he shuffled lower. With numerous sweeps of his tongue, he lavished her nipple, sucked and licked until she was panting.

She dug her fingers into his hair, guiding him to the other breast in need of the same level of devotion.

"Hurry, Valentine," she gasped. "I'm not sure how long I can wait."

"Desire can be overwhelming." As could love, he thought. "Tell me you need me—in your life, in your body."

"I have never needed anything more."

Ava watched him come to stand at the edge of the bed. He dragged his shirt over his head and then unfastened the buttons on his breeches. She watched him yank them down below his hips, watched the solid length of his manhood spring free.

Heavens above!

She should be frightened, but every bit of this man was as spectacular as the rest.

Needing no further inducement to hurry, Valentine undid the buttons on her breeches and tugged. The white drawers she wore underneath stunned him momentarily.

"Breeches can be uncomfortable for a lady" was the only explanation she offered when he gave a frustrated sigh.

"I understand your need for wearing them," he said, while she peeked at his throbbing erection. "But it is yet another layer of clothing keeping me from entering your body."

Ava wiggled her hips as he drew the undergarment down to

her knees. With a final tug, it joined the other discarded clothes on the floor.

Valentine's scorching gaze scanned every part of her naked body.

"Is something wrong?" she said, feeling vulnerable and exposed as he focused on the dark triangle of curls at the apex of her thighs.

"Wrong? For once in my life, everything is right."

Relief coursed through her. She feared his gallantry might prevent him proceeding. Tonight, she wanted to experience the physical bond of love. Tonight, she wanted the sinner, not the saint.

"I want you, Valentine," she said, should he be in any doubt.

"Then you shall have me."

He crawled up to kneel on the edge of the bed, giving her ample opportunity for another glimpse at the length of his arousal —so hard and solid. She expected him to cover her body, to have his thick rod of masculinity press against her intimate place. But he surprised her by spreading her legs wide and moistening his lips as if hungry for a feast.

"Prepare to be pleasured, madam," he said as he bent his head.

He left a trail of scorching kisses from her knee to the top of her thigh. When he moved between her legs, she wondered what he would do, but the sudden kiss pressed to her flesh sent a jolt of excitement straight to her core.

Her heart shot up to her throat.

"Valentine, wait." She threaded her fingers into his hair, trying to stall him.

The lick of his tongue on her aching bud robbed her of the will to fight.

He glanced up at her, those smouldering blue eyes conveying confidence. "I will keep my vow to you, Ava," he said, before delving into the forbidden place she never imagined a man would look at let alone lick and kiss and suck until—

"Valentine."

Like a wild wanton, she writhed against his expert mouth. The coil inside wound tighter and tighter until she wanted to cry out his name, wanted to take him with her on a glorious journey to fulfilment. And then the coil snapped.

Waves of ecstasy rippled through her body.

Her legs trembled as she soared.

Valentine came up on his knees. Lavishing her with attention had done nothing to dampen his own ardour. Had she been a little more daring she might have touched him, but he did not give her time to consider the matter further.

Wrapping his fingers around his manhood as she had imagined doing, he positioned himself at her entrance. She sensed his brief hesitation.

"Don't wait," she breathed. It would be uncomfortable for a time, but she didn't care.

"You're certain?"

"I have never been more sure of anything in my life."

He entered her slowly, withdrew a little and paused after each small nudge to give her a chance to catch her breath. He was so hard, so large, so magnificent, so male.

"I need to push deeper," he panted. "Forgive me if this causes you distress."

There was no time to answer. With a quick, hard thrust he pushed past her virginity.

Ava sucked in a sharp breath as he stretched her flesh. The searing pain tore a gasp from her lips.

Valentine moved to withdraw.

"No." She wanted him. She needed him. "Just give me a moment."

Regret swam in his eyes.

The muscles in his shoulders looked tense as he held himself rigid.

"Kiss me," she said, trying to banish all trace of panic from her voice. "Make love to me."

Valentine wasted no time in obeying her demands. He obliged her every whim, nuzzled her neck when she begged, thrust his tongue against hers when she gripped his hair and forced him to lock lips.

Slowly, he moved inside her, withdrawing, pushing a little harder and deeper each time. The sensation of his warm skin against hers set every nerve tingling. Soon, she forgot the pain and discomfort. The feeling of having him buried deep was like experiencing a piece of heaven on earth. His fluid strokes sparked the flame of desire. It wasn't long before she was writhing and panting to his glorious tune.

"I need to quicken the pace if I'm to find my release."

"Then hurry." Ava wrapped her legs firmly around his hips.

Valentine closed his eyes briefly and groaned as he pounded hard. Ava clutched the muscles in his back and rocked to his pace. When he opened his eyes, she saw a raw look of possession, a carnal need to claim.

With a sudden urgency, he withdrew from her body, pumped his glistening manhood with his hand until his seed spurted onto her stomach.

"You're mine, Ava," he said between ragged breaths.

She recognised the truth in his words.

Lucius Montford Harcourt Valentine belonged to her now.

"Stay where you are," he said, reaching beneath his pillow for a handkerchief to wipe away the evidence of his release. "I have not finished with you yet."

He came to lie beside her, slipped his nimble fingers between her legs, stroked and pleasured her until she came apart once again.

"I've decided I am not letting you leave," he said in jest.

Given the chance, she would have no objection.

Given the chance, she would remain locked in his warm embrace forever.

CHAPTER FOURTEEN

"I am not leaving my wife alone in the dark with a damn stranger." Drake folded his arms across his chest, a clear sign he refused to compromise. He scanned the sea of faces seated in the drawing room—Juliet, Dariell and Ava—before his attention turned back to Valentine. "God's teeth, you suspect this man, Cassiel, of stealing into Miss Kendall's home and threatening to murder her servants."

Valentine swallowed his frustration. He glanced at Ava seated on Drake's blue damask sofa. The wrinkles around her eyes and between her brows conveyed her apprehension about meeting the mystic again.

Two days had passed since Ava sent Mr Cassiel a note asking him to attend Mr Drake's dinner party. The scoundrel replied promptly, telling Ava that, as she would be in attendance, he did not need to meet with the Drakes prior to the event.

"Juliet can say she is unwell and does not wish to take part in the seance." Valentine glanced at the mantel clock as it chimed a quarter past eleven. They had less than half an hour before Mr Cassiel arrived.

"Miss Faversham did the same when we met with Mr

Cassiel," Ava informed them. "She refused to go home and so sat in the hall, reading beneath the light of a candle lamp."

Valentine thought it odd that a woman terrified by a character in a novel would want to stay in a house where the occupants were attempting to contact the dead. Then again, the dead did not get drunk and lose their temper.

Dariell sat forward and gave a curious hum. "This man who communes with spirits, it is important we let him believe he is alone in the room if we are to glimpse his true nature."

Being slight of frame and extremely light on his feet, Dariell had opted to hide inside the window seat during the seance. Fortunately, the Frenchman had returned to town to meet with the actress set to play the role of Lockhart's wife. Then again, Dariell always appeared when needed.

Drake sat forward. "I cannot sit alone in the dark and not know if Juliet is upset or distressed."

Valentine might have mocked him, but he understood his friend's need to protect the woman he loved. For a similar reason, Valentine had revisited the Pit and paid Connor Maguire a handsome sum.

"Please, Devlin," Juliet said from her seat next to Ava. "What if Mr Cassiel has a genuine ability to speak to those who have passed? I want my paternal grandmother to know that I think of her often even though we have never met."

Usually, Drake would berate anyone who believed such nonsense. He was a man who did not mince his words. Most men feared him. And yet with his wife, his gaze softened. "I swear if he does anything untoward we will send for the resurrectionists to take what is left of his body."

Valentine smiled to himself. It seemed Drake would indulge his wife's whims.

"Remember why we are all here," Dariell said, clasping his hands together in prayer as he studied them. "Your expectations, they must be realistic, no? When I meet this man, I will know if his motives are honourable."

Dariell excelled in reading the language of the body. Could he sense the intimacy whenever Valentine looked at Ava? Did he know that Valentine had slipped from the honourable path, had bedded an innocent and had yet to declare his intentions? Ava had remained at Valentine's house since the night he rescued her from the Pit. She had slept in his bed last night, too.

"There is not much time," Valentine said. "Are we all clear what we must do?"

Everyone nodded.

Dariell cleared his throat. "May I ask one question?"

"Of course."

He turned to Ava, who sat with her hands clenched in her lap. "Miss Kendall, you are frightened. Yet I sense it stems from more than the terrible thing this man said about your parents. May I ask what it is about him that makes you tremble?"

Ava gulped. Heat turned her cheeks crimson. She glanced at the other people in the room before finally saying, "I—I find him too familiar."

"Familiar?"

She shook her head. "Please, monsieur, do not ask me to explain."

Valentine's pulsed raced. Something else had happened in his mother's drawing room. If that filthy rogue had put his hands on her, there would be hell to pay. He was about to jump up from his seat and insist they abandon their scheme but Dariell spoke.

"Know, madame, that at no time will you be alone with this gentleman. One word from you and I shall be at your side."

"Thank you, monsieur. I only hope I can put on a convincing display, enough for Mr Cassiel to reveal his true intentions."

"I have faith in your courage, madame."

A growl resonated in Drake's throat. "I do not like this. I do not like this one bit."

The sudden echo of the brass knocker hitting the plate made the ladies catch their breaths.

The clip of the butler's heeled shoes on the hall floor rang like a death knell.

"Cassiel is prompt," Valentine said. "I'll give him that."

Silence descended.

The tension in the air proved palpable.

They were supposed to be enjoying an evening of merriment not sitting like mourners at a wake.

"It will look rather odd if he finds the room deathly silent when this is supposed to be a party," Valentine added. "Does anyone have an amusing story?"

Another brief silence ensued.

"I caught Devlin on all fours growling at Rufus the other day." Juliet chuckled. When Drake groaned, she arched a brow and said, "What? You were."

"How else am I to get the beast off my bed when he pretends he's not heard me?"

"Rufus is their dog," Valentine said, noting Ava's frown.

"A rather large dog," Juliet added. "Though lovable all the same, just like his master."

Drake smiled.

A knock on the door brought Copeland. He inclined his head to Drake. "Mr Cassiel is here, sir."

Valentine's heart thumped wildly in his chest. The man was guilty of distressing Miss Kendall. That was enough for Valentine to despise him.

"You may show him in, Copeland."

They waited with bated breath.

Angelo Cassiel entered the room.

He was dressed all in black except for a blood-red cravat tied expertly around his throat. The contrast was striking, leant towards the macabre for one could not look at him without imagining the cravat was soaked in blood from a gash to the throat.

Cassiel's finely tailored clothes were expensive. Perhaps a spirit had sent a message conveying the place of a hidden legacy. Perhaps Mr Cassiel kept the information to himself and had stolen into the poor person's house and robbed them of their inheritance.

Drake came to his feet and straightened to his full height as he made the introductions. "I am honoured you could find the time to attend our little gathering."

Mr Cassiel's assessing gaze roamed over the guests like the essence of a malevolent spirit seeking the weakest upon which to prey.

"I work on recommendation, Mr Drake." There was a cadence to his voice that was almost holy, like that of a monk who formed his words with great thought and insight. "Lady Valentine was particularly kind during my visit, as was Miss Kendall."

Ava looked up from her lap and pasted a confident smile. "My appreciation of your talent has left me desperate to hear more, sir."

The warm glow of pride settled in Valentine's chest. No one would know that the man's presence made her uncomfortable.

Mr Cassiel inclined his head. "Then I pray I bring you more comforting news this evening."

"Cassiel, it is an unusual name," Dariell said from his fireside chair. "It is what actors call a stage name, no?"

Mr Cassiel's dark eyes flashed with suspicion. "I assure you, there is nothing staged about my ability to hear the deceased," he replied without answering the question.

"I did not imply there was," Dariell countered. "I am merely curious whether you found the name, or it found you."

"The dead found me when I was five years old and have clung to me ever since. I hope that answers your question."

Dariell studied Cassiel for a moment and then rose from the chair. "Well, I must bid you all farewell. As a sceptic, I would not wish to ruin the party."

Mr Cassiel's shoulders relaxed. Oddly, he did not attempt to persuade Dariell to stay. Were men of his ilk not desperate to convert non-believers?

Dariell said good night and left the room. The front door opened and closed, but they all knew the Frenchman had not left the house. Where he had gone and how he planned to hide in the window seat was a mystery.

Drake gestured to Dariell's empty seat. "Please sit down, Mr Cassiel."

The man thanked Drake and took a seat. His naturally sullen features—large pouting lips and heavy-lidded eyes—created an air of unpredictability about his countenance that reminded Valentine of being in his father's presence.

"What a shame your friend could not stay." Mr Cassiel turned his eerie stare towards Valentine, his gaze dropping to the scratch on his cheek. "When a man wanders in the dark, he is but a few steps from tragedy."

Valentine's blood turned cold. The comment related to Dariell's disbelief but his mind jumped to the obvious conclusion. Was Cassiel referring to the night his father tumbled—or threw himself—from the cliff edge?

With a mental shake of the head, he dismissed the mystic's attempt to intimidate.

"Some people prefer to live peacefully in ignorance," Valentine countered.

"And some men never know inner peace, though their confident countenance says otherwise."

Bloody hell!

Could this man read his mind?

"Peace comes from acceptance," Drake said, "not from a word of encouragement from a relative long since deceased."

Cassiel arched a thick brow. "Even when the nature of a loved one's death is uncertain?"

The comment wiped the grin from Drake's face. While he had

come to terms with his brother's death, there was uncertainty about the way Ambrose Drake had died.

"And what of me, Mr Cassiel?" Ava looked the man keenly in the eye. "If my parents wanted to bring me peace why frighten me by revealing that they were … were murdered?"

Cassiel opened his arms wide and shrugged. "I have no control over the messages, my dear. But tonight, with your permission, I shall ask poignant questions in the hope of bringing answers to light."

Ava's face grew pallid.

Valentine wished he could take her in his arms and offer the comfort she desperately needed—take the comfort he needed, too.

"Well," Juliet began, being the only one not unnerved by the mystic's odd revelations. "When shall we begin? I have to admit to being rather keen to hear if you have a message for me."

Cassiel pulled his watch from his waistcoat pocket and examined the time.

Valentine was the only one who appeared to hear Ava's gasp.

She stared at the watch with a look of shock and confusion. "That is a rather unusual watch, sir." The slight tremor in her voice was unmistakable. "Made in Switzerland I believe."

Cassiel thrust the watch back into his pocket, but not before Valentine noted the design on the lid of the gold hunter case. The circle in the centre resembled an image of the sun, each triangular marking around the circumference like the points on a compass. In contrast, the enamel decorating the outer bezel was a vibrant blue.

"Yes," Cassiel replied. "I believe so. It keeps excellent time."

"I knew a man who had one similar," she persisted.

"I gather it was a popular design." The mystic stood. "Now, the hour is approaching midnight. Before I begin, I would like a tour of the house."

Damnation. What if he stumbled upon Dariell?

"Is that necessary?" Drake did not sound pleased.

"You may accompany me. The energy does not flow freely in some places, and so I must assess where to position you to best achieve success."

Was this what happened at his mother's house?

Was this how Mr Cassiel discovered what was worth stealing?

"Then let us get on with it," Drake said, most irritated.

"As you wish."

As soon as Drake and Cassiel left the room, Valentine turned to Ava. "What was it that unnerved you? The fact you recognised the watch? Or had it more to do with the man you knew who owned one?"

Ava's meditative gaze remained fixed on the fire. She shook her head as if trying to drag her mind from a cloud of confusion. "I have seen that watch before." She peeked back over her shoulder at the door before whispering, "Mr Fairfax owned one similar if not identical."

"Your father's man of business?"

She nodded.

Valentine contemplated the information. Perhaps it *was* a popular design, owned by many men. But Mr Cassiel had revealed private information about her parents, and Mr Fairfax had been in Hamilton Kendall's employ. Had the two men corresponded? Had Mr Fairfax divulged family secrets before meeting his demise?

"Another man might tell you it is a coincidence, that there are many watches of a similar design," Valentine began. "But I am inclined to believe there is a connection. I am inclined to think that Mr Cassiel does not need to contact the dead for he is already party to the information."

"You mean from an informant?"

"I mean from a friend or relative who worked with your parents."

Juliet turned to Ava and patted her hand. "Devlin told me

177

what happened to your parents. This must be very distressing for you."

Valentine watched as Ava fought back the tears.

Hell, he would make Cassiel pay if his suspicions proved accurate.

Ava's shoulders sagged. "Part of me wants to run away, to find a distraction. Part of me wants to fight for those who can no longer do so for themselves."

The pain in her voice tore at Valentine's heart. He stood, was about to cross the room and offer comfort when Cassiel and Drake returned.

Valentine's fingers throbbed. Punching Cassiel would bring temporary relief from the anger simmering beneath the surface. But he kept his temper at bay.

"We have found suitable places for you all," the mystic said, moving farther into the room.

From the look of Drake's clenched jaw, he was unhappy with the arrangements.

"Mrs Drake will sit in the study." Cassiel pressed his hands together in prayer and closed his eyes as if receiving divine enlightenment. "Mr Drake is to occupy the master bedchamber."

"And where shall I sit?" If Cassiel could hear voices they would tell him to put Valentine in the coal shed.

"You're to take a guest room. I shall show you which one."

Valentine stepped closer to the fraud. It was whilst staring down his nose at Cassiel that recognition dawned. This was not the man who followed Miss Kendall to the pawnbroker. Cassiel was not the man who attempted to steal the lady's reticule. He was a few inches too tall. Even in this dim light, it was clear to see that his black hair was a few shades too dark. Yet he matched the description of the intruder who stole into Miss Kendall's house.

"I would prefer to remain here, in this room," Ava said, the evidence of her distress still apparent in her voice.

Juliet draped an arm around Ava's shoulders. "Just thinking of her parents has brought on a bout of melancholy."

Cassiel's eyes flashed with a brief look of satisfaction, but then he bowed his head and said, "If that is your wish, my dear."

"It is."

"Then while we are all together, let us recite the prayer now. It will give your loved ones time to gather the strength needed to cross over to the physical plane. It will protect us from those malevolent spirits who may wish to cause harm."

Drake met Valentine's gaze and shook his head.

"Please stand and form a circle." Cassiel ushered them into the centre of the room. He stood behind them, moving to touch each one on the shoulder in turn. "Heavenly Father. Protect us this night from evil forces intent on mischief and mayhem. Protect all those in this house, now and when they depart. Let the power of light surround us to bring forward those who wish to commune with honest intentions. In the name of goodness, we thank you. Amen."

Valentine glanced at Ava and forced a smile. She looked gaunt, a little terrified of what the night might bring. It crossed his mind to put an end to this debacle, but then Cassiel spoke.

"Let us move to our respective rooms. Let us hear the messages from the dead."

CHAPTER FIFTEEN

The room was dark. Blackness invaded every space. The incandescent glow of the snuffed candlewicks had long since faded. Having doused the fire's flames with water—for the spirits moved best when the room was ice cold—Ava saw nothing before her eyes but indiscernible shadows.

The tick of the mantel clock mirrored the thump of her heartbeat.

Every hair on her nape stood to attention.

Mr Cassiel had brought a chair from the dining room and placed it in the middle of the plush Persian rug. He had stood behind her and put his hand on her shoulder, rubbed back and forth in what was supposed to be a gesture of reassurance. Yet something about his manner stirred painful memories of the past. Something about his manner caused nausea to roil in her stomach.

"I sense your mother" was all he said before leaving her alone in the darkness.

Time ticked.

The faint click of the door opening sent a shiver from her neck to her navel.

A grey silhouette moved towards her.

Ava's breath caught in her throat as her heart raced.

"It is I, madame, do not be alarmed," Mr Dariell whispered as he moved to the window seat. He raised the lid and slipped inside.

Knowing the Frenchman was hiding there brought mild relief. The charged energy in the room felt very much like it did on her previous meeting with the mystic. Shadows swayed. One might think that the spirits of the dead filled the gloomy space. But fear played havoc with one's mind.

A host of thoughts filled her head. Would she hear from her parents? Was this all a wicked trick to prey on the weak and helpless?

The tread of footsteps on the stairs drew her attention. A board creaked.

Her ragged breathing grew too loud for her to concentrate on the sounds.

The door opened. She knew the approaching figure was that of Mr Cassiel.

Fear might have choked her again had she not smelt the fragrant tones of her mother's favourite perfume. Hints of frankincense filled the air. An exotic scent bought by her father on a trip to the Arabian Peninsula.

Ava closed her eyes.

Her mother felt close, so close Ava envisioned reaching out to touch her.

Tears splashed on her cheeks as she fought the urge to whisper her mother's name, knowing this was all a cruel figment of her imagination.

Mr Cassiel did not attempt to settle her nerves. He began his strange mantra, the stream of words he repeated over and over and over until she felt herself sinking deeper into the depths of her body. Down. Down. Down, her mind spiralled. As she slipped farther into the distance, her anxiety melted away. A hazy mist appeared, swirling to hinder her vision, surrounding her, carrying her forward now.

"Let me take you back to the night before that fateful day. Back. Back. Back to your last conversation. Do you remember, my dear?"

The cloud dissipated as she stepped through into another dimension. She was no longer in the drawing room on Wimpole Street but walking from the house overlooking the Aegean Sea. She felt hot under the rays of the midday sun, so hot beads of perspiration formed on her brow.

"Something is wrong." Ava spoke with a genuine concern for a moment in time that had long since passed. "I am heading towards the tent near the mine."

"Your mother is worried." Mr Cassiel's words drifted over her. "Her spirit cannot rest."

Somewhere in a distant corner of her mind, Ava heard her mother crying. "My mother is upset because she does not want to return to England. My father insists it is necessary."

"Yes, your father is frightened."

Ava struggled to accept the comment. Nothing fazed Hamilton Kendall. "No. Not for himself, but for his family."

Mr Cassiel fell silent.

"Yes, yes, I will convey the message," he eventually muttered. "Your mother passed suddenly. She cannot rest until she knows you have retrieved their belongings."

The mist returned, a fog of confusion acting as a barrier to this otherworldly place. "I am walking but not moving."

Mr Cassiel continued his mantra in low, hushed tones. "Even if you cannot look with your eyes, you can see with your mind. Ask a question, and the answer will appear to you."

As if commanded by Mr Cassiel's will, Ava silently asked to see her parents. The image became clearer though she had moved forward in time. "Yes, I see them now. I peek into the tent, and my father is kissing her, telling her it is his responsibility to protect his family. Feeling their love, I move away."

"Do not go yet, look around the tent. What can you see? Precious stones? Papers?"

"Nothing. I move away and … wait. I see Mr Fairfax hiding behind the tent. He approaches me and asks if everything is all right." Ava experienced a sudden rush of anxiety. Her heart pounded so hard she thought it might burst from her chest. "I am scared and so answer quickly before running into my parents' tent."

The images faded.

Everything went black.

"Your mother cannot rest," Mr Cassiel repeated in whispered tones. "She wants to leave you her legacy, wants you to continue her work, but she has lost the one thing you need."

The words meant nothing to Ava as she hovered in the darkness.

"You must find this thing that is lost," Mr Cassiel persisted. "You must find it if you want to bring her peace."

"I see nothing," she said, peering into the blackness.

Mr Cassiel continued speaking in a calm voice, offering reassurance and counting in the methodical tone that seemed to wrap around her waist like a rope and pull her up from the dark depths. Upon the count of one she resurfaced, found herself back in the gloomy drawing room far away from the idyllic life she once knew.

The pain of grief filled her chest.

She wanted to go back to the scene with her parents, to keep the memory alive.

"Your mother seeks reassurance." Mr Cassiel moved to stand before her. "She cannot rest until she knows you have taken possession of her personal effects."

"I have," Ava blurted before her rational mind protested. However, she could not speak with the same confidence about her father's precious items.

Mr Cassiel crouched and placed his hands on her knees.

Panic surfaced.

"I will leave you for a short time," the mystic said. His long fingers moved in massaging strokes. "While I am gone, think about what she needs to bring her peace. What is it you would need to continue her work in the Mines of Lavrion?"

Ava stared at the hands gripping her knees. Thoughts of Mr Fairfax filled her mind, ugly thoughts, terrifying thoughts.

A sudden coughing fit came upon her. Despite numerous attempts, she could not clear the irritation from her throat. Mr Cassiel moved to the side table. She heard the clink of crystal, the slosh of liquid.

He returned to her side and offered the tumbler. "Drink this. It will calm your nerves, soothe your throat so we may continue."

A sudden bang from the room upstairs made her jump.

Mr Cassiel stared up at the ceiling. "Rest for a moment. I shall return shortly."

Valentine thought he might go out of his mind if he sat in the dark a moment longer. The silence proved deafening. Every passing second felt like an hour. With this form of torture, a man might lose control of his mental faculties.

Ava was in the room beneath him.

Lord knows what mischief was afoot.

Valentine wasn't sure if Dariell had returned to hide in the window seat, and so all he could do was sit in the darkness and imagine the sheer terror coursing through her veins.

It was a mistake.

He should never have insisted she partake in this charade.

Valentine smacked the floor with the heel of his boot again out of frustration. The crafty sneak might be tormenting Drake or Juliet though he could not imagine Cassiel staying with them for long. Most men struggled to breathe beneath Drake's penetrating stare.

The creak of the boards on the landing sent Valentine's pulse racing. Fear had nothing to do with the sudden rush of blood. Vengeance burned now. He would play Cassiel's game. Allow the mystic to think he had the upper hand.

Valentine remained seated in the chair positioned in the middle of the room.

The hinges on the bedchamber door groaned as Cassiel entered.

"You grow impatient for a message, my lord," he said, closing the door and coming to sit on the edge of the bed opposite Valentine. "Do you have an item of jewellery, a watch or fob I may hold for a moment? Personal effects help to establish a connection."

Having already given Maguire his watch, Valentine would be damned before he gave this thief his seal ring. He wondered what his mother had given. The diamond ring she had worn since her wedding had borne witness to many sleepless nights, many traumatic days. Valentine pulled his most recent purchase—a sapphire pin—free from his cravat and handed it to Mr Cassiel.

Cassiel inclined his head.

"You are a man of many secrets, Lord Valentine," the mystic said in the pathetic voice he used to sound superior.

"As are most men," Valentine retorted.

Didn't everyone have something in their past of which they were ashamed?

Didn't everyone carry guilt over a failed relationship?

The mystic clutched the cravat pin and closed his eyes.

Silence pervaded every corner of the room.

The stillness grew heavier until Valentine felt the weight of it pressing down on his shoulders. An icy chill touched his cheek. Men like Cassiel knew how to taunt and tease the mind.

The mystic started muttering, mumbling. A hum resonated in his throat like the morbid murmurs of the dying.

They were nought but theatrical tricks. Tricks meant to weaken the constitution.

"You were a boy when it started," Cassiel said, his tone soft, slow, though his eyes remained closed. "Too young to understand."

"To understand what?" The sickening feeling came upon him, the same curdling sensation in his stomach whenever he thought about his father.

"That it was his illness that spoke to you. That his violent temper had nothing to do with a lack of love."

Bloody hell!

Valentine considered jumping to his feet and telling this devil of a creature what he thought of his parlour games. But something kept him rooted to the chair. The little boy inside him needed to hear more in the hope one word—*sorry*—might bring an end to his torment.

"Children often have an immature view of the world, a view moulded by their relationship with their parents." The logic of the statement brought temporary relief from the anxiety settling in his chest. "I was lucky enough to have a parent brimming with integrity, a parent I respect and admire."

Honora was strong, dependable, loved with all her heart. His father was unbalanced, irresponsible, too lost in the failings of his mind to appreciate love.

"But despite the light, darkness stalks you like an ominous shadow in the distance," Cassiel said.

"Is it not the same for us all?"

Cassiel's eyes sprung open. For a moment, they held the crazed look he had seen when his father's mood turned sour, when his actions proved irrational, when no one knew what the hell he would do next.

"Your mother has suffered greatly."

"She has," Valentine agreed, despite wishing to tell him to mind his own damn business.

"She has hidden the secret for so long."

Valentine shuffled uncomfortably in the chair. He did not like where this conversation was heading. Were these the random guesses of a clever man using specific words to incite a reaction? Were these the words of a mystic receiving information from a higher plane?

"We are not here to discuss my mother."

"No, we are here because you fear that your father still lives inside you."

"I don't know what you mean," Valentine replied, quick to dismiss the notion that he was tainted, too.

A smirk touched the mystic's thick lips. "Have you not behaved irrationally? Has the madness not extended its claws and dug its nails into your skin?"

The mere hint that Valentine had somehow inherited his father's bad blood caused red-hot fury to rage within. Was that not proof the devil spoke the truth? Was anger not the way evil controlled the mind?

Valentine wasn't sure how Cassiel knew the things he did, but this man was a criminal who thrived on treachery and deceit. Honora must have given away her secrets. She must have given the man the parts of the puzzle for him to piece together.

"There is only one madman in this room." Valentine firmed his jaw. "There is only one man with a propensity for evil, and it is not me."

Cassiel grinned. "The guilty always use threats as a means of defence. Give the matter some thought for I shall leave you alone for a time while I present messages to the other guests."

Valentine's temper had reached the point of no return.

"Messages? You deliver distress. You rouse the devil and allow him to do his devious work."

"What? You are a man of piety now?"

"I am a man of logic." Valentine leant forward. "You told Miss Kendall someone murdered her parents. Why?"

A brief look of shock marred his dark features. He swallowed audibly. "That is what I saw in my vision. That is what the voice of—"

"You're lying." If Cassiel could hear voices from beyond the grave why did he not know of their deceitful intentions? "What purpose might you have for causing her pain? What purpose might you have for breaking into her house and ransacking her room?"

Cassiel shot to his feet. He raised his chin, offered a perfect place for Valentine to land a punch. But he would not hit a man without provocation.

"You have inherited your father's lunacy."

That was the only provocation needed.

The punch came hard and swift. The jab connected with Cassiel's jaw to send the man flying back onto the bed. Valentine grabbed Cassiel by the waistcoat and dragged him to his feet.

"Tell me the damn truth." A strange smell clung to the man's clothes and skin and Valentine resisted the urge to inhale. "Did you enter Miss Kendall's home uninvited? Did you lie to her about her parents?"

Cassiel fought and wrestled to free himself from Valentine's grip. "You have lost your mind."

The mystic could not have said anything more damning.

Valentine dragged him from the room by his blood-red cravat to the staircase. "If I have lost my mind, then I may as well throw you down the stairs. Did you enter Miss Kendall's house?"

Panic distorted Cassiel's dark features. "I have not seen Miss Kendall since … since the night at your mother's house."

"You're lying, damn you." Valentine shook him. "Who told you about my father's illness?"

The door to the master bedchamber burst open, and Drake came charging out. "What the hell is going on here?"

Drake's arrival distracted Valentine momentarily. He loosened his grip on Cassiel's cravat, and the mystic took the opportunity to yank himself free. With no time to lose, he raced down the stairs, slipped down the last few.

"That devil is a damn fraud." Valentine hurried after Cassiel.

Arms flailing, the mystic reached the front door, but he would be lucky to set foot on the pavement before Valentine caught him.

Valentine was on the bottom stair when Miss Kendall came running out of the drawing room.

She threw herself at Valentine, mistaking his rage for distress. "What is it? What did he say to you?"

Valentine looked at Ava, noted the whites of her eyes were bloodshot, noted the dark circles beneath her bottom lids. Her face was porcelain white, her lips drawn thin, and all he could do was pull her into an embrace and offer soothing words of comfort.

Over her shoulder, he watched Cassiel scurry away.

The man would not get far. Come the morning Valentine would hunt him down and drag the truth from the devil's lips.

"The man has evil motives," Ava said. "He poured me a drink, but Dariell advised not to let a drop pass my lips."

Dariell appeared at the drawing room door. "Come. Let us sit for a moment. We cannot tear through the streets at this hour. We should discuss our findings, no?"

Valentine agreed. They should compare notes while the mystic's words were still fresh in their minds.

While Valentine, Ava and Dariell returned to the drawing room, Drake went to the study to fetch Juliet. Once they were all seated, and Dariell had taken it upon himself to light the fire and candles, the Frenchman gave his account of the mysterious goings-on in the drawing room.

"I am no expert when it comes to manipulating the mind, but Mr Cassiel, he does not hear the dead."

Ava gasped. "But how can you be so sure?"

"The man's words sent you into a deep meditative state, a

trance." Dariell sat forward. "If I spoke in a certain way—slow and hypnotic—it is possible to send a person to the far reaches of their mind."

"Trust me," Valentine began, trying to dismiss the theory that Ava had somehow lost control of her senses. "I was fully aware of all that took place. The man was playing games, using information about my family to cause me distress."

"Information about your father?" Drake enquired.

Valentine nodded. "Information few people are privy to."

"I cannot speak for what happened upstairs," Dariell said, "but Miss Kendall's mind did slip back in time. I was here. I heard what she said."

Valentine glanced at Ava who had taken the seat next to a curious-looking Juliet. A mild sense of panic gripped him when he noted the distress in her eyes. "What did you say, Miss Kendall?"

"Nothing of great importance. He spoke about the prospect of me continuing my mother's work." She frowned as if struggling to remember. "But Mr Dariell is right. Somehow I travelled back in my mind to the day before my parents died."

"You were just reliving memories," Valentine said, softening his tone for he had no desire to make her feel foolish.

"But I saw my parents as clearly as if they were standing here. The smell of my mother's perfume filled the room." She inhaled deeply as if hoping she might still catch a whiff of the fragrance. "The scent is rare, purchased abroad."

Drake cleared his throat. "Might the primary note be frankincense?"

"Why, yes."

Drake stood. He crossed the room and offered Ava a small brown vial. "This fell out of Cassiel's pocket during his tussle with Valentine."

Ava's hand shook as she accepted the tiny bottle.

Juliet looked up at Drake and gave a smile full of love and

longing. Drake took his wife's hand and squeezed gently before returning to his seat.

Ava studied the bottle before pulling the stopper and inhaling the contents. She closed her eyes. A tear fell and landed on her cheek. "It is so similar to my mother's scent. In my confusion, it smelt the same."

Valentine watched her. The knot in his stomach wrung tighter with every sniff, every tear.

Propriety be damned, Valentine thought. They were amongst friends, and so he rose from his chair and came to sit next to Ava on the sofa. He draped his arm around her and drew her to lean on his shoulder.

Drake smiled at them before saying, "I think it is fair to say that Mr Cassiel is a fraud, a very clever fraud. The question remains how he knew that was your mother's preferred scent? Did you mention it to anyone?"

"No." Ava paused. "I may have mentioned it at one of our meetings."

"Miss Kendall meets with friends at my mother's house every Friday," Valentine informed.

Silence descended.

"Now I am rather glad Mr Cassiel did not come to visit me in the study," Juliet said.

"He did not visit me, either." Drake's voice brimmed with tenderness. "But we do not need to hear of the past. All that matters is the present."

Juliet smiled at him again, in the intimate way that made Valentine feel as if they were intruding.

Dariell sighed. "Drake is right. And yet Miss Kendall faces a situation that stems from the past but is very much active in the present. I am afraid to say she will have no peace until we discover what Cassiel wants."

"I shall visit him tomorrow." Valentine would relish another opportunity to punch the rogue.

"And I shall accompany you." Drake seemed equally eager to flex his fists.

Ava shuffled in the seat to face Valentine. "But I have no idea where he lives."

There was a moment's silence.

"What do you mean? You sent a letter asking Cassiel to attend the dinner party, and he replied." Valentine saw Ava give the boy the note but had not enquired as to the mystic's address. "You contacted him and made the arrangements for him to come to my mother's gathering."

"Well, yes, though I did not contact him directly."

Valentine frowned.

"Miss Faversham recommended him but was too nervous to suggest it to the group. She found the advertisement in the newspaper. Regarding the party tonight, I sent Miss Faversham a note asking Mr Cassiel to attend."

"Then you have never met Mr Cassiel before that first night?"

"No. Miss Faversham booked the appointment on our behalf."

CHAPTER SIXTEEN

"We must call on Miss Faversham as a matter of urgency."
Valentine sat back in the carriage seat and cursed under
his breath. Ever since his conversation with Cassiel, he could not
shake the sense of agitation writhing beneath his skin. "The lady's
timidity is a perfect mask for her deception."

Ava cast him a disapproving look. "We do not know that Miss
Faversham has deceived us. You have condemned her before
hearing what she has to say."

Valentine snorted. "Miss Faversham set up the initial meeting
with Cassiel." His tone was blunt, sharp enough to take the bris-
tles off his chin in one clean sweep. "The girl is afraid of her own
shadow, and yet she agreed to contact a strange man who delves
into the black arts. The evidence speaks for itself."

They had conspired to steal his mother's ruby, had entered
Ava's house looking for other items of value.

A heavy tension filled the air.

Ava lifted her chin. "And I encouraged her to find her voice,
to find the strength needed to survive as a woman on her own."

"She won't be a woman on her own," he snapped. "The major

will find her a suitable husband, and she will have no choice but to marry."

"How noble of him," Ava mocked. "Of course, I could always invite Miss Faversham to live with me."

Agitation grew to irritation.

It crossed his mind to inform her that, as her husband, he would not have Miss Faversham living in their house, but the need to calm his temper forced him to say, "If that is what you want."

Ava stared at him. Water filled her eyes. She turned to watch the dark shadows whipping past the window.

The pervading silence fed the restlessness within.

He had never felt more alone.

"Tell Sprocket that I wish to return to Park Street." She did not look at him, but he felt the words like a sharp slap to the face.

Had Cassiel cast an evil spell that swallowed happiness, churned it up and spewed it out?

Twenty minutes ago, Valentine had been comforting her on Drake's sofa. Now they were quarrelling about Miss Faversham. But this wasn't about Miss Faversham's duplicity. It was about the boy who feared he might one day wake up to find he'd inherited his father's lunacy.

"It is not safe for you there." Valentine knew what it was like to fear closing one's eyes at night.

She turned her head slowly, struggled to hold his gaze. "It is not safe anywhere. And you cannot take care of me forever." She lowered the window and called up to Sprocket to relay her intentions before closing the window and sitting back in the seat.

Marry me.

That was all he needed to say. But he would tell her the truth about his past before gathering the courage to ask.

"Forgive me if I do not seem myself," he began, laying down his sword to offer a truce.

She glanced at the window as if she had lost interest in the conversation.

"Being alone with Cassiel—" He paused. "Well, the man can play havoc with the mind."

Her mask of indifference slipped. "I imagine he would struggle to unnerve a man with your strength and mental agility."

"It has not always been the case." It was not the case now. Thoughts of the past brought the fears of a weak and helpless boy to the fore. "Cassiel knew something from my past and sought to use it to weaken my stance."

The information sparked her interest. "Did he succeed?"

Valentine sighed. "I think my mood since we settled into the carriage would suggest he achieved his goal."

The scuffle on the stairs had given Valentine an outlet for his fury. Now, he needed another distraction if he hoped to banish the ghost of his father.

Ava swallowed visibly. "And what … what did he tell you?"

"He told me bad blood flows through my veins, too." Valentine inhaled a deep breath. "He told me that I possess the same propensity for madness as my father."

"Madness?" Ava frowned. She shuffled forward in the seat. "But that's ridiculous. You're the sanest, most rational man I have ever met."

The compliment meant more to him than she could possibly know. Usually, words of praise and flattery failed to penetrate. He had heard enough falsehoods from fawning parasites to pay them no heed. And yet Aveline Kendall's opinion touched him on a level he could not quite explain.

"My father suffered from a condition of the mind." There were no words to express the debilitating nature of the illness— both for the patient and his family. "His behaviour was often irrational, unstable. By rights, he was a perfect candidate for Bedlam during his delusional episodes. But my mother chose to keep him at home."

Ava covered her mouth with her hand as her breath came almost as quick as his. "It must have been difficult." Compassion swam in her beautiful brown eyes. "How did you cope?"

Valentine couldn't help but smile when he thought of his mother's courage.

"Honora knew that if someone were to discover the truth it would taint our family name, would make it difficult for me making my way in the world. She cared for him, kept the secret hidden, made excuses when he was unwell, invited close friends to the house when my father was feeling his best."

"Honora is loyal to a fault."

Pride filled his chest when he thought of his mother's sacrifice.

"Her life might have been different, but she loved him."

"And she loves you. Very much."

"Yes."

Silence descended though he could almost hear the loud chatter of her thoughts.

"He died tragically." The words left Valentine's lips as if he were talking about a stranger, someone for whom he held no regard. A cold, clinical approach was a means of protection. "During one rather manic episode, he fell from the cliff on our family estate."

Ava drew in a sharp breath. "Oh, Valentine. I am so sorry." She crossed the carriage to sit beside him, captured his hand and hugged it to her chest. "I know what it is like to lose a parent in tragic circumstances. I know what it is like to feel so helpless you want to run away. Is that why you spent so much time abroad?"

It had taken many drunken nights with his friends, many hours engrossed in business to realise one could not escape the past.

"I left because I did not want Honora to live her life for me. I left to give her freedom, freedom to live, freedom from the haunting memories."

"Then know that since making her acquaintance, she has talked about nothing other than you." Ava brought his hand to her lips and pressed a kiss to his knuckles. He was thankful he had not taken the trouble to wear gloves. "I cannot tell you how thrilled she is to have you home."

"And I cannot tell you how thrilled I am to be back."

It occurred to him that despite a week of turmoil and upheaval—a week far removed from the calm, ordered existence he thought he craved—he had never been happier in his entire life.

"Know that I am always here for you, Valentine, should you feel the need to talk." Ava smiled. "I have admired Honora from the moment we met, more so now I know the hardship she has suffered. She truly is a remarkable woman."

"She is, which is why I have never wanted to disappoint her."

Ava nibbled her bottom lip as she studied him. "And yet you have not married Lady Durrant when you know how much Honora wants to see you settled."

A sharp pang of guilt stabbed Valentine in the chest. But then realisation dawned. Marriage was about love, about loyalty, about trust and friendship. Honora had taught him that. He glanced at Ava seated beside him, gripping his hand to offer reassurance. The prospect of spending an eternity with her did not seem the least bit daunting.

He sighed as he gathered the courage to tell her what she meant to him.

Ava must have mistaken his silence for dejection. Pressing another kiss to his palm, she shuffled closer. "Mr Cassiel is an evil man with sinister intentions. Do not let his silly remarks affect you. And surely Honora must understand why you find the thought of marriage unnerving."

Valentine was about to put her mind at ease, explain that he didn't give a damn about Cassiel, that nothing would make him offer marriage to any other woman but her, not even his respect for his mother, but Ava cupped his cheek, leant forward and kissed him full on the mouth.

"You are everything a gentleman should be," she said, kissing him again, her lips as soft as velvet. "You are the most remarkable man I have ever met."

As always, she tasted of everything that was right with his life.

Valentine slipped his hand up to cup her neck, his fingers delving into her hair in massaging strokes. As her luscious lips met his once more, he was determined to show her that she had quickly become the most important person in his life. With a blinding passion reserved only for her, he made love to her mouth. In the slow, intoxicating way he might claim her body, his tongue swept over her lips before sliding into the warm, wet place that felt like heaven.

Heat pooled low and heavy in his loins.

Ava responded with the same intense level of intimacy. Her tongue tangled with his in a tantalising dance, moved to a sensual rhythm that left them both moaning into each other's mouths.

Mindful that they were in a carriage, Valentine knew they had to stop. Except that her eager hands wandered over his chest, caressed his shoulders, exploring every line of muscle.

Her sudden urgency to touch him fuelled his desire.

Attempting to gather a firm grip on his restraint, Valentine tilted Ava's head back and pressed his lips to the place where her pulse pounded against her throat.

"Valentine," she panted. The word spoke of the hunger, of the craving that plagued him, too. "Don't stop."

Those two words stoked the fire burning in his veins.

"Don't ever stop touching me."

"Hell, Ava. You know how to tempt a man to behave scandalously."

The more he lavished her with attention, the more she begged him to continue. He continued to suck and nip her neck in the erotic way that left her breathless. The yearning inside grew. The throbbing ache of his erection pressed against his breeches. His mind was lost in a heady state of arousal.

Dainty fingers traced a nervous path from his knee up to the top of his thigh. The temptress drew a groan from his throat as she dared to touch the solid length desperate for freedom. Encouraged by his pants of pleasure, she stroked him slowly through the material until his restraint snapped.

"Damnation," he muttered, dragging her across his lap to straddle him. "I said I wouldn't make love to you in a carriage."

Heat smouldered in those dark brown irises. "I would not have you break a vow on my account," she said in the voice of a skilled coquette.

"It wasn't exactly a solemn promise." He held her firmly on his lap while he shuffled forward and drew the blinds. Nothing would stop him having her now, not even his own damn conscience. "I don't imagine it will be comfortable."

"Stop talking. It is your turn to undress."

"Undress? Madam, this will be a wild and reckless mating in a conveyance. There's no time for anything else."

Ava smiled as she shuffled off his lap. "It sounds thrilling, highly exciting."

He had to agree.

While he unbuttoned his breeches and took hold of his throbbing erection, Ava hoisted her skirts up to her waist.

"How is it done?"

"You may sit astride me, or I can bend you over the carriage seat." Lord, he could not believe he was having this conversation. "If we are to behave with wanton abandon, we may as well embrace the role."

"May we try the latter?"

"Without meaning to sound like a libertine, I have no preference as long as I am inside you." Love and lust, it seemed, went hand in hand.

The lady cast him a sinful grin. She turned around and offered him a glorious sight of her soft, round buttocks as she gripped the back of the seat.

Valentine came behind her. He slipped his fingers between her thighs, teased her until she was more than wet and willing. After an awkward fumble, he pushed inside her, so achingly slow the power of it made his knees tremble. There was nothing crude about their joining. The essence of this woman surrounded him, drew him deep to cement the bond that could not be broken.

Slick with the evidence of her arousal, he thrust inside her, deep inside, so deep the loud slapping was like an erotic melody to his ears.

"Do you want to move to a more comfortable position?" he asked, leaning over her to massage the sensitive spot between her legs.

"Not yet," she panted, throwing her head back as her movements became fevered, more erratic.

He played her like a master pianist tinkled the ivory keys— with skill, precision, in the expert way that said the union was destined long before tonight. She came apart calling his name. She muttered something else, and in his desperation to know her innermost thoughts, he imagined he heard the word *love*.

With one more thrust, Valentine withdrew and spilt the evidence of his need for her into his hand. Reaching for his handkerchief, he cleaned away all traces of his recklessness before assisting Ava with her skirts and helping her back into the seat.

It took a few breaths for her to regain her composure. Her cheeks coloured crimson, yet it did not stop her watching him as he tucked his manhood back into his breeches.

"May I ask you something, Lucius?"

It was the first time she had used his given name. He liked the way the word sounded on her lips.

"As long as you've not changed your mind about the position and wish to try the other way." It was too much to expect a man to make love in a carriage twice in one day, though he would have no problem rising to the occasion.

She chuckled. "Perhaps you should see if Mr Cassiel has an opening for an apprentice. You seem to have the ability to read my mind."

As his mind played a mental picture of their amorous interlude, it suddenly occurred to him that the carriage had stopped.

"Any vigorous activity inside will be noticeable now we're not rumbling through the streets." He noted the mischievous glint in her eyes. "You're mocking me. That was clearly not the question you wished to ask."

"No," she said, offering him a smile. "I want to know if it is always like this."

"It?"

"This wonderful thing that exists between us." Ava waved her hand back and forth between them. "Is passion always so overwhelming? So all-consuming?"

"No." Was this her way of asking if she meant something to him? "I have certainly never experienced a feeling like this. What happened at the beginning stemmed from an outpouring of emotion, the consequence of two people sharing a deep and abiding affection. What happened then was that physical lust got the better of us."

"It did," she agreed.

"I want you, Ava, in every way possible." Valentine cleared his throat. He was about to take the biggest risk of his life. "Sometimes it is easier to express one's feelings physically than it is to make a declaration."

She swallowed visibly. "What are you saying?"

Valentine leant forward and raised the blinds. He would have the best light possible in which to judge her reaction.

Ava glanced briefly out of the window. "We've arrived in Park Street." A sudden gasp left her lips, and she pressed her nose to the glass. "Valentine," she whispered, despite the fact they were the only ones in the carriage. "Look."

"In a moment, there is something—"

"There's a man at Honora's front door."

"A man?" The comment distracted him. His mother never entertained gentlemen at home. His mother never entertained gentlemen.

"Pay it no heed. No one will answer at this ungodly hour."

He was right. No one answered. No one needed to. The blighter opened the door and crossed the threshold.

"He is entering your mother's home."

The rogue turned to face them as he closed the door, the light from the street lamp illuminating the left side of his face. Valentine recognised the man instantly. As did Ava.

"Good Lord," she said, just as shocked as he. "Tell me I am mistaken. Tell me that is not Jonathan."

"No, you're not mistaken." Anger banished all romantic thoughts of love. Jonathan *bloody* Kendall was like a thorn buried deep in his backside. "And we are about to find out what the hell he's doing stealing into my mother's house."

CHAPTER SEVENTEEN

An icy shiver ran the length of Ava's back, banishing the heat still simmering in her veins after her illicit encounter with Valentine. The image of Jonathan sneaking into Honora's house had drawn her attention away from whatever the dashing lord was about to say.

"I'm sure there must be a valid reason for his call." The comment sounded pathetic to her ears. What possible reason could Jonathan have for making such a late-night visit? Had Honora unlocked the door in open invitation? Or had he forced it from the jamb moments before they arrived?

"You understand that if he causes my mother distress, I will kill him," Valentine said in the hard voice of a man who would do anything to protect his family. Gone was the smooth, husky tone she had relished mere moments ago.

"Jonathan may be a fool, but he would never hurt Honora."

"Not directly, no. But there is only one reason why he would steal into her house in the dead of night."

Ava scoured the recesses of her mind, trying to find a logical explanation. But Valentine was right. "You think *he* stole the ruby and swopped it for paste." It was a statement, not a question.

"After his recent antics, you must admit the idea has merit. But we will soon know for sure." Valentine opened the carriage door and jumped down to the pavement. "Wait here."

Ava wasn't sure if the command was meant for her or Sprocket. "I am coming with you."

Valentine hesitated for a second before his hands settled on her hips. He lifted her to the ground but did not relinquish his grip. "Tell me that whatever happens here will not change the way we feel, will not change the affection that has developed between us."

Ava sucked in a breath. Her brother's duplicity was bound to make things difficult. But Valentine meant more to her than anything.

"Regardless of my brother's crimes," she said, placing a hand on his chest, "my love for you is not fickle."

He stared at her as his breathing quickened. The beginnings of a smile played at the corners of his mouth. "Ava …"

"Come," she said, pulling away from him. "Heaven knows what Jonathan is doing in there. We cannot delay a moment longer." She captured his hand and drew him across the street.

"Once we have dealt with this matter, there are things I need to say."

"Yes," she said, nerves bringing a sudden bout of nausea to roll around in her stomach.

They came to an abrupt halt outside Honora's front door. The house lay in darkness. Ava strained to listen, though no sounds of distress emanated from within. It did not bode well. Despite all that Jonathan had done to save her from Mr Fairfax, she could not forgive him this.

"Ready?" Valentine's hand settled on the doorknob.

"Ready."

He turned the knob gently, used two hands to prise the door from the jamb. The hinges creaked. Valentine paused, then he ushered Ava across the threshold and closed the door behind them.

Valentine slipped his arm around her waist and drew her close. "We will start by checking the drawing room," he whispered, his mouth pressed to her ear. "That's where Honora keeps the gold goblet she uses to store the ruby."

Ava nodded.

Perhaps he was aware of her trembling legs, of her clammy hands and racing heart. "The truth serves us better than falsehoods," he said before pressing a chaste kiss to her lips.

They approached the drawing room door, but the faint hum of conversation drew them farther along the hall to another principal room, a more relaxed space Honora used to entertain friends.

The deep reverberating tones of a masculine voice mingled with the quiet yet confident voice of the mistress.

Relief settled in Ava's chest as she listened to the incoherent mutterings of their conversation. She touched Valentine's arm. Touching him brought comfort. Touching him gave her the strength to deal with her troubles.

"They sound calm," she whispered, "not at all agitated. Perhaps there is an innocent explanation."

Valentine frowned. "Whatever brings him here, I suspect it involves a certain amount of deception."

He had a point.

Ava noted the tension radiating from the man she loved. How she hoped it was not something to make him doubt his mother's love and loyalty.

In a sudden move, Valentine opened the door and strode into the dimly lit room.

Ava followed.

The couple seated on the chintz-covered couch jumped in shock. Jonathan almost choked on his port while Honora placed her sherry on the side table and came to her feet.

"Lucius, what a pleasant surprise." There was an uncharacteristic tremble in Honora's voice that belied her look of innocence. "What on earth are you doing here at this ungodly hour?" Her gaze dropped to the scratch on her son's cheek. When she glanced at Ava, a satisfied smile formed.

Valentine cast Jonathan a hard stare and her brother shuffled uncomfortably in the seat.

"What am I doing here?" Valentine said, his tone full of reproach. "I might ask the same of Mr Kendall."

"Me? I came to call on my sister, and was worried to find her house empty," Jonathan explained. So worried, he could not look his sister in the eye. "She was not there when I called yesterday, either."

"And so you let yourself into my mother's house at almost three in the morning," Valentine said, avoiding the question of Ava's whereabouts, "and she happened to be up and dressed and waiting to greet you."

Honora chuckled. "Surely you don't suspect us of conducting a liaison. Mr Kendall is young enough to be my son."

"Of course not," Valentine snapped. "Should you partake in a romantic relationship I hope the gentleman might possess a modicum of intelligence."

"Now listen here," Jonathan began though struggled to appear affronted.

"That is exactly what I intend to do," Valentine retorted. "I will listen while you tell me what the hell you're doing here. Since when do people make house calls in the middle of the night?"

Jonathan raised his chin. "A more pressing question might be why the two of you are together at such an hour."

Honora approached her son with outstretched arms and drew him into an embrace. "Come. Sit with us. Share a drink and let us speak about this like mature adults. There is much to discuss."

Ava glanced at Valentine. "We should take a drink. It has been a long night." And a rather exhausting one to boot. She smiled at

Honora. "We attended Mr Drake's dinner party where Mr Cassiel provided the entertainment, hence the lateness of the hour."

"You saw Mr Cassiel again?"

"He broke into Miss Kendall's house while we were rescuing her brother from being beaten to a pulp by Mr Maguire." Arrogance filled Valentine's voice as he delivered the comment like a sudden punch.

Honora appeared unfazed. "Yes, and Miss Kendall has been staying in Hanover Square ever since."

Valentine's eyes widened. "You know about the intruder, about Mr Maguire, about my need to offer Miss Kendall a safe place to stay?"

"Mr Kendall spoke to Mrs Stagg yesterday when she returned to the house to fill a valise."

Heat rose to Ava's cheeks. By rights, she should have approached Honora for help. It would have been the respectable thing to do.

Valentine remained silent for a brief time. "Then know that with regard to Miss Kendall, my intentions are honourable."

"By honourable you mean honest though not necessarily moral?" Honora replied, though she did not seem annoyed or shocked.

"I am standing here," Ava reminded them. They spoke as if oblivious to the fact. "Regardless of how this looks, Lord Valentine is a dear friend who offered his assistance in a time of great need."

Honora touched Valentine affectionately on the upper arm. "My son is the most loyal and trustworthy friend a lady might have."

"He is," Ava agreed.

"But he also carries a position of responsibility that means his conduct is open to scrutiny." One could not mistake Honora's meaning. "I'm afraid Lady Durrant has had a lot to say on the matter."

Valentine breathed a weary sigh. "I never intended to disappoint you, but you know that I cannot make Lady Durrant an offer no matter how hard you try to convince me of her suitability."

A mischievous grin played on Honora's mouth. "I have never thought Lady Durrant a suitable companion for you, Lucius."

Valentine frowned. "But I made a vow."

"A vow to marry. A vow not to let past experience act as a deterrent." Honora glanced at Ava and smiled. "You were the one who mentioned Lady Durrant. I simply went along with the notion, knowing one day you would come to your senses."

"Tell them," Jonathan interjected. "Tell them what brings me here."

Ava considered her brother's tense shoulders, noted the dark circles under his eyes. "Tell us what?"

"Every gossip in the *ton* believes you're conducting an illicit affair," Honora informed them. "By all accounts, Lady Durrant grew desperate and decided to visit you at home, Lucius. Before alighting from her carriage, she watched you escort Miss Kendall inside."

A sudden panic sprang to life in Ava's chest.

Guilt flared when she considered the fact that despite her protestations about having worldly experience, she had become one of those foolish girls whose scandalous activities provided hours of ballroom entertainment.

Valentine shrugged. "I don't give a damn what the gossips have to say. Surely my own mother must know that I take responsibility seriously. Miss Kendall and I will be married."

"I should damn well hope so," Jonathan mumbled.

It took a moment for Valentine's words to penetrate Ava's addled mind. She should be ecstatic at the prospect of spending a lifetime with the man she loved. But something about the comment left her cold to her bones.

Did he want to marry her out of guilt?

Did he want to marry her because his position demanded he act responsibly?

Did he want to honour his vow?

An outpouring of sadness, of disappointment, whirled in her chest, growing in size and momentum the more her mind concocted its imagined stories.

"Would you excuse me for a moment?" Ava did not wait for a reply but turned on her heels and hurried from the room.

"Ava, wait," Valentine called, giving no regard to the fact he had used her given name.

Once out in the hall, the urge to run came upon her. Before her mind protested otherwise, she opened the front door and ran across the street.

"Ava!"

Rain fell, the drops landing like tears on her cheeks as if somewhere amidst the heavens her parents shared her disappointment, too.

The thud of Valentine's boots pounding the ground behind sent her pulse racing. As she reached her front door, he grabbed her arm and swung her around to face him.

"Please tell me you are not running from me," he said, his blue eyes filled with fear and doubt. "Do you not want to be my wife? Can you deny the passion we share?"

Part of her wanted to tell him she was silly. What lady would not want to marry him? Part of her had hoped for so much more.

"How can you ask me that?" Her heart was racing so fast it thumped against her chest. "Have you not heard what I said? I love you. I have given myself to you, the only man with whom I could ever share such an intimacy. Does that not tell you everything you need to know?" She dashed tears and raindrops from her cheek. "For an intelligent man, you surprise me."

A smile formed on his lips. The frown on his forehead faded and his eyes shone with a brilliance she had not witnessed before.

"What?" she snapped. "You find the fact I have bared my soul amusing?"

"No, Ava. I find the fact you love me makes me grin like a mule eating briars."

Still feeling a tad confused, she said, "Well at least one of us is being open with our feelings. But despite the fact Society may deem me the great whore of Babylon, I cannot marry you, Valentine."

His amusement faded. "You love me. Nothing else matters."

"It is not *my* feelings that are called into question."

Was the man being deliberately obtuse?

Was it just that he wanted to hear her repeat her declaration?

Valentine slapped his hand to his chest, covering his heart as if mortally wounded. "You doubt the depth of my feelings? Did I not tell you, moments before we spotted your brother breaking into my mother's house, I had something I wished to say?"

He had said that.

He had said that they shared a deep affection.

"You did," she confessed. "What was it you wanted to say?"

Valentine stepped closer, his muscular body pressing her against the door, reminding her of the first night he kissed her in the mews. He cupped her cheek, and her heart quickened again beneath his touch.

"There is no other woman in the world for me, only you. You stole my heart the moment I underestimated you on the battle-field. You claimed my soul the moment you lowered your guard and turned to me for help. I am in love with you, Ava. Nothing would make me happier than if you consented to be my wife."

The surge of emotion brought tears to her eyes. "You do?"

"I do." He pressed his body against her, kissed her with a passion that conveyed the full extent of his feelings. "I have seen you strong, courageous and fiercely independent. I have seen you cry in my arms, seen fear mar your perfect features. I have heard your moans of pleasure, heard your voice raised in anger, and I choose it all. Everything. Every laugh. Every tear."

Something between a laugh and a cry burst from her lips. She wrapped her arms around his waist, relished the unique scent that clung to his clothes, to his skin. Love filled her heart, so bright, so intense, so powerful.

"And I love the honourable gentleman and the scandalous libertine. I choose them both. I choose you, Valentine."

They shared a kiss as hot and as wicked as the one they shared that night in the mews. Soon their breathing grew short and shallow. Had she a key to hand, she would have dragged him by the cravat into her house, though she doubted they would have made it past the stairs.

Valentine straightened and took a step back. "Thank the Lord it is three in the morning and your neighbours are about their beds."

Ava glanced at the house across the street, to find Honora and Jonathan staring at them through the drawing room window. "Not all the neighbours are abed."

Valentine followed her gaze. "I almost forgot about our interrogation."

"Interrogation?"

"For once in my life I find myself questioning my mother's honesty. They share a secret," he said, nodding to the two people still staring. "And I'll be damned if I'll leave here before knowing what it is."

CHAPTER EIGHTEEN

Valentine stared at the guilt-ridden faces of his mother and Jonathan Kendall as they sat together on the couch. After a moment of celebration, where he informed the pair that Ava had consented to be his wife, he resumed the role of judge and jury.

"You say you owed our father a debt," Ava said from the chair next to Valentine's, positioned purely to appear more intimidating. The low table between them acted as a barrier to prevent Valentine from launching forward and throttling Jonathan Kendall.

"A debt it has taken me almost eighteen years to repay," Honora confirmed.

"May we know what it is?" Valentine asked with some impatience. It was hard to focus on the task when love for the woman at his side filled his thoughts.

Honora turned to Jonathan Kendall. "Trust that Valentine will protect her until we resolve this matter." When Kendall nodded, she focused her attention on Valentine. "Hamilton Kendall once came to my rescue when your father suffered from his first disturbing episode. We were at a ball, and Hamilton offered his assistance. I told him then that I considered myself in his debt. As the years passed, I never expected he might seek to remind me of my vow."

A wave of regret swept through Valentine. He would have liked to meet Ava's father. If only to ask what the hell had happened to Jonathan when it came to inheriting family traits.

"My father came to you when he purchased the house across the street?" Ava asked. "That was the last time he came home before he died."

Honora smiled. "When Hamilton realised I occupied the house opposite, he paid more than the market value to ensure you would have a home close to friends."

Ava gave a contented sigh. "He was always thoughtful like that."

"Hamilton asked me to keep something safe for him. He gave me a sum of money—even though I refused the offer numerous times—and told me that upon news of his death I was to hire an agent to keep a watch on his man of business."

"Mr Fairfax?" Ava shivered visibly upon mentioning the name.

"Indeed."

"Father suspected the man had devious intentions that went beyond his designs to marry you," Jonathan interjected, "and he was not wrong."

Ava sucked in a breath.

Valentine was thankful Fairfax had perished in the mine else he might have had to track him down and beat him black and blue.

"While I would not wish death upon anyone," Ava said, "I am rather glad he met his end."

A look passed between Honora and Jonathan that cast doubt upon the statement.

An icy chill ran the length of Valentine's spine.

Ava gripped the arms of the chair so tightly it looked as if the bones might pierce the thin skin covering her knuckles.

"Despite the agent's reassurance, Mr Fairfax did not die in the mine." Jonathan spoke softly, as though he knew the fact would cause his sister great pain. "Mr Fairfax is alive and well and behaving as deviously as Father predicted."

"Alive?" Ava gulped. "Oh."

Valentine attempted to piece together the snippets of information. "Are you saying Hamilton asked you to safeguard something fearing what Mr Fairfax might do?"

Honora straightened. "Just before Hamilton returned to London, he bought another five-year licence to mine in a particular spot on the coast of Greece. Few people are granted permission. I have that licence." She paused and swallowed deeply. "He also gave me a … a rare ruby on the understanding that I would keep it a secret from his children until such a time as the agent proved that Mr Fairfax was no longer a threat."

Honora tried to hold Valentine's gaze, but a flicker of shame flashed in her eyes.

Valentine knew why. "So Hamilton did not sell you the ruby as you claimed?"

"No," she said, briefly lowering her gaze, "but you understand why it was important that I not mention it to anyone."

"Not even to your son?"

"Not even to you, Lucius." Honora winced as if the words pained her.

"I see."

"You must understand, had Hamilton not come to my aid in the ballroom, everyone would have learnt of your father's illness. I trusted him to keep our secret, and I afforded him the same courtesy."

Valentine accepted her reason for withholding the truth—*lying* was too harsh a word. But what about the theft of the gem? Did Mr Fairfax know Honora had the ruby? If he was the one responsible for stealing into the house and making the swop, why was Valentine instructed to investigate his mother's friends?

"What of the paste replica sitting in the goblet in the display cabinet?" Valentine said. Judging by the way his mother shuffled uncomfortably in the chair, he did not have to say anything more.

Jonathan Kendall's pained expression served as forewarning, for Valentine knew that Honora's next comment would invariably cause him distress.

This time, Honora held Valentine's gaze. "*I* had the paste replica made, fearing Mr Fairfax might discover its whereabouts." She coughed to clear her throat. "The real ruby was not stolen but is stored at the bank."

Valentine sat in stupefied silence.

The world he knew tilted, leaving a sudden imbalance.

What astounded him most of all was not that his mother had concocted a story based on a vow she had made in the past, but that she had involved him in this invented tale. Why?

"I know you're disappointed, Lucius."

"Disappointed?" Hell, this was the first time in his life his relationship with Honora had ever been called into question. "You lied. To your own son. You led me on a merry dance."

Honora flashed a mocking grin. "Hardly. Other than attending the meeting here the other day, you have made no enquiries into the stolen gem."

Anger bubbled in Valentine's chest.

"No, because I have been assisting Miss Kendall in her efforts to save *that* fool." He stabbed his finger at Jonathan Kendall. "To save *that* fool from ending up dead in a ditch." He shook his head and exhaled. "Besides, the damn thing hasn't even been stolen."

Ava shuffled her chair closer to Valentine and placed her hand on his forearm. "Honora would not have lied to you without a justifiable reason."

Valentine cast Ava a sidelong glance. "I understand her reason. It hurts that she felt she could not trust me."

"I know." Ava offered a weak smile.

"My father once told me that if I ever found myself in trouble,

I was to seek your mother," Kendall interjected.

Valentine gritted his teeth. He refused to listen to a man with the brains of a trout. "Don't tell me you have been pestering my mother to pay your damn debts. I hope you received the long lecture about family and responsibility."

"Won't you at least allow him to finish," Honora chided. She rose from her seat and moved to the console table to refill her glass with sherry. "Perhaps then you might have a different opinion."

The fool had gambled away his inheritance, disrespected his father's name, trampled over the years of hard work. The buffoon showed little regard for Ava's welfare, did not protect her as a brother should. Valentine doubted anything would change his opinion.

"Then please continue." Valentine gestured for the man to speak. "Feel free to enlighten us."

Honora appeared at Valentine's side. She thrust a tumbler of brandy at him, offered Ava a glass of sherry. Perhaps they needed a drink in preparation for whatever nonsense Kendall was about to spout.

"The debt I owed to the Maguires was not a gambling debt," Jonathan began.

Valentine arched an arrogant brow. "You mean the debt you now owe me."

Jonathan sighed and dragged a hand through his mop of dark hair. "I do not have a gambling problem, but it serves me for Fairfax to think that is the case."

"You don't?" Ava sat forward. "Then why are you pawning your belongings? Why did you sell Mother's ring?"

Jonathan hung his head and rubbed his chin.

What could be so damning that he found it difficult to speak?

Honora crossed the room and placed a tumbler of brandy on the table in front of Kendall before dropping back into her seat.

"Your brother borrowed money from those ruffians at the Pit, ignorant to the exorbitant rate of interest," Honora said, clearly aware of Kendall's dealings with the Maguires. No doubt she knew of Ava's attendance and of Valentine's involvement, too. "Money he used to pay Mr Fairfax. The scoundrel is blackmailing Mr Kendall." She cast Kendall a sidelong glance and shook her head. "Oh, if only you would have sought my help sooner."

A heavy silence descended, almost suffocating in intensity.

The colour drained from Ava's face as she stared wide-eyed at her brother.

Valentine sat back in the chair as if someone had slapped him to his senses, while Kendall's cheeks turned crimson.

"Mr Fairfax is in London?" Ava's voice trembled.

What the hell had this blackguard done to make her fear him so?

"No. I meet him at the coaching inn near Frimley," Jonathan explained. "As long as I pay him the agreed sum, he assures me he will not venture farther north."

"Frimley?" Ava's hand shook as she gripped the stem of her glass. "But that is only thirty miles away." She brought the glass to her lips and drained it of sherry before shuddering visibly.

"I have hired a runner to watch him in my absence."

With a host of questions filling his head, Valentine wasn't sure which one to ask first. Why did Kendall not just shoot the rogue and dump his body in the Thames? And why had Kendall called Valentine out when he had more important problems?

Even for a man with some intelligence, it still proved baffling.

Valentine cleared his throat. "May I start by asking about the threat that prompts you to pay the blackmailer?" No sooner had the question left his lips than he felt Ava's penetrating stare search his face. "What hold does the man have over you?"

Perhaps Fairfax had witnessed fraudulent business deals.

Jonathan looked at Ava, his eyes softening with what appeared to be compassion.

"Does it have something to do with me?" Ava suddenly asked.

A nervous silence hung in the air while Valentine awaited an answer.

After exhaling a weary sigh, Kendall said, "It is not so much that Fairfax holds a secret, but that he has made threats regarding the safety of my family."

"You mean me," Ava blurted. "Fairfax has threatened to hurt me."

"He has." Kendall's tone was full of regret.

For the second time this evening, a fury to rival that of the devil's burning rage burst to life in Valentine's chest. If Kendall did not have the courage to snuff out this blackguard, Valentine would. He would see to it that Fairfax hadn't a breath left in his lungs let alone enough to make despicable demands.

Through the chaos of his mind, a thought struck him. He turned to Ava. "Might I be right in thinking you once thought yourself in love with Mr Fairfax?"

Hell, it killed him to utter the words, no less imagine that her heart once pined for another. So much for the calm, rational approach. The sooner he dealt with Fairfax, the better, for his heart was liable to give out.

"Not in love with him, no," she answered honestly. "Perhaps it was more of a mild infatuation, one quashed when I realised his intentions were far from honourable."

Valentine saw the truth in her eyes, eyes that still held a hint of fear. "And he harmed you in some way?"

Ava gulped. "He tried to force a wedding, if you understand my meaning."

The blood froze in Valentine's veins. "Then there is little point discussing the blackmail because I am going to kill him anyway."

Honora gasped. "Lucius, do not lower yourself to this man's standards. There must be another way to get rid of him."

"Fairfax wants the licence Father secured to access the mines," Kendall said. "By all accounts, Father promised him a partnership. He also demands the return of the ruby he says was promised to him upon our father's death. Payment for his services."

"But that is ridiculous," Ava protested. "Father would never —" She stopped abruptly. A frown marred her brow. Numerous times she shook her head as the worry lines grew more pronounced.

Valentine touched her arm. "What is it?"

"Mr Cassiel mentioned the mine. He said that my mother couldn't rest, that she wished us to continue her legacy, and asked what was needed to work in the Mines of Lavrion."

Valentine contemplated the information. One might think that Cassiel did possess powers of an otherworldly nature. But the watch, the vial of frankincense, all the questions relating to the same topic, cast doubt in Valentine's mind.

"One might think that he did hear the voice of my mother," Ava added, mirroring Valentine's fleeting thought.

"Or one might think he is employed by Mr Fairfax to discover if you know the whereabouts of the licence." Valentine studied Ava's face, knew the moment she accepted his explanation as being the rational one.

"Mr Fairfax is a man of great cunning," Honora said. "We must deal with him, and quickly."

First thing in the morning, they would call on Miss Faversham. A woman with such a nervous disposition would break easily. Once they knew the whereabouts of Cassiel, Valentine would deal with that problem before advancing on Fairfax.

But there were still a few questions bouncing back and forth in Valentine's mind.

"Aside from all of the problems with Fairfax, Mr Kendall," Valentine said in a hard tone for he would have a truthful answer. "Why would you add to your troubles by calling me out?"

Honora huffed. "You speak of that silly duel." She looked down her nose at Kendall. "Go on, tell him."

An embarrassed flush coloured Jonathan Kendall's cheeks. He

snatched the tumbler and downed a mouthful of brandy. "Lady Durrant paid me to call you out." His shoulders sagged, and his grey eyes brimmed with mortification. "At the time, I was desperate to meet Fairfax's weekly demand, though Portia thinks I am addicted to the gaming tables."

"She paid you?" Ava asked incredulously. "And you took that woman's money?"

Valentine knew of Portia's deviousness but had not realised how low the lady would stoop.

"Mr Kendall came to me the day before the duel, when he finally found the courage to take the advice given by his father," Honora said, shaking her head at the fool sitting at her side. "I assured him that Lucius had too much integrity to shoot a man without cause and that all he had to do was delope."

Valentine supposed he should be flattered that his mother had faith in his character despite the fact she hadn't trusted him with the truth.

"Lady Durrant did not want Valentine dead." Ava sounded annoyed. "The woman wanted to make him jealous. A blind fool could see that."

"I played her game," Kendall said, "for my own ends."

Valentine gritted his teeth. "And all the time you were playing games, scrambling to pay the blackmailer, lying to conceal the truth from your sister, you left her vulnerable to an attack from unexpected quarters."

Kendall dragged his hand down his face and sighed.

"Hence the reason I told the tale about the theft," Honora said.

"Told a tale, Mother? You sent your son on a fool's errand."

Honora lifted her chin and with an air of hauteur said, "Someone had to watch Aveline while her brother made a trip to Frimley, while he attempted to find the funds to pay those rogues at the Pit. He refused all offers of financial help and so what else could I do?"

Valentine eyed her suspiciously. Did his mother have another motive for throwing him in Aveline Kendall's path? Did she hope he might come to admire the lady as she did?

"Are there any other secrets either of you wish to divulge?" Valentine said when the long-case clock in the hall finished chiming four. If they were to make an early start in the morning they needed sleep, although sleep would be the last thing on his mind once Ava stripped out of her clothes and slipped into bed beside him.

Honora looked at Kendall and shook her head. "Will you help Mr Kendall, Lucius, help him bring this villain to justice?"

Valentine did not need time to contemplate the question. "I will do whatever is necessary to protect Miss Kendall."

"Excellent." Honora clapped her hands and came to her feet. "Then let us part and get some much-needed rest. We can resume this conversation in the morning."

"A sensible idea," he said in a mocking tone.

"I am glad you agree." Honora crossed the room. "Aveline, allow me to escort you upstairs to find a suitable bedchamber."

Valentine jerked his head back.

Ava glanced at him, and then at his mother. "You want me to stay here tonight?"

"Of course." Honora arched a brow. "You cannot stay with Lucius. Gossip is rife. I refuse to give Lady Durrant more reason to spread vicious rumours about my family."

Ava nodded. "Very well."

What else could she say?

It pained Valentine to think of sleeping without her tonight. He needed her in his bed, needed the closeness, the heightened level of intimacy that existed when two people were in love.

"When this is over, I might tell Lady Durrant what I think of her meddling," Ava said.

"When this is over," Valentine replied as a plan formed in his mind, "we shall show Lady Durrant how wrong she was to assume you are anything less than a lady."

CHAPTER NINETEEN

"How are you progressing with the reading task, Miss Faversham?" Ava spoke softly, avoiding the real questions burning in her mind, for she doubted they would get anything from the girl if she crumpled to the floor a blubbering wreck.

Despite it being rather early in the day for a house call, no one turned away a viscount. While Honora took tea with the major and Mrs Faversham in the drawing room, Valentine and Ava occupied the sitting room at the rear of the house.

"I am on the second volume of *The Monk*. Mrs Madeley has the first volume, and then I think she is to pass it on to you, Miss Kendall."

"And what are your thoughts on the novel so far, Miss Faversham?" Valentine asked, staring at her over the rim of his teacup.

Matilda's bottom lip trembled, and she could not hold Valentine's gaze. "On the novel? Oh, it is not for the f-fainthearted, my lord. Particularly when one shares a n-name with a character."

"Particularly when that character is corrupt and responsible for Ambrosio's descent into sin," Valentine added, setting his teacup and saucer on the side table. "Deception is a trope rife in gothic novels, rife in everyday life, too."

"I'm afraid I rarely venture from the house, my lord," Miss Faversham said. "Reading about such things in n-novels is the limit of my experience."

"That surprises me." Valentine sat forward. He appeared calm, in complete control of his emotions, much like the day of the duel when he forced his way into Ava's hackney cab and spoke so openly about love.

Matilda's eyes widened. "Oh, and why is that?" She was about to take a sip of tea but froze with the cup a few inches from her mouth.

Perhaps Matilda expected a compliment about being more confident than she gave herself credit. She most certainly was not expecting Valentine to broach the subject of the mystic.

"You have no qualms contacting an unmarried gentleman. One might wonder how you came to make the acquaintance of Mr Cassiel."

The china cup clattered on the saucer as the girl's hand shook. She paled. Silence descended when she failed to respond.

"Well?" Ava said, keen to encourage Matilda to answer. "Did you not say you found his advertisement in the newspaper?"

"Yes." Matilda nodded, setting her drink back on the tea tray. "That is correct."

"Which newspaper?" Valentine enquired.

"Pardon?"

"Which newspaper prints such an advertisement when most people find the notion of contacting the dead offensive, against Christian beliefs?"

Matilda tried to force a smile. "I cannot remember."

"Did you want to contact the dead?" Valentine pressed.

Ava recalled Matilda's reluctance to participate. And yet, now she came to think of it, the girl had not seemed fazed by the mystic even though his appearance might be considered unusual.

"You had met Mr Cassiel before that night," Ava said. It was the only explanation to account for Matilda's lack of reticence around the gentleman. "It was your suggestion we hire him."

"No." Matilda shook her head.

"We met with Mr Cassiel last night," Ava said, knowing she had to tell a tale to draw the truth from Matilda's quivering lips. "He mentioned you were acquainted prior to that first meeting."

"Yes," Valentine added. "He persuaded you to approach Miss Kendall with the idea of a seance."

The girl looked to be drowning under the weight of questions, drowning from the knowledge that she could not save herself no matter how long she held her breath.

"We are in love," she suddenly blurted. Matilda gasped as if the words eased the searing pain in her lungs. "We met in the bookshop, meet there when Mother permits me half an hour to peruse the shelves."

Ava's frustration dissipated.

Miss Faversham was a victim of deception, too, it seemed.

"Angelo is in need of money." Matilda glanced over her shoulder to the door. She lowered her voice. "We are to elope once he has saved the necessary funds."

Valentine relaxed back in the chair. No doubt he thought the gesture might encourage Matilda to speak more freely. "And so he prompted you to find him work, knowing you meet at my mother's house on a Friday."

"I didn't think it would do any harm," she confessed. "As enlightened ladies are w-we not looking to further our minds?"

"We are," Ava said. Matilda would suffer greatly once she learnt the truth about the mystic. Clearly, the thought of escaping her parents' home proved too tempting to resist. "Though that does not explain why Mr Cassiel broke into my house, or the fact Mrs Stagg said you were his accomplice."

Matilda froze. Her breath came in rapid pants.

"We know what Mr Cassiel was looking for," Valentine said.

The girl hung her head. A sniff turned into a sob. Her shoulders shook from the sheer force of her release. "I didn't w-want to do it."

"Why would you treat my belongings with disrespect when I have been nothing but kind to you?" It hurt to think of the hours Ava had spent trying to restore Matilda's confidence only to feel the sharp stab of betrayal.

Matilda raised her gaze. Her eyes were bloodshot, rimmed red. "I knew nothing of his plans. Y-you have to believe me. He left a note in the garden, in the usual place, and I snuck out of the house to meet him on the corner of Mount Street." A sob choked her throat, forcing her to gasp.

"You could have refused to enter Miss Kendall's house," Valentine said coldly.

"He told me to wait outside the house while he spoke to Miss Kendall. I didn't know he had forced his way inside … not until I heard a commotion and ran to investigate. Then it was too late."

"I want his address," Valentine demanded in a voice that would make the strongest man crumple. "I want it now. Else I shall stride into the drawing room and inform your parents that you are guilty of aiding a criminal."

It was as if Satan had risen to poke her with his fiery trident. Miss Faversham jumped from the chair, her whole body trembling so fiercely she struggled to catch her breath. "What will you do to him?"

"We want to ask him some questions about his associate, that is all," Ava said, trying to get through to the girl. "We believe a friend or family member may have influenced him."

She dashed the tears from her eyes. "You think Angelo was forced to act so dreadfully?" Hope clung to every word.

"That is what we are attempting to establish," Valentine said in a calmer tone.

After a brief pause where Matilda muttered to herself, she finally said, "Head to Cheapside. You will find Angelo in Coleman Street."

"And the number?" Valentine stood. Clearly, he was in a hurry.

"Don't tell him I told you," Matilda blurted.

Valentine straightened to his full height. "The number."

"Five, Angelo lives at number five."

❀

It was noon by the time Ava and Valentine reached Coleman Street with Mr Drake in tow. Valentine insisted on calling for his friend, explaining that should anything untoward happen, he would not leave Ava at the mercy of the blackguard Cassiel.

"Do we have a plan?" Mr Drake asked as they navigated the busy street, dodging wild dogs and filthy children eager to earn a penny.

They had left Valentine's carriage in Basinghall Street for they did not wish to alert Mr Cassiel of their arrival.

"I thought we would knock on the door and wait for a reply," Valentine mocked.

"What, before beating him to within an inch of his life?" Mr Drake looked rather pleased at the prospect.

"Something like that."

They came to a halt outside Burton's barber and wig-making shop.

"This is number five." Valentine glanced up at the three-storey building. "Cassiel must lodge in a room above the shop."

"It might make it more difficult to gain entrance," Ava said as a cold shiver ran the length of her spine. Mr Cassiel had a strange command over her senses. The thought of seeing him again left a lump in her throat.

Valentine and Mr Drake looked at her and smiled.

"Trust me, we will gain access to Cassiel's room," Valentine said before pushing open Burton's door.

They all entered the shop.

One of the gentlemen seated on a wooden bench—there were five men in total—looked up from his newspaper and scanned Valentine's pristine attire before sighing.

The fellow shook his head and turned to the man seated beside him. "Looks like we have a longer wait than expected. The quality always move to the front of the queue."

The barber loomed over a man reclining in a chair near the window. He swept a lethal-looking razor the length of the poor fellow's neck. Razor in hand, he glanced at the door, his eyes growing wide as he, too, perused their clothes.

"May I help you?" The barber wiped the blade on the white sheet draped over his customer's clothes before approaching them.

Ava grimaced upon seeing the spots of blood splattered over the sheet. Thank the Lord she had no need to feel the scrape of a blade at her throat.

Valentine whipped a card from his pocket and flashed it to the barber. "I seek access to the apartments above. I seek a gentleman by the name of Cassiel."

Having glanced at the only piece of information on the card he deemed important—Valentine's title—the barber bowed awkwardly. They all leant back to dodge the man's sweeping arm for he seemed to forget he brandished what those in the rookeries called a weapon.

"There's no one lodging here by that name, milord."

All eyes in the room were upon them as silence descended.

"You're certain?" Valentine withdrew a few sovereigns from his pocket and thrust them into the barber's open hand. "The gentleman has ebony hair, thick eyebrows. He favours black clothes and a red cravat."

The barber pursed his lips and narrowed his gaze in thoughtful contemplation. After a time worthy of a few sovereigns, he had a sudden epiphany. "Yes, I think I know the fellow. He lodges with

Lilly on the top floor." The barber gestured to a door on the far wall. "Though she'll still be abed."

"Then I had best wake her," Valentine said. He placed a guiding hand on Ava's back as they crossed the room and exited the shop via the door. They climbed the wooden staircase, found only one door at the top and so knocked.

Beyond, the room was silent.

Giving a huff of impatience, Drake hammered his fist until they heard a woman's shrill voice calling for them to wait.

The door flew open.

"Do you have to knock so loudly?" The blonde-haired woman rubbed the back of her hand across heavy-lidded eyes. "Anyone would think the house was ablaze."

They had definitely dragged her from her bed. Why else would she answer the door wearing nothing but a thin chemise?

"You are Lilly I presume?" Ava said, ignoring the sight of the young woman's nipples protruding through the flimsy shift. "We are looking for Mr Cassiel. It regards a matter of great importance."

"I might be Lilly. Who's asking?" The woman opened her eyes fully. After blinking numerous times, she stared at the hulking figure of Mr Drake. "Well, ain't you a big fellow." One could not mistake the admiration in her voice. She glanced at Valentine. "Lord Almighty, have I died and gone to heaven?"

Ava knew how Lilly felt. Valentine was an exceptionally handsome man. But he was her man, and Lilly could put her eyeballs back in their sockets.

"We seek Mr Cassiel," Valentine said, looking Lilly keenly in the eye.

"He ain't here."

Ava forced a smile. "You mean he is out?"

"No, I mean he left this morning and ain't coming back. Maybe you should ask the dead where he's gone as they know more than I do."

Valentine muttered a curse.

The thought of Mr Cassiel roaming free to cause mischief left an empty feeling in Ava's chest. What if he was at her home in Park Street, threatening her servants, tearing the place apart? What if he stalked Jonathan, watching him, waiting for the perfect moment to pounce? What if he had written to his employer, Mr Fairfax, seeking his assistance?

Ava touched Valentine's arm. "We must hunt for clues as to his whereabouts," she said in a hushed voice. "I cannot rest until we understand the part he is playing here."

Regardless of the fact they were in company, Valentine cupped her cheek. "Rest assured I will do everything in my power to bring you peace."

How she wished they were alone. She would kiss him deeply to show her appreciation, to thank him for being strong and dependable.

Valentine turned to the woman ogling them at the door. "How much to grant me access to your home? How much to tell me everything you know about the man named Cassiel?"

A smile touched the woman's lips.

Money opened doors. Anyone who worked for a living understood the need to forgo loyalty if it meant filling their stomachs and keeping warm come winter.

"His name ain't Cassiel. I can tell you that for free." She wrapped her finger around a lock of blonde hair and cast a coy grin. "Ten pounds, and you can rummage through what's left of his belongings."

So Mr Dariell was right when he accused the mystic of using a fake identity.

"Agreed." Valentine retrieved a note from his pocket. "Here's twenty pounds. I want you to show me his belongings, tell me what you know of his movements these last few days."

Lilly accepted the note. She checked the amount and then

hastened away with her windfall, leaving the door open, an invitation to enter.

The apartment comprised of a large room with a rickety poster bed in one corner, a wing-back chair flanking the fire and a small table with two wooden chairs. The place was so cold one might freeze to death in their bed. The material panels hanging from the bed frame were once blue and now looked a dirty, muted grey. Washing—a chemise, a man's shirt and white stockings—hung on a rope tied from one bedpost to a nail in the wall.

A small basket of wood by the fire drew Ava's attention. The broken pieces looked familiar. She picked one up and examined the grain.

"I told him they were too good to burn," Lilly said, locking the money away in a box she kept under a floorboard near the bed. "I was supposed to take them to the pawnbroker, but he smashed the pretty box when he came home last night."

"The vanity box?" Ava's heart missed a beat.

Lilly nodded. "He burnt the sloped desk, too."

"Do you know how he came by the items?" Valentine said.

Lilly shrugged. "They've been here for a week or more."

A hard lump formed in Ava's throat. Her stomach lurched at the thought she may have been at home asleep while Mr Cassiel crept around her house. Her mother kept her private papers inside the writing slope. Had Cassiel been hunting for the licence?

"He took most things with him," Lilly continued. "Though he left the morbid clothes he wore when entertaining the nabobs with his tricks." She gave a curt nod. "No offence."

"So you agree the man is a fraud," Mr Drake said, unsurprised.

"He's an entertainer, like me. Oh, he knows how to put on a good show."

"You're an actress?" Valentine said as he wandered about the room, examining the threadbare furnishings.

Judging by the fact Lilly continued to parade about in her

undergarments, Ava suspected Valentine was being polite. There was every chance Lilly worked the streets.

"I'm an actress, a dancer, anything the manager wants me to be," Lilly replied.

"You said Cassiel was not his name," Ava said. She hoped his real name might provide a clue as to his connection with Mr Fairfax.

"George Black is his name. Black of name, black of heart. That's what I said to him when he left without so much as a by your leave."

George Black?

Ava scoured her mind, trying to recall a connection to her father, to anyone who worked for him.

"Has he always been a mystic?" Valentine enquired. He came to stand before a wooden chest in the far corner of the room. For some strange reason, he inhaled deeply. "Does this belong to Mr Black?"

"I've only known him this last month." Perhaps embarrassment forced her to add, "When the rent's shared it leaves more to spend on coal." Lilly crossed the room to stand beside Valentine. "There's nothing in there but his silly costume. He said black made him look more devilish."

"May I look inside?" Valentine asked.

Having paid twenty pounds for the privilege, Ava would insist upon it.

Lilly knelt down and raised the lid. "I'll take his clothes to the pawnbroker." She pushed the black garments to one side and delved deeper into the chest. "Mr Burton downstairs might buy the wig, whiskers and eyebrows."

"The wig?" Drake stepped closer to the chest.

Ava froze. She did not want to examine the rogue's belongings. But what if she missed a vital clue?

"George liked to dress for the role. Why he wore those disgusting things on his face is no one's guess." Lilly pulled the bushy black brows out of the chest. "Mouse skin, that's what they're made from."

A sense of trepidation caught hold of Ava and held her in its firm grasp. "What colour is Mr Black's hair?" she said as Lilly pulled out the black wig that brought images of the mystic flashing back into her mind.

"Brown."

"He wore these shoes, too." Lilly handed them to Valentine.

He studied them for a moment, turned them over in his hand. "Is there a reason for these wooden blocks?" Valentine removed a small wedge and handed it to Mr Drake.

"Men use them to make themselves appear taller," Drake said, examining the item. "Though I have no need of them myself."

Valentine placed the shoes back in the chest. He drew his hand down his face and sighed.

The tension in the room grew with each new revelation. Every piece of the disguise stripped from Cassiel, left a clearer image of a man who seemed just as familiar.

Valentine reached into the chest and dragged out the bright red cravat. He brought it to his nose and inhaled. "This smells like a mixture of animal fat and some medicinal ointment."

Ava wanted to move closer, to be of assistance, but her feet remained rooted to the spot.

"George used that to cover his scar. The ointment helped stop the irritation. He had a soft wax for his face and then patted it with powder. Gave him skin as pale as a ghost."

"His scar?" Ava's voice was barely a croak.

Lilly nodded. "Oh, he had many, from the mining accident abroad."

A heavy, suffocating silence descended.

The room tilted and swayed before Ava's eyes.

Lord, no!

She did not want to think what that meant.

Had a ghost from her past—the wicked man who haunted her

dreams—donned a disguise to continue his torment? It was not a coincidence that Cassiel insisted on dim lighting, that he conducted his seances in the dark. She felt the truth of it deep in her gut. It explained the discomfort she felt in Cassiel's presence. Dressed as Cassiel, Mr Fairfax had touched her, laid his hand on her shoulder, gripped her knees.

Nausea roiled in her stomach.

Valentine met her gaze.

In a second, he was at her side, his strong arm wrapped around her shoulder.

"Thank you for your assistance, Lilly," he said. "We have learnt all we need to know. But if I can ask one more question."

"For the price you paid you can do what you like."

"Would you happen to know if Mr Black has relatives in Frimley?"

Lilly frowned. "No, but he stayed at the coaching inn just outside Frimley. He said the rabbit stew was the best he ever tasted. Better than any of the food he had in Greece."

CHAPTER TWENTY

"I don't like this. I don't like this one bit." Mr Drake sat back in the carriage and watched as Valentine tucked Ava's hair into the white wig purchased from Burton's barber and wig-making shop. "God's teeth, the man is unstable."

"I don't like it, either," Valentine replied. His fingers shook as he pulled Ava's wig into position. He had insisted on the disguise to hide her identity.

"There is every chance Mr Fairfax had something to do with my parents' deaths," Ava said, noting the panic in Valentine's eyes, the same panic that coursed through her veins, too. "He will continue to hound me unless I do something to stop him."

It had taken the best part of the three-hour journey to convince Valentine as to the merit of her plan. In the guise of Mr Cassiel, Fairfax had met both men and would bolt for the hills as soon as he locked eyes with them. Ava was the only one who had a chance of speaking to the rogue, of luring him out of the coaching inn so that Valentine could deal with the scoundrel.

Ava knew what that meant.

Valentine would kill him.

Valentine would forever have the man's death on his

conscience. Ava loved him too much to let that happen which was why she had kept part of her plan secret.

"I intend to speak to him, to tell him we know nothing of the licence and that we cannot help him. When I storm out of the inn, he will surely follow."

Hidden in the shadows—for darkness was already upon them—Ava had peered through the window to see Mr Fairfax seated at a round table in front of the fire. Her legs had almost buckled in shock.

"Rest assured, I shall watch your every move," Valentine said. "Should I sense you're in any danger, I will charge in there as if the devil is at my heels. Is that understood?"

"It is." Ava forced a smile. "There is nothing to fear. What can he do in a room packed with patrons?"

Mr Drake shook his head. "I still don't like it."

"It is the best solution."

Mr Drake narrowed his gaze as he considered her words. "Then before you go, let me tell you that you are the woman my friend has been waiting for, the one he deserves. You would die for him. I see it in your eyes."

Mr Drake did not know how close he had come to speaking the truth. There was every chance she would lose her life tonight. But she could not think about that now.

"And she knows I would give my life for her in a heartbeat," Valentine replied though he kept his gaze fixed on Ava.

Ava inhaled deeply before she lost courage and changed her mind. "Ten minutes is all I shall give him. Be ready and waiting in the courtyard."

As she reached for the door, Valentine took hold of her arm and drew her around to face him.

"Close your eyes, Drake," he said as his mouth came crashing down on hers.

He kissed her as though it might be the last time—with love, with passion, with a profound tenderness that touched her soul.

"Take no risks," Valentine pleaded. "If you're worried, promise me you'll leave."

"I promise. Now you must let me go." A sudden surge of emotion brought tears to her eyes. She turned away and exited the carriage. Raising the hood on her travelling cloak, she marched towards the White Hart Inn.

❀

People glanced up from their mugs and tankards at the sound of someone entering the inn. Mr Fairfax was no exception. He studied her for longer than most, narrowed his gaze suspiciously as she moved towards him.

"Mr Fairfax," she said, trying desperately to keep her voice calm and even. It took every effort to look at him. "Forgive me for not enquiring after your health sooner." She gripped the top rail, pulled out the chair and sat down. "My brother has only recently informed me that you survived the mining accident in Lavrion."

Ava studied him beneath the glow of candlelight while he sat in stunned silence.

How had she not noticed the similarity with Mr Cassiel? Yes, his hair and side whiskers were much lighter, his brows thin, his lips pale. Indeed, the absence of thick brows altered the shape of his forehead. Still, in the depths of her soul, she had known to be wary. Now she understood why she felt so terrified in the mystic's presence.

"Aveline, you look as beautiful as ever. The white wig is rather becoming."

Oh, she was immune to his sycophantic flattery.

"What a shame your actions do not match your lofty praise."

Mr Fairfax smiled. "Well, I doubt you came here to make polite conversation. Did Jonathan tell you what I want?" He sipped ale from a mug as he stared at her intently.

"The same as what you've always wanted. Access to the mine. A share of my parents' business. For some reason, you think it is your due."

Arrogance flashed in his eyes, eyes that did not seem as dark and menacing as she remembered. "Your father wanted a partner. He let me believe he would reward me for years of loyal service."

"And yet he failed to grant what you believe you deserved. There must have been a reason for his reluctance."

He stared at her as he drummed his fingers on the table in the annoying way she remembered. "Perhaps I was lapse in my accounting. Perhaps your father's spies corrupted his mind against me."

Talk of her parents brought grief to the surface. She placed her clasped hands on the table for fear of reaching over and slapping the scoundrel until he admitted the truth.

"My father distrusted your motives, and he was right. But you have no right to make demands on his estate. No court of law would support such a claim."

He reached across and touched her hand. Every fibre of her being recoiled in disgust. "We are not in a court of law, Aveline. I make my own rules. You know that."

As he leant closer, she saw the scar peeking above his cravat, saw the faint pockmarks on his cheek that he had hidden with wax, powder and thicker whiskers. The sight brought thoughts of the accident to the fore.

"Did you k-kill my parents?" Ava did not want to hear the answer, and yet she longed for the truth. Uncertainty played havoc with the mind, led one to concoct horrific stories. "You did. There is no point denying what I know is true."

Mr Fairfax's hand slipped from hers as he sat back in his chair. Still, she felt cold to her bones. He contemplated the comment for some time.

"Hamilton tried to kill me." He snorted as if the incident was amusing. "Your brother told him of our little tryst in my room. He called me to the mine and attacked me."

Painful images invaded her mind. Horrific images no one should associate with kind, loving parents.

"Did you kill them?" she whispered through gritted teeth.

"Not directly."

"What sort of answer is that?" Anger pushed grief aside.

"I may have pulled a pistol, may have shot the rocks above their heads. How was I to know the area was unstable? How was I to know the roof would collapse?"

Ava closed her eyes. Tears welled.

How was it possible for her heart to break all over again?

Her parents were together when they died, she told herself. Neither would have wanted to live without the other, and so she had to find comfort in that.

"Then tell me how you're alive." The loathing in her voice conveyed the depth of her disdain for this man.

"I crawled to the next tunnel, but your father stopped to help your mother." The hypocrite had the gall to make the sign of the cross. "Luck was on my side."

"But you were presumed dead."

Mr Fairfax shrugged. "My injuries were such that I lost my memory for a time. Someone from a nearby village found me and took me in. I spent a year there until I made a full recovery." He raised an arrogant brow. "Then I decided to return to claim the bounty your father denied me."

Ava had heard enough. She wanted this man out of her life for good. He was dangerous, a liar, a deceiver. And she could not risk him appearing again in the future, not when she had children.

"Then I shall make you an offer," she suddenly said, knowing it was foolish, but she had to do something. "One I am sure will prove tempting. My friends are waiting outside to kill you, so I would think carefully before making a decision."

Fear wiped the amused grin off his face. His frantic gaze shot to the window and he muttered a vile curse. "Let me hear your terms."

It was too late to rescind now. She had to move forward with her plan.

Ava sucked in a breath. "I call you out, sir. I seek satisfaction for the deaths of my parents. I seek recompense for the vile way you treated me, for the torment you have caused my brother."

"Are you challenging me to a duel?" he asked incredulously.

Ava raised her chin. "I am. There is a field to the north, a few minutes' walk from here. Should you agree, I will meet you there in half an hour."

Mr Fairfax jerked his head back. "You wish to duel in the dark?" he whispered.

"Bring a lantern. The winner will take possession of the licence to the Mines of Lavrion, will take ownership of the ruby."

Ava had no desire to return to Greece. There was talk of the area being unstable due to a conflict with the Ottoman Empire. And her home was with Valentine now.

Valentine.

She dreaded telling him of her plan.

"You have them in your possession?" Mr Fairfax's greedy eyes widened.

"I do."

Mr Fairfax rubbed his chin while he contemplated the dilemma. "And Lord Valentine is waiting outside?"

Ava nodded. "Along with Mr Drake."

A sinister grin darkened his features. "What is to stop me taking you hostage and planning my escape?"

Ava came to her feet. She gripped the table, made the action appear threatening rather than an aid to help her stand. "I am leaving. Make your decision."

"How do I know Lord Valentine won't shoot me before the duel?"

"I give you my word we will follow the code of honour."

Ava turned to walk away, but Mr Fairfax jumped from his chair and grabbed her hand. "I accept the challenge," he whispered, "though you will need to provide pistols."

A rush of fear almost made her cast up her accounts. "Oh, I think I can manage that."

CHAPTER TWENTY-ONE

The bleak look in Ava's eyes as she left the inn tore at Valentine's heart. He straightened as he moved from his hiding place in the shadows, as he waited to pounce on Fairfax and drag him off into the woods behind the coaching inn.

Valentine raised his hand to signal Drake, who was waiting on the opposite side of the cobbled courtyard. Fairfax would chase Ava's heels, desperate for more information about the licence.

But Ava did not walk to the carriage as planned. She came striding over to Valentine.

"There has been a change of plan." Her bottom lip quivered as she spoke.

Valentine slipped his arm around her waist and pulled her close to calm the shaking that had taken command of her body.

"I understand," he said, knowing he had asked too much. "You do not want the man's death on your conscience."

"It is not that."

"What then? Did he provide evidence to support his claim? Were you mistaken when you suspected he had a hand in your parents' deaths?"

Ever since Ava had learnt that Fairfax and Cassiel were the

same man, she had feared the worst. Why else would Cassiel say that her parents were murdered?

"No." Ava raised her chin and exhaled deeply. "Fairfax confessed. He caused the mine to collapse. From what I understand from his cryptic clues, he embezzled money. My father must have found the evidence in the accounts."

Valentine pursed his lips. "I am sorry. It must have hurt to hear his admission of guilt."

"Jonathan told my father of Mr Fairfax's plan to ruin me, to force a wedding." The sudden cold indifference in her tone unnerved him. "My father attacked him, and Fairfax swears he acted in self-defence."

"And you believe that to be the case?"

With no witnesses to the crime, the blackguard could say anything.

Ava arched a brow. The forlorn expression he'd seen a minute earlier was replaced with a confidence, an arrogance he'd witnessed when first meeting her on the duelling field.

A crippling sense of trepidation held him by the throat.

"I don't know what to believe," she said. "But know that I love you more than life itself. I love you enough not to let you sully your hands on that scoundrel."

Valentine's heart swelled against his ribs. Despite all Fairfax had done, Ava's only thoughts were for him.

"I do not trust him, Lucius. What if he appears at some point in the future, to hurt my family, to seek revenge?"

Confused as to what she wanted, Valentine said, "What are you proposing we do?"

Ava hesitated before cupping his cheek and kissing him once on the lips. "I have challenged Mr Fairfax to a duel. Set to take place in thirty minutes in the field a little farther along the road." She pointed north. "The winner takes the licence and the ruby. Though I intend to put a lead ball between his brows."

Shock rendered Valentine speechless.

The searing pain in his chest as his mind played out the scene caused one knee to buckle. Bile bubbled in his stomach. Panic choked his throat. His head spun until he struggled to see straight.

Sheer terror forced him to say, "How can an intelligent woman be so bloody stupid? Tell him you made a mistake. Tell him I'll give him five thousand pounds to disappear for good. Tell him … just tell him something, damn it."

Ava placed her hand on his chest though Valentine could not remain still. He swung around, punched the air, dragged his hand down his face and wished he could turn the clock back to the moment they first rattled into the courtyard of the White Hart Inn.

"No," he said as he whirled back to face her. "Get into the carriage and wait for me there."

"You are not my husband yet, Valentine."

"And I doubt I shall be your husband at all if I permit such recklessness."

A tense silence ensued, a silence permeated with mumbled curses.

"Fairfax took advantage of me," she said, sounding just as determined as he. "Jonathan prevented him from stealing my virginity, but he would have used me given the chance. For that alone I deserve vengeance. And I refuse to let you pay the heavy price on my behalf."

Images of her standing alone in a field, scared and vulnerable, flashed into his mind. Anger surfaced. He would be the one to put a lead ball through Fairfax's cold heart.

"Then I will be your second," Valentine insisted.

"You may name yourself my second, but you will follow the code of conduct."

Drake strode over to join them, and Valentine was glad of the distraction.

"Am I to understand Fairfax wishes to remain in the inn?" Drake narrowed his gaze. "What is it?"

Valentine gave a mocking snort. "Ava challenged Fairfax to a duel, set to take place tonight. The one standing receives the licence and the ruby."

Drake's expression darkened. "I can only imagine the conversation when she told you." He turned to Ava. "Valentine will never allow you to risk your life. If Juliet were standing here, I would bundle her into the carriage, tie the rogue to the axle and drag him fifty miles along the road."

Ava arched a brow. "You do not respect the fact your wife has her own opinion?"

Devil take it, the lady was brave.

No one challenged Devlin Drake.

It took Drake a moment to answer. "Not if it means I might lose her." He seemed to consider the comment. "But I would respect her wishes to a certain extent. I would work to find a compromise."

After a brief pause, she said, "I am prepared to make certain concessions."

Thank the Lord.

"Then permit me to act on your behalf," Valentine pleaded.

"No. I have the skill to shoot in the dark."

The dark!

Bloody hell!

He had not even thought of that.

"We should discuss this somewhere else before Fairfax sees us," Drake said.

"There is no need," Ava replied. "I told him you were waiting outside to kill him. I told him that the duel was his best option if he hoped to gain possession of the mine."

Another tense silence ensued.

Fairfax was no fool. He had a slim chance of escaping the duelling field alive. If he shot Ava, Valentine would kill him, regardless. Fairfax's only option now was to run, to bide his time before returning with a fresh plan of attack.

Relief coursed through Valentine's veins.

' "I have a suggestion," Valentine said. Fairfax would not head for London, so his only option was to venture south. "Let us wait across the road and see what the rogue does. If he heads north, we will follow him and assume he is heading for the duelling field."

Drake arched a brow. "And if he heads south?"

"Then he'll be unfortunate enough to meet well-dressed bandits on the road." Valentine focused his gaze on Ava. "Are you in agreement?"

"I am," she said without hesitation.

Having crossed the road to hide amidst the shrubbery, they stood and watched the door of the coaching inn. Long minutes passed. A carriage arrived to block their view of the courtyard. Consequently, they almost missed Fairfax sitting astride his horse. With his hat pulled low, he nudged the animal into a canter as he turned onto the road heading for the coast.

"The man is cunning enough to know he had no chance of winning on the field," Valentine said, exhaling the tension he'd held since Ava mentioned the duel. He could handle whatever came next as long as she wasn't staring down the barrel of a pistol.

"He has always been a coward," Ava said as they moved out of the shadows and hurried across the road towards Valentine's carriage.

They were about to enter the courtyard when a man on horseback charged past them as fast as windy flames devoured a hay barn.

Valentine cursed the fool.

"Heavens above!" Ava grabbed Valentine's arm. "I may be mistaken, but that rider looked like Jonathan. Did you tell him we were here?"

Valentine had left a note with Honora when Ava returned home to change clothes and fetch her cloak. "I informed him of our intention, yes."

Her eyes grew wide with panic. "Then we must go after him before he does something he may live to regret."

Valentine seemed to spend every waking minute chasing Jonathan Kendall's coattails. The man was unpredictable, acted without thought or logic. But there was no denying he cared for his sister, and so Valentine ushered them into the carriage and ordered Sprocket to give chase.

They held on to the leather straps as they bounced and swayed along the narrow lane. A thump on the roof above forced Valentine to yank down the window.

"Do you have the men in your sights?" he called up to Sprocket.

"They're just a bit farther ahead, milord."

The wind whipped Valentine's face as he thrust his head fully out of the window. The glare from the carriage lamp made it impossible to see more than a few feet in front. A sudden biting chill on the back of his neck alerted him to the fact that Ava had lowered her window, too.

"I think I see them," she called out amidst the violent rumbling of the wheels and the rush of wind whistling through the conveyance. "Jonathan is riding alongside Mr Fairfax."

Valentine leant further out to gain a better view.

Two black shadows moved and swayed in the distance as their horses pounded the dirt. The animals galloped so closely together one mistake would see both men thrown from their horses. Valentine would not want to be the one riding close to the edge, for the road dropped away to the left, dropped down sharply into a ravine.

"What? No!" Ava cried. "They're fighting. It is too dark to identify which one is Jonathan."

Valentine agreed. The collars of both men's coats touched their chins. Seated in the saddle, they were of a similar height and frame. He could do nothing but watch them push and kick and grab each other's coat sleeves as they raced along at breakneck speed.

It crossed his mind to load his pistol, to aim and wait for a clear shot of Fairfax, but even he lacked the skill to fire accurately under such terrifying conditions.

With each rider trying to wrestle the other from his horse, it came as no surprise when the man on the right slipped from the saddle.

Ava gasped. "Jonathan!" she called despite not knowing if the rider hanging on by the reins—and with one leg still draped across the saddle—was her brother or Fairfax.

Just when Valentine thought he might predict the outcome of the battle, the rider seated upright took his gaze off the road to beat his opponent to the ground. Obsessed with victory, he failed to notice the low-hanging branch until it smacked his head. The force of the impact knocked him clean off the horse and sent him tumbling down into the ravine.

"Jonathan!" With her voice choked with emotion, Ava repeated her brother's name numerous times. "Oh, please don't let it be him."

Sprocket brought the carriage to a grinding halt.

As soon as the wheels stopped turning, they were all out of the carriage and racing towards the scene. Both horses continued galloping along the lane. Not knowing who the rider was attempting to regain his seat on the saddle, they all peered down the dark ravine, looking for a body below.

Sprocket approached with a lantern held aloft.

"Come a bit closer to the edge," Valentine said to the coach-man. The bank leading down into the valley was not too steep to navigate. "Hold the lantern while I climb down."

"Is that wise?" Ava appeared at his side and clutched his arm.

"How else will we know if he's alive?"

If it was Jonathan, Valentine would do everything in his

power to save him. If it was Fairfax, he would ensure the fellow never made it out of the ravine.

"Sprocket must have a rope under his seat," Drake said.

"I don't need a rope. Just keep the lantern high." Without another word, Valentine stepped off the edge of the road onto the grassy verge that petered down into the valley. He slipped numerous times on dead bracken as he crabbed sideways down to where a man lay sprawled on his front.

Valentine grabbed the still man's arm and turned him over, relieved to find the cold, lifeless eyes of Mr Fairfax staring back at him. Crouching beside the body, Valentine checked for a pulse.

"It's Fairfax," he shouted up to where Ava and Drake stood waiting with Sprocket. From what he could tell, the impact had snapped the rogue's neck. "He's dead."

Valentine wasn't sure if they heard him, but as he began his ascent back up the steep hill, he saw Ava fling her arms around a figure too small to be Devlin Drake.

As Valentine neared the top, Drake offered his hand and hauled Valentine to safety.

"I presume he died of his injuries," Drake said, brushing dirt off Valentine's coat. "Or did you have to help him along?"

"My hands are clean. But I would have made sure he didn't live to cause my wife further distress." Protecting Ava would be his life's mission. Making her laugh, helping her to fulfil her dreams would be top of his agenda, too.

"Your wife?" Drake smirked. "Did I miss the ceremony?"

"Of course not. But I will marry her once I've pestered the archbishop for a licence."

A surge of emotion forced him to swallow deeply. He glanced at Ava. Happiness radiated from her like a bright beacon. She turned to him and smiled, and he felt the power of it deep in his chest.

"And is she in agreement?" Drake asked. "Then again, I

cannot imagine there is a woman in the world who wouldn't want to marry you."

The comment proved too much. Water welled in Valentine's eyes. He tried to speak, but the lump in his throat prevented him from making a sound.

Drake gripped his shoulder. "That's how you know she is the one for you, my friend. I am not afraid to admit that I cried when I realised the depth of my feelings for Juliet."

Valentine coughed to clear his throat. "No doubt you're eager to return home rather than watch me turn into a blubbering wreck."

"On the contrary, this is one moment I don't want to miss. Who would have thought Lucius Valentine would feel anything for a woman other than indifference?"

CHAPTER TWENTY-TWO

T he wedding took place five days later in the chapel on the grounds of Valentine's country estate near Covehurst Bay. It was a quiet, informal affair, not what the *ton* would expect from a member of the aristocracy, but the only people who mattered were there.

Ava loved that Whitecliff House overlooked the sea. Inhaling the fresh, salty air brought back happy memories of her parents and their time in Greece. She had sensed Valentine's reluctance to return, learnt from Honora that he had not been back since the night his father died. Even so, Valentine wished to concentrate on their future now and not wallow in past pain.

"Three weddings in the space of a month," Lord Greystone said as they sat before the roaring fire in the drawing room, exhausted after a wedding breakfast that Mr Drake struggled to finish. "All we need now is for Dariell and Lockhart to marry."

The Frenchman arched a brow as a mischievous glint flashed in his eyes. "Remember that Society must think Lockhart is already married."

Thankfully, Jonathan had retired to his room, and so they could speak freely.

"The lady playing the role of his wife must be a skilled actress," Ava said.

What if the woman despised Lockhart? How does one feign a look of love and intense longing? She glanced at Valentine and met his heated gaze. In a moment, she would make an excuse to leave the room knowing her husband would follow.

"Surely you don't expect this actress to share his bed?" Lydia, Greystone's wife, said.

"Knowing Lockhart, she will have no objection," Valentine added.

Dariell relaxed back in the chair. He steepled his fingers together and sighed. "I am afraid to say that the actress proved unsuitable for the part. Most unsuitable indeed."

Mr Drake sat forward. "But I thought Lockhart had made arrangements to return to town next week?"

"He has."

"Then who will play the role of his wife?"

A smile touched Dariell's lips. "I have the perfect lady in mind. She owns the property Lockhart is renting. Neither know that their destinies are entwined."

"Then I suspect Lockhart has more than a few surprises in store," Valentine said.

Dariell inclined his head. "Indeed."

The other men in the room looked at their wives and mumbled in agreement.

After taking a sip of her champagne, Honora said, "So you are all returning to town next week?"

"We must support Lockhart in his effort to clear his name." Valentine glanced at Ava. His blue eyes flashed with apprehension. After the problems with Mr Fairfax, they had hoped for more time alone.

"Perhaps now is a good time to tell you that I shall not be returning to town." Dariell's declaration came as a shock.

"You won't?" Lord Greystone frowned.

"My fate lies with the Darlings in Falaura Glen." Dariell raised his hand before anyone had a chance to speak. "Do not ask me about it now. All will become apparent in due course."

Silence descended.

The Darlings in Falaura Glen.

It sounded like a magical place, a place of lush green meadows, rambling roses and a babbling brook. Even in the dead of winter, Ava imagined people found it enchanting. A haven they did not want to leave. Despite having spent two days at White-cliff, Ava felt a similar sense of belonging. This would be their home when not in town. They would raise their children here. She might even craft jewellery from a room overlooking the sea.

Ava's heart fluttered at the prospect of spending a lifetime with Valentine. She rose to her feet, eager to have five minutes alone with him. "Please excuse me for a moment."

The gentlemen stood.

Ava was in the hall when she heard Valentine make his apology, too. She waited for him, captured his hand and drew him into the study. Once inside, he turned the key in the lock and pulled her into an embrace.

"Does this remind you of our first kiss in the mews?" he said, pressing her back against the solid oak door.

Before she could answer, his tongue swept over her lips and penetrated her mouth.

Ava clung to him, fought the urge to rip off every item of clothing to leave nothing but his toned, naked body. The ache between her legs throbbed as he devoured her, drank so deeply she was close to finding her release despite the fact he hadn't touched her yet.

"Oh, Valentine. I need you. I need to feel you, all of you."

"Love, continue talking like that, and this will be a rather reckless mating over my desk."

"Have we time?" she asked as a delicious image of him thrusting inside her took hold.

"We can be quick, though there will be no time to undress."

"Then hurry."

Valentine continued kissing her as he guided her towards the desk.

"I want to spend every day with you," she said, watching him unbutton his breeches as she pushed aside papers, gathered up her skirts and shuffled onto the edge of the large, imposing desk.

"Life with you will be an adventure." Valentine entered her body in one slow, intoxicating slide. "Ah, you definitely want me, Ava."

"I have wanted you from the day we first met."

"And I want you so badly I am willing to act like a libertine on my wedding day."

Ava swallowed a moan when his thumb massaged her intimate place and he thrust deeper. "I like the libertine."

"Then consider this preparation for when we attend Lady Carmichael's ball next week. When we seek vengeance on the gossips."

"Yes," Ava panted as the coil inside wound tighter.

And that was the last comment either of them made for some time.

Lady Carmichael's ball was an ostentatious affair with jugglers, acrobats, a performing monkey—although Valentine took care to avoid the wild creature who hopped on people's shoulders—and a flowing fountain of champagne. Everyone who was anyone was in attendance tonight. Spiteful gossips included.

Valentine had arrived with Drake and Juliet while Ava came with Honora and Lady Cartwright. Having neglected to post an announcement of their wedding in *The Times*, and with Honora being under strict instructions to remain tight-lipped, Valentine and Ava received no hearty handshakes of congratulations.

Just like the night at Rockford's ball, Valentine sensed Ava's presence in the ballroom. Numerous times, he sought her out simply to smile and lock gazes. Love filled his heart. Happiness flowed through his veins to bring a level of calmness he had never known.

Portia Durrant hovered around him like a bee on a honeypot. He spoke to her about Lady Carmichael's extravagance, excused himself when the topic turned to the Kendalls. The urge to put Portia in her place, to inform the lady that his wife outranked her, proved overwhelming. But there was only one way the lady would feel true embarrassment, and so he had to stick to the plan.

Valentine removed his pocket watch and checked the time. "Will you excuse me? My presence is required elsewhere." Valentine offered Drake a wide grin.

"Ah, it's time for your ten o'clock liaison in the library," Drake replied.

Excitement bubbled in Valentine's chest at the prospect of holding Ava close, of kissing her in the sensual way that made him lose all grasp of sense and logic.

"You know what to do should Lady Durrant fail to take the bait."

"Indeed." Drake smiled. "I shall ensure the lady gathers her cronies and comes to find you."

"Good luck," Juliet said. "I wish I could be there to see Lady Durrant's face when she learns Ava is your wife."

Valentine touched Juliet affectionately on the arm. "I'm sure she will regale you with the facts over supper."

Valentine left his friends and prowled the perimeter of the dance floor to give Portia ample time to follow his movements. Once confident he had the lady's attention, he pounced on Ava.

"Lord Valentine," Ava said, her eyes brimming with affection, "I did not expect to see you here this evening."

"Did you not?" he whispered playfully in her ear. "Am I to

understand from your sensual tone that you're pleased to see me?"

"I am always pleased to see you."

He offered his arm. "Then perhaps you might like to take a stroll. It is too cold to venture into the garden, but Lady Carmichael has a large collection of gothic novels in her library."

"Gothic novels?" Ava threaded her arm through his. "How interesting. I am told the erotic is a popular trope."

"Perhaps it is a subject you might care to investigate."

"Is that wise?" she said, failing to suppress a giggle. "Some say that a libertine lurks behind your gentlemanly facade."

"And you, my love, have the skill of a courtesan when it comes to pleasuring your husband."

"Then lead the way. Perhaps we might learn of a new position to add to our growing repertoire."

"I draw the line at donning a robe and playing the mad monk," Valentine said as he led her through the crowd and out of the ballroom.

The beady eyes of the circling vultures watched their every move.

Soon, they would swoop down ready to rip Ava's reputation to shreds.

A few people passed them in the hall. No one stopped them slipping into the library.

Excitement and the pounding thrum of lust captured him the moment he entered the dark, deserted space. His thoughts turned salacious even though he knew this was merely a means to teach Lady Durrant a lesson, a means to restore Ava's good name, and not a reason for him to plunge into his wife's willing body.

Ava braced her hands on her hips. "I imagine this will work better if they catch us in a clinch."

Valentine closed the gap between them. He captured her hands and drew her to the middle of the room, to where they had a perfect view of the door. Despite portraying an air of confidence, he recognised the nervous hitch in her voice.

"I prefer to use the word *embrace*. It expresses the depth of my love rather than implying something more licentious." He slid his arm around her waist and pressed a chaste kiss to her lips.

Ava smiled. "You lured me here under the pretence of hearing erotic stories," she teased.

Valentine arched a brow. "And tonight, when we are away from here, I shall tell you a tale that will curl your toes."

Ava cupped his cheek. "Then I pray the ball passes quicker than a whirlwind."

Valentine kissed her again, in the slow, sensual way that was like a mating of souls.

"Do you think Devlin will—" Ava began, but upon hearing a noise outside the door, Valentine placed his finger on her lips.

"Hush, love, someone is here." Noting the slow turn of the doorknob, he glanced at Ava. "Look at me as if you're desperate to tear the clothes off my back."

Ava arched a brow. "That won't be difficult."

They remained locked in an embrace until three women burst into the room, leaving the door wide open to cast a modicum of light over the scandalous scene.

Portia Durrant was accompanied by Mrs Wainwright—a notorious gossip responsible for many a ruination—and Mrs Titterington, whose name was so opposed to her stern disposition.

"Oh!" Portia exclaimed as they all looked upon Ava as if she were the devil's spawn. "Is Lady Carmichael aware that you're using her library as a bordello?"

"A bordello?" Valentine scoffed. "Madam, it seems your wild imagination has got the better of you. Now get out, close the door and be on your way."

Portia flicked her red hair and raised her chin. She turned to the other two vultures out to scavenge on her leftovers. "Did I not tell you they were conducting an illicit affair? I think this proves my point."

"Indeed," Mrs Wainwright said disapprovingly. She focused her attention on Valentine. "I doubt your mother would approve of you carrying on with this gal." She stared down her pointed beak as if hungry for him to discard Ava's ruined carcass for them to feed and feast.

"May I ask why you have involved yourselves in our private affairs?" Ava said with the confidence of an aristocrat.

Portia glared. "Because there is a place for a man to court his mistress and it is not amongst respectable Society."

Ava inhaled deeply. She kept her calm composure while Valentine's blood boiled.

"And what about a man who wishes to court his wife?" Ava said. "Are a married couple not permitted to sneak into the library to share a moment alone?"

A stunned silence filled the room.

Despite blinking far too many times to count, Portia gave a wry smile. She turned to her friends and chuckled. "Some people will say anything to save face. I recall no mention of a wedding in the broadsheets. Do you?"

Mrs Wainwright and Mrs Titterington failed to respond. Both matrons appeared somewhat uncomfortable and shuffled back towards the door.

"We did not make a formal announcement." Valentine's stern voice echoed through the room. "But allow me to present my wife —the Viscountess Valentine."

"Your wife?" Mrs Wainwright choked on the words.

"I suggest you offer her the respect befitting her station," he demanded, "else there will be hell to pay."

Portia stood rooted to the spot, her face as pale as Lady Carmichael's bust of Apollo.

Both matrons hurried forward. They curtsied whilst offering

their felicitations followed by profuse apologies for their dreadful mistake.

Ava accepted their congratulations with good grace. She was wise enough to know one did not make enemies in the *ton* unless absolutely necessary. Besides, when Lockhart returned it would serve them well to have a few allies amongst the ranks.

Throwing Portia glares of disdain, both ladies left the room.

Ava took hold of Valentine's arm as they made to return to the ballroom. Portia Durrant stood rigid as they passed.

"It seems I have something to thank you for," Ava said, stopping briefly to address Lady Durrant. "Had you not paid my brother to call Valentine out, we might never have met."

They did not wait for a reply but left the woman stewing in her misfortune.

When they entered the ballroom, the strains of a waltz captured Valentine's attention.

"Would you care to dance?" he said, desperate for an opportunity to hold Ava in his arms.

Ava smiled. The satisfaction gleaned from putting Portia in her place still sparkled in her eyes. "What about your careless footwork?"

"Will you not make allowances for your husband?"

"I would do anything for you."

The comment warmed his heart.

He drew her onto the floor, his pulse racing as he took her in his arms. As they whirled about in perpetual circles, he gazed at her intently, his whole body alive with powerful pulses of love. The depth of her emotion swam in her eyes, too.

"I cannot help but wonder how this glorious thing happened," she said as he pulled her a little closer than deemed appropriate. "Mere weeks ago I had only heard your name, and now I love you more than I ever thought possible."

"In that regard, I must disagree with Epictetus."

She gasped, and her bewitching eyes widened. "You disagree with a great philosopher?"

"Did he not say that no great thing is created suddenly?"

She considered the question. "He did, but then we must assume he did not meet the love of his life on a duelling field."

"Or wrestle with a monkey to protect her from a rogue."

Ava chuckled. "Perhaps Epictetus never experienced a passion so consuming it forced him to behave recklessly."

The comment brought the memory of their lovemaking in a carriage flooding back. "You seem to like it when I'm reckless," Valentine said, moistening his lips.

"Yes," she sighed, "though it is hard to be reckless when married."

"On the contrary, I am about to show every gossip in this room how much I love you. I am going to kiss you, Ava."

She blinked. "What? Here on the dance floor?"

"Yes," he said, pulling her so close their bodies touched, "on the dance floor of all places."

THE END

Thank you!

Thank you for reading *Valentine's Vow.*

Will Lockhart persuade Miss Darling to play the role of his wife?
What fate awaits Dariell in Falaura Glen?

Find out in *A Gentleman's Curse*
Avenging Lords Book 4

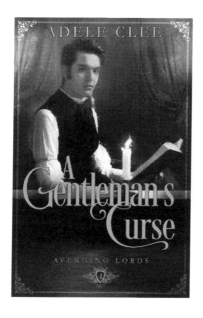

Coming soon!
A Gentleman's Curse

Printed in Great Britain
by Amazon

33014673R00151